I0525849

AIRSHIP 27 PRODUCTIONS

Mars McCoy-Space Ranger Volume Two

Mars McCoy & The Curse of the Star Lance © 2013 James Palmer
Mars McCoy & The Chaos Horde © 2013 Van Allen Plexico
Reaching for the Stars © 2013 Ron Fortier

Published by Airship 27 Production
www.airship27.com
www.airship27hangar.com

Interior illustrations © 2013 Shannon Hall
Cover illustration © 2013 Michael Youngblood

Editors: Ron Fortier & Van Allen Plexico
Associate Editor: Charles Saunders
Production and design by Rob Davis

Special acknowledgement and thanks to Mark Maddox who designed the Mars McCoy
logo and the look of the "Black Bird."

ISBN-13: 978-0615838090
ISBN-10: 061583809X

Printed in the United States of America

10 9 8 7 6 5 4 3 2 1

Mars McCoy
Space Ranger

TABLE OF CONTENTS

From their hidden asteroid base, "the Black Hole," the Space Patrol dispatches its Black Bird ships and crews to the most dangerous corners of the galaxy.

They work in the service of the Empire of Man, newest members of the vast Galactic Alliance that includes dozens of strange and bizarre alien races.

Operating among the "Fringe Worlds," the 144 Rangers of the Space Patrol selflessly protect Humanity—and all others who desire protection—from the multitude of deadly threats that fill the universe.

In their tiny, two-person Black Bird ships, Captain Marshall "Mars" McCoy and his comrades keep their weapons hot and their tempers cool—as action and adventure await at every turn!

Mars McCoy and the Curse of the Star Lance

by James Palmer

"'m glad this patrol duty is almost over," said Marshall "Mars" McCoy. "This is boring. There's nothing happening for parsecs in any direction."

In the seat next to him, his beautiful, statuesque copilot, Lieutenant Betty-12, surveyed her instrument panel. "You'd rather be in danger?"

"I'd rather have something to do," said McCoy, leaning back in his pilot's seat. There were no course adjustments to make for the moment, so he stared ahead through the viewport instead, the stars winking at them like pinpricks in velvet.

"This system has been at peace for some time," said Betty-12, concentrating on her controls. "Thanks in no small part to us and the rest of the Space Patrol."

McCoy sighed. "I know. I just wish something would happen. However minor."

"Well," said Betty-12, "perhaps we should be grateful for the relative peace and quiet. In any case, we are now done with our sweep of this sector. Your orders?"

McCoy gave a sly grin. "Betty, my dear, let's head for home. Lay in a course for the Black Hole. Prepare to enter null space."

Just then the Null radio flickered to life. "Helloooooooo?" said an urgent voice, filled with static.

McCoy glanced at his copilot. "Can we clean that up?"

"I'm trying," she said, tapping buttons and working the radio's controls. "I don't understand it. The signal goes through null space, so it should be crystal clear. Unless..."

McCoy immediately knew what Betty-12 was getting at. "Null space feedback," he said. Betty-12 nodded.

"Whoever it is, they're close," said McCoy. "Start a short range scan. I want everything. Infrared, gamma, the works."

"Scanning EM band," said Betty, working her instruments. The screens of Black Bird Five flickered and bleeped as the ship scanned their immediate area for anything that could send a distress signal.

"If it's this close, why didn't we find it earlier?"

"Maybe because it wasn't here earlier," said Betty-12 without looking up from her instruments. "I have something. A series of short, regular radio bursts."

"Could be a pulsar," McCoy mused.

"No. Because you're not dead from radiation." Betty-12 looked at him, her blue eyes sparkling. She was a robot, a machine, and could take levels of radiation that would cook McCoy in his Space Patrol uniform.

"OK. Then what?"

"It's a ship. But that wasn't the source of the distress call."

"Show me."

Betty-12 pressed a series of buttons and the small screen that divided the two halves of the command console lit up, showing a tiny ship.

"Looks like an ore hauler," said McCoy. "Pirates?"

"Not in such a small craft, and not without support. They would not need help."

McCoy nodded, rubbed his stubbled chin in thought. "True. But I've heard of space pirates using the old distress signal trick to free would-be Samaritans of their vessels. And their lives."

The null radio crackled and buzzed again.

"There are no other ships in this vicinity," said Betty-12, consulting her instruments. "Detecting faint vital signs of at least one humanoid life form."

"Let's get over there and check it out," said Mars. "Get on the horn to the Black Hole, let them know what's going on."

"Horn?" Betty-12 asked, arching her right eyebrow and staring at McCoy quizzically.

"It's an old Earth term. Never mind. Tell Commander Verne we'll be a little late."

McCoy brought Black Bird Five in closer. The other craft was not much larger than the Space Patrol vessel. It was bulky, gray and free of insignia or identifying serial numbers. But there were no pirate markings either.

". . .elp me. . ." came a faint cry from the null radio. Betty hit the com button. "This is Black Bird Five calling unidentified craft. What is your situation?"

". . .countered . . . erelict," came the tinny, far away voice. "Boarded . . .et up claim beacon." More static. "It's the . . . -ar . . . -ance."

"Can you repeat?" Mars shouted into the null radio.

". . . *Star Lance* . . ."

A chill ran down McCoy's spine. If the name registered with Betty-12's robotic memory, she didn't show it.

"Prepare to be boarded," she told the radio. "We're coming to rescue you."

The null radio answered with static.

"There's a lot more wrong with their radio than null space feedback," said McCoy as he brought the Black Bird closer. "Do you know the ship he was talking about?"

"The *Star Lance*," Betty-12 recited from her memory banks. "Experimental class Navy Cruiser. Disappeared with all hands on its maiden voyage twenty-seven years, eight months, five hours and forty-seven minutes ago."

McCoy shook his head. Until she started talking like that, he could almost forget his beautiful copilot was a machine. "Uh, yeah. That's the one. I didn't think she really existed. The Navy doesn't like to talk about her, and everyone who claims to have found the wreckage ends up dead."

"Not this time," said Betty-12, her deft hands working her controls. "Should I radio the Black Hole and tell them about the *Star Lance*?"

"No. I don't want Voroshilov overhearing." Voroshilov was the Navy's liaison to the Space Patrol, but as far as McCoy was concerned, liaison was a fancy term for *spy*.

McCoy hit the forward thrusters, slowing Black Bird Five and preparing to dock with the distressed vessel.

An emergency rescue of this nature wasn't overly complex. They had to dock with the vessel, open the hatch and extract the pilot. But McCoy knew that danger was always just a hearbeat away.

"People say the *Lance* is cursed," said McCoy, bracing for the metal-on-metal thump as Black Bird Five merged with the hull of the damaged ship.

"I don't believe in curses," said Betty-12. "Docking rings engaged."

Mars McCoy released his seat restraints. "Let's go and say hi."

Betty-12 grabbed a first aid kit as she followed McCoy to the rear of the Black Bird. McCoy leaned down and tugged on a handle, which released their hatch with a hiss.

Suddenly the ship rocked violently, knocking McCoy and Betty-12 to the deck. The Black Bird's warning siren went off. So did the null radio.

"Get out of here!" came the frightened voice they first heard minutes earlier. It was crystal clear now, and full of panic. "She's gonna blow!"

"What?"

Betty got up quickly from where she had fallen and glanced at the readings on her console, her keen robot eyes zeroing in on the data.

"Their engines are overheating," she said without emotion. "Something's wrong with the ship's null engine."

"Let's get him out of there," said Mars, tugging on the doomed ship's hatch. It wouldn't budge.

"Let me," said Betty-12, reaching down into the opening and tugging at the thick hatch. The hatch opened with a scream of screeching metal.

McCoy dived feet first into the opening, his boots hitting rickety deck plating six feet below. Betty-12 watched him from the opening, as expressionless as if she was watching grass grow on some lush green colony world on a sunny afternoon.

There were more sirens going off on this ship, louder, more urgent. Billowing smoke clouded McCoy's vision, and his nostrils were filled by the acrid smell of burnt wiring.

"Hello?" he called, his voice echoing in the small space.

"Over here."

McCoy peered through the smoke and saw a man lying under a hunk of metal. Mars scowled into the smoke. "Betty!"

McCoy heard a thud behind him as Betty-12 dropped into the damaged ship. Without a word she grabbed the piece of metal and lifted it effortlessly while McCoy dragged the ship's pilot out from under it.

"Th-thank you," said the pilot. He was young. Short sandy blond hair stuck out from his head, and wore a grey tunic and matching trousers. "The ship . . . is falling apart."

"What happened?" Asked Betty-12.

"Later," McCoy barked. "We've got to get him out of here before his ship comes down around our ears."

Betty-12 helped the man to his feet and, with considerable effort, they lifted him through the opening into Black Bird Five. Betty-12 slammed the hatch shut while McCoy gave full power to the thrusters. "That ship is gonna blow any second," he said. "Soon as we're clear, I'm skipping into null-space."

"Roger," said Betty-12, who was busily securing the injured pilot to one of the Black Bird's bunks.

The ship exploded with a flash, the force rocking Black Bird Five as it became enveloped in a rainbow of light, entering the safety of null-space.

"How's our passenger?"

"I am still assessing his injuries."

The pilot tried to sit up, but Betty-12 put a restraining hand on his chest. "Easy. You are injured."

The pilot sat up, grey eyes stared widely at his savior. "You're a robot," he said.

"Yes. How did you know?"

The pilot grinned. "You're too pretty to be a real woman." After that brief state of coherence, the pilot fell back on his bunk, coughing.

"Ship . . . fell to the . . . curse."

"Shhhh," Betty-12 soothed.

"All I could see were stars," said the young man. "So many stars. They changed. The stars changed!"

"What's your name, pilot?" asked McCoy.

"Rand. N-Nathan Rand."

"What happened out there?" Betty asked, opening the first aid kit.

"D-don't know. The *Lance* . . . rippled. Like a pond when you throw a stone into it. My ship got too close."

"That doesn't make any sense," said McCoy.

"Stories were right," said Nathan Rand. "Ship . . . cursed."

"You're all right now," said Betty-12. "Just take it easy."

Nathan Rand passed out then, leaving Mars McCoy and Betty-12 in silence as they headed home.

"You two want to tell me what happened out there?"

Commander Herbert George "H.G." Verne glared at Mars McCoy and Betty-12 as they stood at attention in his office. He leaned back in his chair, crossing his arms. They could hear the whir of the servos in Verne's mechanical right arm as he moved it across his chest and tucked it under his left arm.

"A ship was in trouble and we saved the pilot," said McCoy. "We don't know why the ship blew. Unless it was the curse."

Commander Verne glanced self-consciously at the door, which he had locked after it closed moments ago.

"I don't want to hear any talk about ghost ships and curses," Verne said, pointing his metal index finger in McCoy's face. "These space jockeys are superstitious enough as it is."

"With all due respect, Sir. I think we have a bigger problem." Betty-12 looked at their commanding officer.

"Oh? Do enlighten me please, Lieutenant."

"The *Star Lance*, Sir. It existed at one time, and was lost. It was carrying a top secret drive and classified weaponry."

"That the Navy would love to get its hands on again," Verne finished, his mood darkening even more than it had been after Black Bird Five's arrival. "Not to mention the Orgum-Ree, and every space pirate in the Fringe. If we can believe the stories."

"We have to check Rand's story out, Commander," added McCoy, running his hand through his unruly red hair.

Verne nodded, mulling this over. "We can't keep it under wraps for long, either. That pilot is down in sickbay babbling away about his precious *claim*. Not to mention the curse."

Verne looked at McCoy, then Betty-12. "I want you two to go back out there and find the *Lance*."

"And this talk of a curse?"

"There are no such things as curses. Besides," He softened, gave McCoy a fatherly wink. "If there was a curse, it looks like you and your copilot broke it."

"How did we do that?" asked Betty-12.

"By coming back alive."

McCoy shook his head. "OK. We'll check out the pilot's story. He ranted the coordinates the whole way back. But what do we do when we find it?"

"Call me and sit tight," said Verne. "I'll call the Navy. Eventually. But we need to guard it against anyone else finding it. We'll move the Black Hole to its location if we have to. Now get out of here." He thumbed a button on his desk, unlocking the door with a ping.

Betty-12 exited first.

"I'll bring you back a souvenir, Commander," said McCoy, grinning.

"I'd rather you didn't. Now move."

"Yes, sir."

As they walked to the hangar bay and the waiting Black Bird Five, McCoy noticed their fellow Space Rangers, and even a few Spacers First Class, staring at them as they passed, speaking to each other in hushed tones

"Good news travels fast," whispered McCoy. "Let's go. The sooner we can confirm Rand's story the sooner we can get this over with."

Ten minutes later they were leaving the hollowed out asteroid that was Black Hole headquarters. Once they were at a safe distance, they engaged the skip engine and slipped into null space.

Commander Verne didn't have to wait long for news to get out.

A nurse that was ministering to the pilot's injuries heard him rambling about the *Star Lance*. Not knowing exactly what he was ranting about, and having not yet received Commander Verne's gag order, she let it slip to a member of the maintenance crew, a Spacer First Class who was just getting over a case of Valuvian flu and had come in for a follow up visit. This Spacer had scarcely returned to his refueling duties in hangar bay two when he told four others what the nurse overheard. In a confined, isolated space, even one the size of the Black Hole, that was all it took to get the rumor mill going.

Even though no one aboard the Black Hole frequently talked to the Galactic Navy, Space Patrol liaison Lieutenant Commander Sergei Voroshilov was shrewd enough to figure out that something big was going on that he didn't know about, and that would not do. As soon as he finished the day's paper work (the Galactic Navy required copious records of the Space Patrol's goings on, in triplicate) he headed for Commander Verne's office.

Verne's office door opened at the Russian's approach.

Verne wanted nothing more than to dive into the nearest escape pod and head anywhere. The gravity well of a gas giant would be preferable to his own office at this moment.

Voroshilov stood in the open doorway for a few seconds, as if trying to read the secret in Verne's hard features. Then he stepped inside.

"Somebody here is keeping a secret."

"There was a slight burst of Hawking radiation near the coordinates the pilot gave us," said Betty-12. "I'm laying them in now." The Black Bird Five was still skipping through null space, headed toward the vague coordinates the pilot Nathan Rand gave them before drifting off into incoherent babbling.

"Why would the *Star Lance* be giving off Hawking radiation?" McCoy asked.

"I do not know, but I have a feeling we are about to find out."

The Black Bird Five emerged from null space within a few thousand kilometers of the coordinates. They were dangerously near Sector 12's

Oort cloud. Ahead of them out the viewport, Mars McCoy and Betty-12 could see dozens of blacker bulges against the blackness of space, while Black Bird Five's radar lit up hundreds more of the dirty snowballs that made up this system's ring of comets.

"Our friend must be a comet miner," said McCoy. "He never expected to find a ship out here. I'll bet he got too close before he knew what he had."

"I am detecting no signs of it now," said Betty-12. "No infrared, no radar blip, no radio bursts. It's like it was never here."

"The Oort cloud could be occluding it. We'll have to go in there."

"That is very dangerous."

McCoy sighed. "I know. But it has to be done. Prepare for evasive maneuvers."

"Roger," said Betty-12, her hands on the controls.

Slowly, cautiously, Mars McCoy guided Black Bird Five into the cloud of comets.

Lieutenant Voroshilov took a seat opposite Commander Verne's desk, his squat frame making him look even shorter than his five feet six inches. He continued to stare at Verne across the desk, like a boxer sizing up an opponent before the first round.

Verne swallowed hard. "What can I do for you today?"

"I have heard rumors," Voroshilov's thick Russian accent made the comment sound more threatening than it probably was, but this thought didn't comfort Verne in the least. He decided to play dumb, at least for now.

"What kind of rumors?"

"I think you know, Commander Verne," said Voroshilov icily. "And if this is something the Navy should know about, you need to tell me. Now."

Verne leaned back in his chair and breathed a heavy sigh. "Look. I don't know what you're talking about. If you'll excuse me, I'm very busy." He glanced down at some unimportant paperwork he had pushed around on his desk all day.

"The Navy will not be pleased that the Space Patrol is keeping secrets."

Verne sighed, tapping the metal fingers of his right hand on his desk. "It's nothing. McCoy and Lieutenant Betty rescued a ship pilot who had some crazy story. I sent them to check it out."

"What kind of crazy story?"

"Something about a ghost ship."

Voroshilov started, then grew silent. "Space is vast. There are many ghost stories."

"Yes there are," agreed Verne. "Would you like to tell me one?"

Voroshilov shrugged. "Not today."

"Then I guess we have nothing more to discuss."

Voroshilov nodded and stood. He left Verne's office without another word.

Verne leaned back in his chair and watched the Navy man go. *Good*, he thought. *Now it's his turn to sweat a little. The* Lance *was beyond top secret, in spite of half the galaxy swapping stories about its disappearance. If he would rather stay silent about what he knows than get useful intel the Navy would love to have, then that's his choice.*

Still, he did not like the thought of sending two of his best people into something they did not know about.

Navigating the comets that tumbled through space mere kilometers from Black Bird Five wasn't as easy as McCoy hoped, but it was challenging enough to appeal to his adventurous nature. Betty-12 manned the controls as she always did, showing no emotion. She could be walking down a maintenance corridor on the Black Hole for all the expression she showed. McCoy concentrated on the flight controls, relying on sight as much as the instruments; they were close enough to the dirty balls of ice that he could see them through Black Bird Five's forward viewport. Betty kept her robotic eyes on the instruments and weaponry. If a smaller comet got too close before they had time to maneuver away, she had standing orders to blast it into its constituent elements.

"Any signs of our quarry yet?" McCoy asked after they had been navigating through the comet field for an Earth standard hour.

"Not yet," said Betty-12. "Nothing but comets as far as the eye can see, and the sensors can detect."

McCoy grinned at his copilot's attempt at levity. "If she's in here, we'll find her. I'll bet our pilot friend got so excited he got too close to one of these snowballs. That's why his ship blew up."

"His ship's hull was fully intact," said Betty-12. "Comet impact does not explain what happened to his vessel."

"Well," said McCoy. "I guess that just leaves the curse."

"You humans are too superstitious," said his lovely copilot.

"Maybe. But I've heard plenty of stories about ships that encountered the *Star Lance* and were destroyed, and of crewmen that met with some violent end after returning home from their encounter. Stand by for emergency starboard burn." He hit the thrusters and the ship tilted wildly to the right as a ball of ice and rock twice as large as Black Bird Five soared past them.

"That was way too close. We'd better find that thing quick. These guys are getting thicker the further in we go."

"I just might have something," said Betty-12, glancing at her screen. "Twelve point one mark eight. Do you see it?"

"I don't see anything."

Betty-12 pressed buttons. "Going to infrared. There was something there for thirteen nanoseconds."

"You can measure time in nanoseconds?"

"Can't you?"

McCoy chuckled. "If you see it again for longer than thirteen nanoseconds, give me a holler."

"There it is again. This time at twenty-seven oh four mark two."

"That's nowhere near the first coordinates," complained McCoy as he piloted the Black Bird in the direction Betty-12 indicated.

"I know. But it's there."

"Well, then so are we."

What they saw defied all logic.

Ahead and above them was the largest ship Mars McCoy had ever seen. It was a long, dark needle with a bulge of drive clusters at one end, drifting at an odd angle among the comets that filled the Oort cloud. She was clearly battered and broken; large holes lined her bulk big enough to drive a Navy destroyer through. Comet shards and other debris drifted through those sections, like dust motes in a cathedral. The outer hull was severely charred and pockmarked by micrometeorite impacts from years in space.

"I hope there's enough left of her to get registry info for confirmation," said McCoy.

"Mr. Rand was obviously able to ID her. That should not be a problem."

McCoy moved them in closer. The comets were beginning to thin out, pushed aside by the *Lance's* defense fields, which had remained curiously in operation during its years adrift.

Finding it easier to maneuver, McCoy's curiosity was winning out over

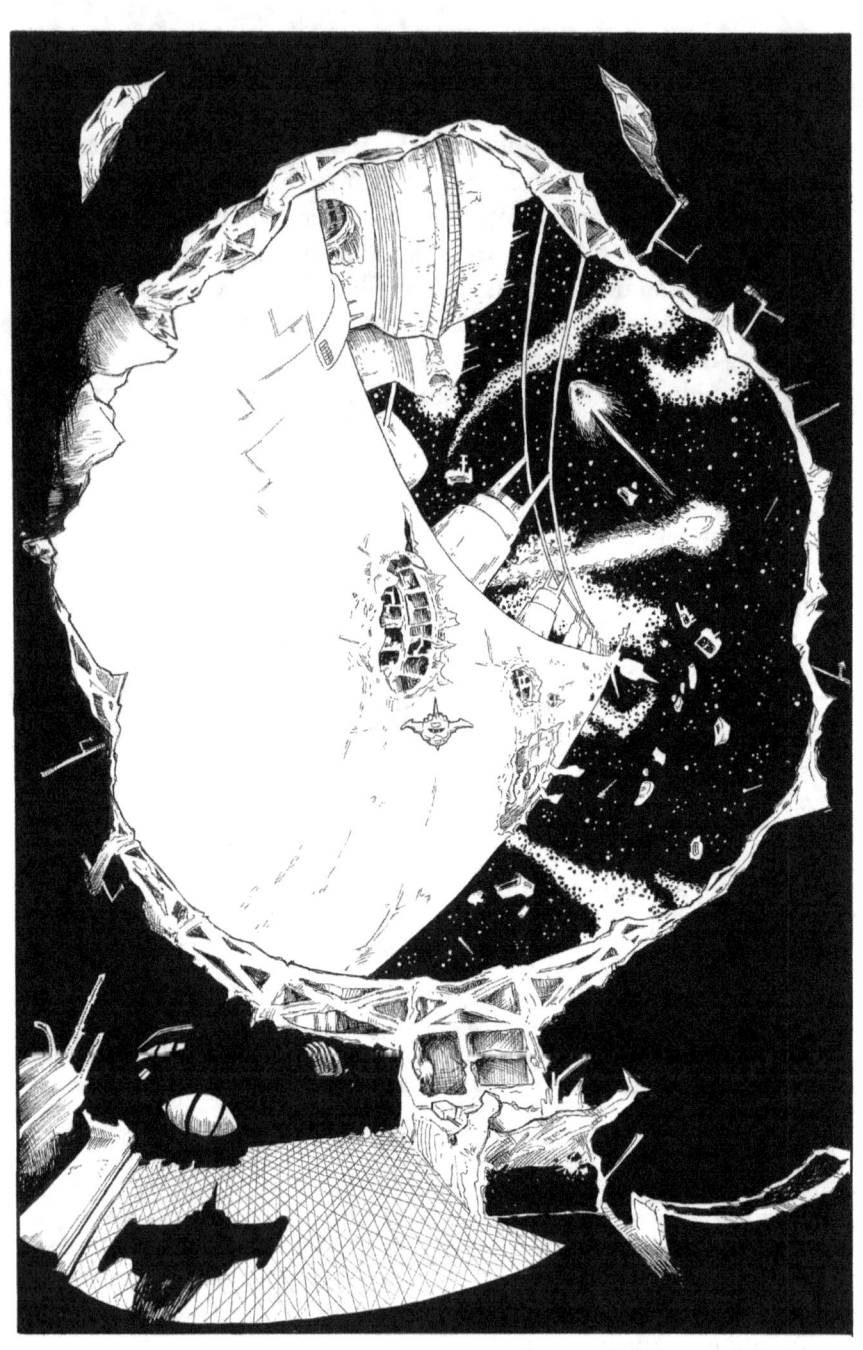

Ahead and above them was the largest ship Mars McCoy had ever seen.

his desire to avoid the curse, and he edged the ship closer.

"Look at her," he said. "She must have been some ship. I'll bet the Navy went nuts over losing her."

"They'll soon have her back."

McCoy frowned to think that the bureaucrats of the Galactic Navy would be getting their hands on it. The *Star Lance* was the stuff of legend, bigger than the Navy. Bigger than all of them.

"We have confirmation," said Betty-12. "Magnification of the hull shows a serial number still intact and legible. It is the *Star Lance*."

"Where have you been all this time?" McCoy said in a low voice, as if he was whispering to the ship. If Betty-12 noticed this strange human behavior, she didn't comment.

"Your orders, Captain?"

"Just like Verne said, contact him and hang tight."

"I'll raise him on the null radio now."

"Good," said McCoy. "In the meantime, let's check this baby out. From a safe distance, of course."

McCoy hit the rear thrusters, edging Black Bird Five closer to the derelict vessel.

"I am detecting null space distortion," said Betty-12, staring at her screens. "Also EM activity, especially on the radio end of the spectrum."

"The null space distortion could explain why Rand's null radio was acting up," said McCoy. He gritted his teeth and pushed the Black Bird closer. He thought about the rescued pilot and his ruined ship and wondered how he could keep them from suffering the same fate. Faint light from the system's distant sun limned the derelict in a ghostly glow. Seeing it here, like this, in one of the most unlikely of places gave McCoy an idea.

"Where was the *Star Lance* when it disappeared?"

Betty-12 paused, checking her internal memory banks. "It disappeared after entering null space, just after it left Hyben Station."

"And they got all the way out here in twenty-seven years?"

Betty-12 understood where he was going with this. "Drifting as it is, even at sub-light velocities, would take the *Star Lance* at least two hundred years to reach its current coordinates."

"Exactly. I think I know why so few people have ever stumbled onto her before."

Betty-12 nodded. "The null drive is still operational."

"Yes. That also explains why people all over the galaxy claim to have spotted her. She keeps skipping in and out of normal space."

Mars hit the com button on the null radio. "Black Bird Five to Black Hole. Come in, Black Hole."

"Black Hole here. What can we do for you, Captain McCoy?"

"Get Commander Verne on the double. I have a private, his ears only message."

"Roger."

While they waited, McCoy scanned the derelict *Star Lance* with his naked eye, admiring the Navy's handiwork. For a bunch of bureaucrats, they had created the deadliest piece of flying steel he had ever seen. The *Lance* was listing horribly, punched through with holes, but everywhere McCoy could still see signs that this had once been a grand ship, and he wondered why the Navy never commissioned another to replace it.

McCoy and Betty-12 watched as the ship rolled past them, the light of this system's distant star illuminating shattered conning bubbles, gun turrets bristling with blast-cannons, and protrusions containing sensor arrays. A small comet about the size of Black Bird Five caromed soundlessly off one of the sensor nodules, sending ice bits flying that shimmered like sparks of electricity.

"She's a real beauty, isn't she?"

"I do not understand the question. The *Star Lance* is perfectly symmetrical, if that's what you mean."

McCoy scowled. "What is taking them so long to get Verne on the radio?"

"It's this null space distortion. I suppose we were lucky to get through at all.

"B-black . . . to ack Bird . . .," the null radio sputtered as it came to life.

"Black Bird Five here," said McCoy. "We have found the *Star Lance*. I repeat. We have found the *Star Lance*."

"Holding position," said Betty-12. "The null space distortion is waning here."

More static from the null radio. Then, "Sit tight, McCoy." It was Commander Verne's voice. "We're . . . inging the lack Hole . . . you."

"Did I hear that right? He's bringing the entire Black Hole here?"

"That is what I gathered."

"Roger that, Commander."

"That's probably a good idea," said McCoy. "We've got pirates."

"What? Where?"

McCoy pointed off to their right; a rainbow spiral of light, the telltale sign of null space distortion, had just appeared, ejecting a familiar and lethal-looking attack cruiser.

"It's the *Purge*," said Betty-12, noticing the ship's telltale pirate markings.

"The Star Tigress!" shouted McCoy. "She must have gotten Rand's distress signal too. This makes things much more interesting."

"Their blast-cannons are energized," said Betty-12, checking her instruments.

"Wait," said McCoy. "Don't we even get a hello?"

"I don't think Captain Yin is in the mood for pleasantries. Recommend evasive maneuvers."

McCoy glanced at his copilot. "You think?"

The *Purge* fired its forward blaster-cannons, the yellow beams of energy searing through space just ahead of them, melting comet fragments instantly in their wake.

"Whoa," said McCoy. "That was close enough to blister the paint."

"They are hailing us."

"Put it on screen."

A small section of Black Bird Five's viewport vanished and was replaced by the darkened interior of the pirate ship. Framed in the middle of the viewer was the beautiful face of Captain Sonya Yin, her long blue-black hair twisted into a tight ponytail. Her eyes widened when she saw just who she was dealing with. "McCoy," she hissed. "We have legal claim to this wreckage."

McCoy shook his head. "Sonya, Sonya, Sonya. When did pirates start making legal claims?"

Captain Yin visibly bristled at McCoy's use of her first name, but said nothing.

"This is property of the Galactic Navy, and therefore is exempt from any salvage claims made against it. Besides, everyone who ever found it died or went insane. You want to be next on that list?"

"If anyone dies here today, McCoy, it will be you. Now stay out of my way or get your molecules scattered among these comets."

McCoy tousled his thick red hair and gave his best boyish, devil-may-care grin. "As fun as that sounds, I think we'll pass."

Sonya Yin gave a long, icy laugh. "Such bravado. You're all alone out here, McCoy. It's just you and your robot."

"That won't be the case for long, my dear," said McCoy. Out of viewer range, he gave a subtle hand signal to his copilot, who stared unbelieving at him for a second before punching in a few commands on her console. The lovely face in the viewer scowled at him. Then, strangely, Captain Yin gave a savage smile.

"Then I suppose we must speed up our salvage operations. Goodbye, Mars McCoy."

The viewer flicked off abruptly. "Punch it!" yelled McCoy as he grabbed the controls.

He pushed full power to the Black Bird's thrusters, the coordinates Betty-12 had entered seconds ago taking them into a section of the *Star Lance* that was open to space.

Captain Sonya Yin glared after the tiny ship as it disappeared into the derelict battleship. The blaster fire her gunners sent toward the Black Bird's location passed harmlessly through space and destroyed a large comet fragment. "You'll not get away that easily," she hissed through gritted teeth. "Move us alongside."

"But, Captain," whined one of her crew—a little Ban called Weenzil.

"What is it?"

"The *Lance* is leaving." He pointed toward the readouts on the massive console in front of them. The telltale early signs of null space distortion were erupting into being around the dead vessel. By the time Yin looked out their viewport, the *Star Lance* was gone.

It took the crew of the Black Hole three hours to find out the *Star Lance* had been sighted. Voroshilov wasn't pleased, even though he suspected as much from Verne's comment about a ghost ship and his unwillingness to give the Russian the details. But when he contacted Navy Headquarters, his superiors kindly thanked him and told him to keep them informed. Which was a nice way of saying, "Don't bother us with crazy talk about ghost ships." Smiling, he called back his superiors at the Navy with the news that the *Star Lance* was found once again. This time, possibly for good.

Mars McCoy and Betty-12 were surprised to see how much of the *Star Lance* was still intact. They were inside what appeared to be a large cargo hold. A few ships sat silently in their docking clamps, looking as if they had never been flown. Nearby, held tightly beneath heavy netting, were stranger objects McCoy couldn't identify.

"I detect some power fluctuations," noted Betty-12. "Sections of this vessel are still operational, including basic life support and gravity."

"Great. That's a comfort, at least."

"The null engines are engaged," Betty-12 went on. "We have skipped out of normal space."

McCoy guided Black Bird Five into a docking area, clamps in the floor automatically slamming around the ship's landing gear. "That explains why the *Purge* isn't firing on us or following us in. This hold is certainly big enough."

"Any survivors?"

Betty-12 checked her instruments. "No life signs."

Then McCoy got an idea.

"What if we could fly this thing?"

His robot copilot looked at him. "That is unlikely. According to the stories, this ship has an experimental drive. We don't know how it works."

McCoy shrugged. "We'll learn."

Within seconds, McCoy was out of his seat and donning his space suit, all thoughts of the alleged curse gone from his mind. After a moment, Betty-12 stood and did likewise. As a robot, she didn't really need it, but the helmet would allow her to talk to McCoy in the airless cargo hold.

Suddenly, McCoy felt a wave of dizziness wash over him. The ship shook for a second, but nothing rattled, no gear was knocked out of place. His vision blurred, as if reality itself was rippling like a pond into which a stone has been thrown, just as the pilot Rand had described.

"Did you feel that?"

"Yes," said Betty-12. "Another skip, perhaps?"

"I've never felt a skip like *that*."

Just then the viewport of Black Bird Five was flooded in bright, white light. It was coming from the entryway to the cargo hold. A small figure stood in the center of that light.

"I thought you said there were no life signs aboard."

"There were none." Betty-12 walked back to her copilot seat, glanced at the console. "Now, the readings are...mixed."

"Mixed?"

"Yes. Uncertain."

Mars shrugged and checked his blaster pistol. "Then let's go say hello."

They exited the ship, blasters drawn. Large sections of the hangar bay were open to space, but the artificial gravity was working. The figure before them did not move. The light that engulfed the cargo hold was very bright, but not painful to look at. It illuminated the cargo stowed beneath the thick netting, and McCoy glanced at it as they walked past. It appeared to be an assemblage of asteroids, with glints of dull metal poking through the black crust. Sections of the metal protruded from the rock at right angles. It looked old, and manmade.

As they closed on the dark figure they began to make out more details. It was humanoid, with pale yellow, metallic-looking skin, and it stared at the Rangers with huge, pupil-less golden eyes. Around it an aura of energy shimmered faintly.

"A Faash'Tan," said Betty-12.

The being nodded, as if he heard her through her helmet in the airless cargo hold. When they finally got close enough to see the alien in complete detail, he smiled at them and nodded. The voice they heard next seemed to come as much from inside their heads as from their helmet radios or from the airless void. "Greetings, Mars McCoy."

Mars frowned, studying the odd being. A faint memory tugged at his thoughts, and with that memory there came a name.

"Monaik?"

The Faash'Tan nodded again.

"Why do I feel like I should know you? And—what are you doing here?"

"I came to this *now* to deliver a message. You are in danger."

"Huh?"

"You are out of *space* now, and out of *time*."

"What?"

"You don't have much time. You are out of the *now*."

Mars glanced at at Betty-12. "Do you have any idea what he's talking about?"

The statuesque copilot shook her head.

"They see, but they do not understand. I came to this *now* to tell you this ship is dangerous. You are not Faash'Tan. You do not understand how to move through *not-space* and *not-time*."

"Monaik, what in the Twelve Moons of Almagurdi are you babbling about? Stop the riddles and tell it to us straight."

McCoy could now hazily recall other encounters with this being; he also remembered why the Faash'Tan's cryptic visits annoyed him. It was always like this with Monaik; you could never get a straight answer. Of course, what could he expect from a member of a race that had left the physical constraints of the universe behind when McCoy's ancestors were still painting cave walls? A people who flitted about space without ships as easily as mankind could walk across a room?

"We have skipped into null space, haven't we?" Betty-12 asked, hoping a more direct line of questioning could get a straight answer.

The Faash'Tan shook his yellow head. "Not null space. *Not-space.*"

"Oooookay," said McCoy. "This is getting us nowhere. Monaik, why are you here? What do you want?"

"To warn you."

"Wait," said Betty-12. "I understand. We are in a region of the space-time continuum the Faash'Tan call *not-space.*"

Monaik nodded. "Not-space isn't safe. You are not alone here. The crew of this ship found out too late."

Monaik looked down at the grey deck plating, shuffled his strangely booted feet.

"You tried to warn them," Mars said.

The Faash'Tan nodded. "Was not meant to be."

"When?"

Monaik looked up at him. "Now. There is only now. You are in danger. You are not alone here."

"Who is here with us?"

Monaik looked at Betty-12, then back to McCoy. "You have an old Earth saying. Ghosts in the machine. Beware the ghosts in the machine, Marshall McCoy."

"Huh?"

"If we are in danger, we can't stay here," Betty-12 interjected. "We must take control of the ship and skip back into normal space."

McCoy nodded, glancing at his copilot. "Agreed. Monaik? Do you know where the bridge is on this thing?"

But when he looked back, the alien was gone.

Now that the word was officially out, the Black Hole was on the move. Commander Verne was busy shouting commands while Voroshilov communicated with his superiors in the Navy, coordinating their response. Both men did everything they could to stay out of the other's way.

Meanwhile, others were making plans of their own. On the planet Brigand, the space pirates buzzed with the news, and made preparations for the greatest haul in history, while an Orgum-Ree vessel skipped into null space near their homeworld, on the way to sector twelve's Oort cloud.

Cautiously, Mars McCoy and Betty-12 made their way toward the point of the *Star Lance*'s needle, where they felt the bridge must be. It was slow going. Sometimes they would get halfway down a dark corridor only to find it blocked off by a twisted bulkhead too heavy for Betty-12 to move. Other times they would find the next few meters ahead of them opened to vacuum, though some sort of energy field continued operating to keep these areas sealed off, like a tourniquet for an amputated limb.

Nothing felt right. McCoy couldn't put his finger on it, but he knew that something was strange and different. He didn't need Monaik to tell him that they weren't in normal space—or even null–space. He also had the feeling they were being watched. "How much farther do you think it is?"

"Unknown," said Betty-12. "We are not exactly working from a map here."

"Was that another joke?"

Just then the ship shook; a jarring shudder that reverberated through the vessel like the shiver of a giant. McCoy could hear strange sounds too, echoing through the walls and coming up through his boots to his ears.

"What do you think Monaik meant about us not being alone?"

"I do not want to be here long enough for that to be a concern."

"Let's keep moving, then. The sooner we get to the bridge, the sooner we can figure out what's going on."

Another shudder almost knocked them to the deck. Betty-12 grabbed McCoy's gloved hand and helped to hold him steady until it passed.

"Perhaps after twenty-seven years, this vessel is merely falling apart," she offered.

"Sure, that's a comforting thought. Let's hang on to that, shall we?"

The lights in their suits picked out a partially open door to their left. Betty-12 used her robot strength to slide the door open, and their suit lights picked out what kept it from closing completely.

On the floor was a space-suited figure, its arm sticking through the now fully open doorway.

Betty 12 knelt to examine the corpse, turning it over. The bubble helmet was smashed, and what was left of the doomed form was little more than a mummy. Leathery skin stretched tightly over a skull cracked open like an egg, the face a ghastly rictus of frozen agony.

"Humanoid," said Betty-12 emotionlessly, while Mars McCoy stood back in horror, his eyes scanning the rest of the room. He let his suit lights illuminate what appeared to be a large galley or mess hall. Metal tables and stools were upended or tossed into corners, their legs bent and mangled. Among them were dozens of bodies.

"Some of these aren't wearing spacesuits," said McCoy.

Overcoming his initial shock and revulsion, he stepped over the threshold and inspected the bodies more closely. He recognized the Navy colors circa thirty years ago. "Some of the ship's crew. But who are all these other guys?"

There were space-suited bodies slumped and piled among the other remains. A few he recognized, such as a four-armed figure that could only be a Trenago. Others were completely unknown to him, and would be to anyone in the Empire of Man. He walked toward a large, hulking shape, in a suit of some heavy grey material with a large black bubble helmet that blocked the intrusion of McCoy's suit lights. The suit was covered in strange markings and had shoulder pads covered in lethal-looking spikes. The front of the suit was ripped open as if by sharp talons. McCoy gulped. Despite his training and experience, he wouldn't want to meet this guy in a dark alley on Brigand, but something had torn him open like a ration packet.

"Whoever this person was," said Betty-12 of the corpse in the doorway, "he wasn't Navy."

"There are a lot of people here who weren't Navy," said McCoy. "They must have stumbled upon the *Lance* just like that pilot we rescued."

Betty-12 nodded. "Your orders?"

"Let's keep going, find the bridge before whatever did this comes back."

As they started to leave the galley-turned-charnel house, McCoy's right boot came down on something hard and metallic. He stepped back to shine his suit lines on it. It was a mechanical hand that had been ripped violently from its owner. "Let's go," said McCoy.

The chime in Commander H.G. Verne's office rang. Annoyed, he jabbed the comm button with his thumb. "Yes?"

"It's the pilot we rescued, Sir," said a woman's voice. "You wanted to be advised of his condition."

"And?" Verne snapped.

"He's dying."

Verne headed for sickbay, with Lieutenant Commander Voroshilov hot on his heels.

Nathan Rand looked worse than when he was brought in, his eyes sunken and staring wildly, his sweaty face ashen. His arms were extended toward the asteroid rock ceiling, his fingers bent into cruel talons.

"*They are in danger!*" the patient shouted.

"What's he going on about?" Verne demanded.

"He's been like this for the past five minutes," said the nurse. "His vitals are dropping. We're trying to stabilize him but..."

"*Outside time. Outside space!*"

The nurse dialed up a sedative on the life support console at the pilot's bedside and poised her hand over the inject button. "I'm going to sedate him."

"Beware the ghosts. *Ghosts in the machine!*"

"Wait," said Voroshilov, grasping the nurse's hand in his iron grip. "Let him speak."

"But he's in pain, Sir." The nurse glanced hesitantly at Verne since Voroshilov wasn't her commanding officer.

Verne looked at Voroshilov. "This is pointless. The guy's feverish. He doesn't know what he's saying."

Voroshilov narrowed his eyes and looked at the ranting pilot. "Who is in danger?"

The pilot continued staring at the ceiling, his face a mask of agony. But he heard and understood the question. "Captain McCoy...and that pretty copilot."

"In danger from what?

The pilot's look of comprehension turned once again to madness. "Lurkers beyond time. Eater of space!" He grabbed Commander Verne by his uniform front, pulled him toward him. "Ghosts. The Lurker in Darkness!"

Then the pilot's body convulsed, his back arching in pain. "*Beware the Lurker beyond the stars! The Eater of Space!*"

Verne pulled himself free as the nurse hit the inject button, but there

"Beware the Lurker beyond the stars! The Eater of Space!"

was no need. The pilot was dead.

"What happened?" yelled Verne.

The nurse checked her readouts. "Massive heart attack "

Voroshilov turned and walked out of the sickbay.   Grumbling, Commander Verne followed.

"You mind translating that mumbo jumbo for me?" he said, catching up to the Russian.

"I do not know what you are talking about."

"Don't give me that." Verne grasped the shorter man's shoulder with the iron grip of his mechanical arm, twisting him about. He was met by a cold stare.

"You know more about this than you're letting on, and if two of my people could be in danger because of it, I want to know."

"If Captain McCoy is in danger it is only because he acts rashly, and without thought."

"What do you know about the *Star Lance*?"

Voroshilov looked down at the floor, then back at Verne. Then he looked around quickly and stepped closer to Verne.

"I was in the running to be an officer aboard the *Star Lance*," he said in a low voice. "I've seen some of the specs. Most of them were classified beyond top secret, especially those dealing with propulsion, power and weapons systems. Only crew assigned to those areas would learn the details, and then only after they were aboard."

"And?" whispered Verne.

"I saw enough. The *Lance* contained alien technology. Highly advanced."

Verne nodded. "We've all heard the stories. What else is new?"

Voroshilov shook his head. "The stories say that we used Faash'Tan technology. This isn't true. We don't know what it is. We found a remote alien planet, the remains of a long dead, highly advanced civilization. Makes what Faash'Tan tech we've seen look like an old Earth internal combustion engine."

"The Navy lost a lot when she disappeared," said Verne. "They'll want it back."

Voroshilov nodded. "And other races will want it as well."

Now it was Verne's turn to nod. "I've already thought of that possibility. I sent McCoy and Lieutenant Betty-12 to find the *Lance* and sit on it until we get there."

"If pirates or the Orgum-Ree find out it was spotted, your people will need help."

"Call who you need to," said Verne. "I'm moving the Black Hole to Sector 12's Oort cloud."

"You'll help us retrieve the *Lance*."

"I'll help rescue my people, if it comes to that. If the Navy gets its top secret toy back, so much the better. Now let's get going."

McCoy and Betty-12 finally reached the bridge. It was intact, and flooded with the same white light they had seen earlier.

It was coming through the forward viewport, an almost all-consuming whiteness punctuated here and there by black motes.

"It is like space in reverse," said Betty-12. "White space and black stars."

McCoy nodded. "So this is what not-space looks like." Turning to his copilot, he said, "How soon can we be underway?"

Betty-12 was already walking around the large bridge, looking over the controls. "I do not know. There is power to many of these consoles, but I am at a loss as to their purpose."

McCoy glanced around, nodding. He had been on board his share of Galactic Navy vessels, but he had never seen a bridge quite like this one. The *Star Lance* was experimental in every way, it seemed. "Well, let's do the best we can. If we can just shut down the skip engine, return to normal space, we'll let the Navy sort it out."

"I believe I have identified those controls. Along with some alien circuitry."

"Alien? You mean Faash'Tan."

"Negative. This is more advanced than what we know of Faash'Tan technology."

"That isn't much." McCoy plopped himself down in the captain's chair. "We've got gravity. What about life support?"

"We have basic life support. Oxygen and heating are fully operational."

"Good," said Mars, removing his helmet. "I was getting claustrophobic." He sniffed the air cautiously. It was a little stale, but breathable, and the temperature, while cool, was comfortable. "You know, I'm wondering why we have any power at all. Even a Navy battle cruiser can't go twenty-seven years without refueling. And what about that force field around the damaged areas?"

"Perhaps those are some of the experimental, top secret features."

The *Lance* shuddered once more, a jarring motion that sent a section of the ceiling over the right rear area of the bridge crashing to the floor and sparks flying.

"We need to know what's causing that," said McCoy.

"If I had to guess," said Betty-12, pointing toward the viewport, "I would say *that* is the cause."

Mars followed her gaze toward the viewport and saw something there that chilled his blood.

When the Black Hole exited null space it was not alone. A Navy battle group of five attack cruisers formed a defensive perimeter along the outer edge of the Oort cloud, while a hundred thousand kilometers away three Orgum-Ree destroyers and four pirate vessels waited just outside the Oort cloud.

"This should be interesting," muttered Commander Verne darkly. "Voroshilov!"

"Da."

Verne winced, turned around. "It looks like the entire Fringe knows about the *Star Lance*."

"Yes. But the Navy will crush our opposition and reclaim the *Lance*."

Commander Verne shook his head. "It's going to be an absolute bloodbath to get to that point. All personnel! Battle stations!"

The hangar bay was filled with running men and women, both human, alien and robot, rushing to their fueled and ready Black Birds and preparing for takeoff.

Voroshilov barked similar orders to his comrades aboard the Navy frigates and battle cruisers that hovered within just a few thousand kilometers of the three massive Orgum-Ree ships, their strangely shaped spires and protrusions bristling with weaponry.

One of the pirate ships skipped away into null space, its cowardly captain no longer lured by the easy pickings an unprotected, derelict *Star Lance* would offer. The rest of them closed in fast, hitting one of the Orgum-Ree ships with blaster-cannon fire.

"The pirate ship *Pulse* is deeper within the Oort cloud," said the Black Hole's tactical officer. "We're not picking up any other ships."

"Not even a Black Bird?" asked Verne worriedly.

"No Sir."

Verne sighed. "Thank you, Lieutenant. Voroshilov. How do you want to play this?"

"The *Star Lance* is top secret classified property of the Galactic Navy and *cannot* fall into alien hands."

"You mean enemy hands."

"Yes, of course."

Verne narrowed his eyes at the Russian. The man had always been a xenophobe, but it might get the better of him here. "Launch all Black Birds. I want the *Star Lance* secured."

With a roar of thrusters every Black Bird aboard the Black Hole launched into space, blaster cannons at the ready. The Orgum-Ree ships responded in kind, opening up to belch forth swarms of insect-like vessels that spit a blaster fire.

"Tell the Navy to get chatty with the Orgum-Ree homeworld," said Verne, "or we're gonna have an intergalactic incident on our hands."

Voroshilov nodded, still barking commands and answering questions from unseen parties, holding an earbud in his right ear.

The Orgum-Ree launched smaller vessels, sleek craft that looked lethal to the touch. One of the Black Birds disappeared in a blossom of fire, seconds before an answering volley from that ship's wing man sent the Orgum-Ree attackers into oblivion.

"This is going from bad to worse really quick," said Verne, pacing the Black Hole's command center, his boots thudding heavily against the deck plates.

"The Orgum-Ree are demanding we share the *Star Lance*'s technology with them," said Voroshilov, his hand touching the earbud inside his right ear.

"They are, huh?" said Verne, annoyed. He knew what the expansionist Orgum-Ree meant by *share*.

Voroshilov nodded. "They think we are going to use the *Lance* to destroy them."

"That's crazy! We've had good relations with them for a hundred years."

"We've had *strained* relations with them for a hundred years," Voroshilov corrected.

Verne stared at Voroshilov for a long moment. He knew they had to keep the *Star Lance* out of enemy hands, especially pirates. But what they were doing here could spark an interplanetary war, and he didn't need that on his conscience. He also didn't need some Navy lackey to tell him their relationship with the Orgum-Ree was tenuous at best, and that most of the mantis-like aliens would rather eat a human than look at one.

"Let's destroy the *Lance*," he said at last. "That will show the Orgum-Ree that we can't destroy them with something we don't have, and those blasted space pirates will no longer have a target for their greed. Then we'll blast *those* thugs back to Brigand."

Voroshilov shook his head slowly. "My orders are to retrieve the *Star Lance* intact."

Verne grumbled. "Very well. It's Navy property, so it's their show. But I'm not going to put my men in danger just so the Navy can have their toy back."

Voroshilov scowled and went back to coordinating with the Navy fleet. The velvet blackness outside the Black Hole's viewport was alive with blaster fire and tiny dots exploding as they were hit. The Navy vessels clearly took the lead, firing on the Orgum-Ree and pirate ships with equal ferocity. Verne hoped this wouldn't turn into a galactic incident followed by years of war, but he was glad for the extra firepower.

"Where is McCoy?" he asked the busy command center.

McCoy stood frozen, staring at the horror that looked back at them through the viewport.

It was an enormous eye—or, more aptly, a hideous caricature of an eye. A vast grey bulk was shoved against the viewport, which held a gigantic pus-white orb that took up the center portion of the viewport. It quivered as it fixed them in its inscrutable gaze. McCoy had never been so frightened. He felt like the ant being stared down by a petulant child with a magnifying glass. The eye appeared blind, but it looked upon them with such malevolence that McCoy *knew* with every fiber of his being that he and Betty-12 were being watched.

"It appears Monaik was right," said Betty-12 without emotion. "We are not alone."

Then, strangely, suddenly, the thing vanished.

"Either we both really saw something," said McCoy. "Or we're both going nuts."

"Robots cannot go nuts."

"That doesn't make me feel any better. I want to know exactly what happened here."

"We should be able to pull the ship's logs," said Betty-12. "Whatever happened to the crew and the ship couldn't have happened all at once."

"Let's do it. The Navy keeps meticulous records; this ship would have been no different, no matter what strangeness they ran into."

McCoy sat in the captain's chair and reviewed the console before him. A diagram of the ship was lit up, showing sections of the hull that were breached. These areas were outlined in red, and McCoy surmised that this indicated the force field which seemed to protect the rest of the ship from the vacuum of space, while letting Black Bird Five pass through. But there were other strange things he didn't recognize as being part of any ship he was familiar with.

"Lieutenant."

Betty-12 walked over next to him and looked at the diagram.

"What do you make of this?" McCoy pointed to the section containing the engine room, where a small white dot pulsed and flickered.

"A power source?"

McCoy nodded. "Could be that experimental drive the legends mention. I sure would like to get a look at that thing."

"It is not essential to our mission. I'm sure the Navy would take offense."

"I know. I'll get the ship's logs called up; you work on getting us out of wherever we are."

"Aye," said Betty-12 and went back to work at the navigation console.

McCoy familiarized himself with the captain's console, which really wasn't much different from the usual Navy or Space Patrol technology he knew. Another minute and he had found the last thing the captain had worked on.

The viewer flickered to life, replacing the weird white light streaming through the viewport with the interior of the bridge.

A tall, middle-aged man with a military buzz cut stood before the log recorder camera.

"Ship's log," he said. "This is Captain John Bryson. It has been almost thirty-six hours since the anomaly—as our science officer has termed it—occurred. We don't know where we are, or how to get back, but we know that we are in a region of space, perhaps an area of the space-time continuum, that is unknown to science."

The captain paused, lifted his left arm at the elbow, flexing his artificial hand. McCoy gasped. He stepped on that same mechanical hand in the mess hall.

"Our science officer believes what happened has something to do with the experimental drive we were testing as part of our mission. The alien technology we reverse-engineered makes use of a quantum singularity for power, and there were unforeseen side effects to using this power source."

Captain Bryson looked down at the floor, lost in thought. "We will try shutting down the drive, to see if that returns us to regular space. With any luck, my next log entry will be done with the *Lance* safely in space dock. Bryson out."

"I know what that dot on the engine room diagram is," said Betty-12.

Before McCoy could ask what she meant, another log began playing.

"Ship's log, Captain John Bryson speaking. Our attempt to shut down the singularity has failed, but the ship has skipped, at least temporarily, into regular space. We are now attempting to make contact with someone who can help us, but there is a great deal of null space distortion emanating, we believe, from the singularity."

The log broke off suddenly, and was quickly replaced by the next entry on the list, which was posted three days later.

"We skipped again. We are in a unknown region of space. The positions of the stars don't match our charts, and the ones that do are so far from where our charts say they should be that our science officer, Lieutenant Tracer, believes we may have skipped through time as well. I am inclined to believe him, as the stars are redshifted as well. I think we have skipped to the end of time. The crew is uneasy, and my officers and I fear mutiny."

The next log began, showing a very different officer. He stared, red-eyed, looking as if he hadn't slept in days. He was unshaven and his body shook nervously as he talked, his voice a stage whisper.

"It has been . . . I don't know. Months. Years. Does it even matter anymore? My crew, my officers, have all turned against me. My science officer has immersed himself in the alien tech. It has totally consumed him. He has a strange light in his eyes, and he speaks sometimes in an unknown tongue our ship's translator can't decipher. He brings others to his cause. They huddle in groups of three or four in the corridors, and there are symbols and markings on the walls of their crew quarters, and in the engine room. They look like circuit diagrams, and they are scrawled in metallic ink. When the lights dim during the day crew's sleep cycle, the diagrams have a faint glow. I think Tracer tapped into the ship's power source with them somehow, and they are doing something to the ship... to the crew.

"At first, we thought Tracer was coming down with space psychosis. I put him on light duty and the ship's physician put him on anti-depression meds. Then I found him in his quarters scrawling numbers on his walls. Prime numbers. He didn't stop until he listed every prime number he could think of. The man was always brilliant; now I fear he has gone mad. God and the Emperor help me, I thought he would get better. We needed him. I put him back on duty. Oh, God!"

Captain Bryson paused now, putting his good hand to his forehead and mopping sweat from his high brow.

"I don't know how Tracer turned them against me. He told them he saw something in his quarters. Something that frightened him and gave him hope at the same time. He said he knew what happened to the aliens on that long-dead world where we found the singularity technology. He said they weren't dead. He said he knew how to get us home, and that if we helped the aliens, they would help us."

Captain Bryson paused again, as if collecting his thoughts.

McCoy glanced at Betty-12, who busied herself with the engine controls while she kept an eye on the viewer. Her face showed no emotion. McCoy envied her emotional detachment.

Captain Bryson mopped his brow again and continued. "There is talk of an Eater of Space. Tracer saw it in his quarters, and now others have seen it as well. Tracer said it could take us home, and he spent every moment dissecting the alien tech. I tried to stop him, throw him in the brig, but my officers and men-at-arms had already turned against me. They confined *me* to quarters instead.

"The ship continues to skip in and out of null space, going God knows where, while the crew busy themselves with carrying out Tracer's insane wishes. They gather in the mess hall, which is near my quarters, and I can hear them chanting sometimes in that alien tongue Tracer sometimes spoke in the beginning. I can't sleep when they do that. But what's even worse is what they say in Standard English. I can hear them saying 'Eater,' 'Eater,' Eater'."

"They are going to come for me. I know. Eaters need food. Someone's coming!"

The ship's log had come to an end. There were no more entries. The viewer flicked off, leaving them with a clear view of the strangeness outside. McCoy was pleased that the thing they had seen earlier was still nowhere to be seen.

"The captain went nuts."

"It sounds like the entire crew became insane," observed Betty-12.

"So," said McCoy, eager to change the subject. "Can we get out of here?"

"Unknown. We can probably get the thrusters going, assuming enough of them are still intact, but the skip engine is already unstable. Even if we can leave *not-space*, as Monaik called it, there is no way to be certain where we will end up."

"I'm more worried about being anywhere that thing outside is. Set a course for anywhere but here."

Betty-12 turned and stared at her commanding officer, not comprehending. Then she nodded and sat down at a console, pressing buttons.

There was a shudder far to their rear, and McCoy was pleased that even in a ship this size he could still feel the familiar vibration of a ship's thrusters.

"Nice job, Lieutenant," said McCoy.

"That wasn't me," said Betty-12. "The thrusters engaged on their own. Something else is operating the *Star Lance*'s thrusters and feeding it navigational data."

McCoy ran to Betty-12's side at the helm. "Can we stop it?"

"Negative. Controls are not responding. Skip engine is engaging."

They watched through the viewport as the familiar rainbow-colored hole opened in front of the ship and enveloped it. When the light faded they were in what appeared to be normal space.

"I wonder if the science officer, Tracer, hardwired this puppy to work from the engine room," said McCoy.

"It is a possibility," said Betty-12.

"Maybe we can shut it down from there."

McCoy picked up his helmet and placed it over his head, listening for the telltale snap and hiss of the environmental seal closing itself, while Betty-12 did likewise.

"Make sure your blaster is ready," said McCoy. "We don't know who or what we're going to find down there."

Betty-12 checked the diagram of the *Star Lance* before they left the bridge, memorizing the way to the engine room. As they made their way through now-familiar sections of corridor, McCoy noticed how much easier it was, because they knew which paths were clear of obstructions, at least for now. In minutes they were back at the mess hall with its pile of bodies. Without looking at the decades-old carnage within, they turned right at the next junction, continuing onward toward the engine room.

McCoy started feeling edgy, the short hairs on the back of his neck tingling. He placed a ready hand on his blaster.

"Betty, ever get the feeling you're being watched?"

"I have heard other humans speak of this phenomena. Do all members of your species believe they are psychic?"

Something lunged from the shadows, slamming into Betty-12 and knocking her to the deck.

McCoy instinctively drew his blaster as an ungodly screech pierced the darkness. He trained his suit lights on the blackness ahead of him, but saw only more darkness. Betty-12 was sitting up now, her gaze focused on the grim corridor ahead.

"Are you all right?"

"I am undamaged." Betty-12 quickly stood, here eyes scanning the darkness ahead of them.

"It's gone," said McCoy.

"It's there."

Betty-12 pointed to the path in front of them, her mechanical eyes doubtlessly discerning what McCoy's human eyes could not. "It's watching us."

McCoy squinted into the gloom. His suit lights could make out nothing ahead but a section of corridor lined with dusty, dented storage lockers. "I don't see anything."

"Even so, it is there." She drew her blaster. "Clearly the creature we saw outside the ship isn't the only denizen of not-space."

McCoy nodded. "I wonder why we're just encountering them now."

"Perhaps they were attracted to the ship when it appeared, and had time to reach it since it has lingered here."

"I don't want to take any of them back with us," said McCoy. "Come on. We're ready for him now."

They walked side by side, helmet lights scanning every turn and bend and opening large enough to conceal any would-be attacker. Except for a quick thudding as of scurrying feet, they found no sign of the creature following its attack on Betty-12.

"I think it attacked out of fear," said the robot.

"Let's be careful, though."

"Agreed."

They had traveled another hundred yards when all hell broke loose.

The inky black, comet-strewn vacuum outside the Black Hole's viewport

"Something lunged from the shadows…knocking her to the deck."

was alive with blaster fire.

The pirates, oddly enough, were the ones with the weakest stomachs for fighting. They had the numbers but were unable to form a cohesive attack formation, and had to dodge not only the Space Patrol, the Navy and the Orgum-Ree, but also each other in their mad attempts to obtain the ultimate prize: the *Star Lance*. One ship skipped back to Brigand the second both the Navy and Orgum-Ree ships fired on it. Another tried to make a break for the comet field and the treasure it contained, but were pushed back by the Patrol's quick cordon of the area. No one dared skipping through null space to the *Star Lance*'s coordinates. Skipping into a comet-riddled Oort cloud wasn't a good idea under any circumstances.

"Someone get me McCoy!" Verne snapped.

"He isn't answering!" someone called back in the crowded command center. Verne took a deep breath, his eyes glued to the viewport and the frightening scene unfolding there. He hoped McCoy was all right.

Again, the thing attacked.

It lunged from the shadows, hitting the robot copilot and knocking her blaster from her hand to skitter across the deck.

McCoy aimed at the darkness and fired, the yellow energy blast piercing the gloom as it lanced down the hallway to strike a ruined bulkhead a hundred feet in front of them. Again they heard that terrible screeching as McCoy knelt to help his copilot to her feet.

"Thank you," she said tersely.

McCoy retrieved her blaster from where it fell and handed it to her. She checked its charge and moved forward. Her suit was slashed along her right shoulder, but she was otherwise unharmed.

"I think it is playing with us," she said. "As an animal plays with its food."

"We're not on the menu," said McCoy.

"According to the ship's diagram, there are several rooms running off this corridor," said Betty-12. "Crew quarters. Plenty of places to hide."

"Roger that."

McCoy aimed his blaster into every room they came upon, his suit lights picking out overturned bunks, mangled storage lockers, and more suited bodies. Betty-12 did the same, covering the left side of the hallway.

Neither found any signs of the creature.

"Whatever it is," said McCoy, "it's shy."

Betty-12 nodded, leveling her blaster on an overturned locker that looked big enough to conceal what attacked them. Again, nothing.

McCoy kicked absently at a white space helmet, which rolled and spun around. The human owner's mummified head was still inside.

McCoy gritted his teeth. "What in the worlds happened here?"

Betty-12 glanced at the helmet and the decapitated head inside. "We are close to the engine room."

McCoy nodded, consciously stepping around the helmet.

Then they saw what Captain Bryson had muttered about in his logs. Lines drawn on the walls and the floor. They looked like circuit diagrams, and glowed faintly in the gloom. Red emergency lights flared.

"We're getting close," said McCoy. "In an emergency, most of the power on a Navy vessel gets diverted to where it's needed most. Life support and engineering."

"I believe these drawings are actual circuits," said Betty-12. "They're tied into the ship's power. The captain said they were drawn in metallic ink."

"They're like nothing I've ever seen before," said McCoy. "Alien?"

"Perhaps."

Blasters held high, Mars McCoy and Betty-12 crept closer to the entrance to the engine room, a wide, triangular opening that glowed faintly from within. Their ears were filled with the rhythmic thrumming of the ship's thrusters, the hum of the engines; louder here than in any other part of the ship. Cautiously they entered the engine room, and discovered a world alive with green fire.

The entire engineering section was filled with a weird green light that glowed sickly, emanating from some far corner behind a wall of equipment. Everywhere they could see the circuit diagrams scrawled on the walls, connecting to each other and looping back in on themselves in a strange tapestry of madness.

"The light is a force field," said Betty-12.

"For the singularity," said McCoy.

Betty-12 nodded.

"Twenty-seven years ago the Galactic Navy created a microscopic black hole. We need to shut it down."

A large shadow crossed their path and something black lashed out, knocking them both to the decking.

McCoy heard the outer lining of his suit tearing and reached up with his free hand, clutching his chest. The front of his protective suit fell away in tatters.

"Betty."

"I am all right, Captain."

McCoy got to his feet and helped Betty-12 to hers. Her suit was slashed as well, and McCoy could see shimmering circuitry beneath.

"You're not."

"A flesh wound," said Betty-12. "Look out!"

A sledge hammer with claws hit McCoy squarely in the back, sending him flying. He hit the engine room floor and his helmet slammed against the metal, causing a hairline crack to open near the neck coupling. Behind him he heard the same high-pitched screech they had heard earlier.

McCoy flipped around and for the first time got a clear view of the horror that attacked them in the corridor.

The thing was a shifting, shapeless mass. A long, eyeless head jutted from the center, white needle teeth flashing, while long arms ending in talons reached out for them before dissolving back into the mass. It was like a living tar pool, a seething pit of malevolence.

McCoy fumbled for his blaster, which he'd dropped when he hit the floor. He fired at the creature as it lashed out at Betty-12, hitting the dark mass dead center.

The creature let out another high-pitched screech and flowed backward, but its molecules held together. The blaster's typical disintegrating effect did nothing to the monster.

Betty-12 leveled her blaster at the creature and fired, the searing beam hitting it on the bullet-shaped head. Again it cried out, again it poured backward, but its molecules held together.

"Our weapons are useless," said Betty-12.

"I wouldn't say useless," said McCoy, standing. "They obviously hurt it. They just can't kill it."

The thing raged as it tumbled over a bank of equipment, its mass flowing in between some of the metal duct work. A sickening, burning smell came to McCoy through the crack in his helmet.

"We need to shut down the singularity," said Betty-12.

"Right." McCoy had almost forgotten what they had come here to do; he was so transfixed with the creature. Where did it come from? What planet's evolution gave rise to such monsters? But he had no time for such thoughts now.

Betty-12 skirted around the creature, which struggled to reform its head and talons. McCoy did the same, using the tangled maze of duct work and equipment as a barrier between himself and the creature. He never took his eyes off of it.

The creature coalesced into a more solid form and stepped from the maze of duct work. It had taken the form of a large humanoid, the insignia of a Space Ranger clearly etched into its shiny black body.

"It's a chameleon," said McCoy, firing again.

The thing was ready. The center of its body recoiled from the beam, making a perfectly round hole for the blaster beam to pass through harmlessly. *This is why nobody could kill it*, thought McCoy.

"If you've got any ideas," he said to Betty-12, "now would be a good time to share them."

"Let's ask him."

McCoy looked toward the greenish light of the containment field. Inside it was a long cylindrical shaft that came to a point halfway to the floor. Another shaft rose up to meet it, coming to a point less than an inch from the top shaft, like the tips of enormous nails. Somewhere between the two points floated a microscopic, invisible black hole.

But even more wondrous than the ship's power source was what looked back at them through the containment field.

Sitting cross-legged on the floor was a dead man.

It wore a rotting Galactic Navy uniform. The leathery skin of its face stretched taught over angular cheekbones, its eyes now dried orbs that stared at them sightlessly. The shrunken lips were peeled back from too-white teeth that glowed green in the ghostly light of the force field.

McCoy had seen plenty of dead men, especially on this trip, but there was something very different about this one. It was breathing.

They watched as the chest expanded and contracted slowly, as if air were being forced in artificially rather than being drawn in by the lungs. Something rattled in the chest. McCoy noticed the insignia and epaulets of a Navy science officer. "It's Lt. Tracer," he whispered to Betty-12, remembering the captain's log.

Then the head moved, and the dead orbs that were once eyes appeared to stare at them.

"Did you enjoy playing with our pet?" it said, its voice raspy, like dry leaves blown by an autumn wind.

"Pet?" said McCoy, turning to the creature, which stood two feet away, looking at them with its night-black ersatz face. "That *thing* is your *pet*?"

Something like an insane approximation of a laugh issued from deep inside the corpse. "*Pet* is one of your terms. To us it is more of a servant. A servant who likes playing with its food too much."

"What's this all about, Tracer? What are you trying to—"

"The one called Tracer is no longer here."

"Then who are you?"

"*We* are the Ch'Thoon," answered the corpse. "We are using this body to communicate with you in your primitive language. Your pathetic universal translator cannot parse the True Tongue."

"The Navy reverse engineered your technology."

The corpse nodded. Then it looked back at them. "Yes. For amoebae, you are very clever."

While McCoy interrogated the talking corpse, Betty-12 studied the containment field controls. A warning claxon sounded as the containment field winked out of existence.

McCoy drew his blaster, leveling it at the mummified head of the corpse. "What are you doing aboard this ship?"

"This is *our* ship. It was built using our technology. We did not die out as your Navy believed. By activating this ship's drive, they unknowingly opened the door for our return."

"Return?" asked Betty-12. "Return from where?"

"The Outer Dark. Our planet died. We did not. Climate changed. Temperature increased. Oceans rose against us. Ice encroached. We left our bodies behind."

"They transcended their corporeal bodies," said Betty-12. "Amazing. They are quite likely more advanced than the Faash'Tan."

Tracer's corpse erupted in that cruel mockery of laughter again. "We learned of the Faash'Tan from your minds, your records. We are as far beyond them as they are beyond you; as you are beyond your homeworld's primates."

"If you're so smart," said McCoy, "You'd know better than to insult the intelligence of someone aiming a blaster at your head."

"You cannot kill what is already dead, Ranger."

McCoy decided to test that theory. He fired. The destructive beam angled away from Tracer's head flowing instead into the space above the corpse, where the beam spiraled briefly before disappearing into thin air.

McCoy released the trigger.

"The singularity," said Betty-12, and McCoy realized the tiny black hole that powered the *Star Lance* had sucked in the blaster beam. They wouldn't be destroying the alien-possessed corpse with their blasters. He had to try something else.

"Foolish creatures and your useless weapons," the corpse breathed. "Man will be the first to fall when we return."

"You've been flicking in and out of normal space for almost thirty of our years." said McCoy. "If you could invade us, you would have done it already."

The corpse stretched the thin skin of its face into a ghastly parody of a smile. "Quite true. For primitives, your species has proven resilient and unpredictable."

"The crew wouldn't help them," said Betty-12. "Not at first."

"Not without *assurances*," the corpse breathed. "In the beginning, their only thought was to return to normal space. But we needed a few things before we were ready."

"Those strange artifacts in the hold," said Betty-12.

"Yes. Artifacts left by us when we still traveled the stars as you do. Weapons we will use to destroy your childish Empire."

"Did you kill Tracer?" McCoy asked.

The corpse nodded its head slightly. "An accidental byproduct of merging our superior minds with his primitive one. He wanted ultimate knowledge. We gave it to him. At a cost."

"Some trade." McCoy glanced at Betty-12, who was transfixed on the space where the tiny singularity floated, invisibly belching X-rays and Hawking radiation and the Emperor alone knew what else.

"Can we shut it down?"

Betty-12 looked at McCoy. "Unknown. The Empire of Man has nothing like this. It is completely beyond our science."

"And your understanding, robot," said Tracer's corpse. "We are the Ch'Thoon. And we will use this ship to return to normal space and inhabit your primitive human shells. We will rule the galaxy forevermore."

"You're doing a bang-up job so far," said McCoy.

"As we said," the corpse replied, a trace of annoyance in its unearthly voice, "we had difficulties. The void being we summoned to bring us bodies fell out of our control. It killed everyone aboard. And everyone who came after."

McCoy glanced behind them at the night-black monstrosity in its human shape, presently glaring at them.

The corpse laughed its dry laughter. "Who are you to order us? We are the Ch'Thoon. We roamed the galaxy before your kind discovered fire. Your precious Emperor will house our minds, and we'll rule with his hands."

Betty-12's fingers worked the control consoles near the singularity, calling up engine specs and working on shutting down the *Star Lance's* strange power source.

"The skip drive is stuck in the on position," she said, hitting buttons and flipping levers.

"The power source cannot be shut down, robot," said the corpse. "We control it. We are its masters. Not you."

"We can change that," said McCoy, growing annoyed with the aliens' arrogance. He holstered his blaster and turned to help his copilot, wishing he hadn't snoozed his way through black hole physics at the Academy.

"What are we looking at here?"

"These are the controls that generated the black hole initially," said Betty-12. "I'm sure of it. It also provides it with enough matter and energy to keep it from evaporating, while keeping it microscopically small so it doesn't suck the entire ship into it."

"That's a good thing. What else?"

"When we shut down the force field, we also shut down the containment field that keeps the black hole in place. It could fall into the ship and destroy it."

"And get bigger from all the matter it would consume," added McCoy.

Betty-12 nodded. "These controls are fused. We can't shut it down."

McCoy nodded. "We'll see about that."

McCoy looked around the engine room. Then he saw what he was looking for on the far wall. Pulling his blaster, McCoy walked over to a set of glowing lines scrawled into the metal engine room bulkhead.

"What are you doing?" demanded the corpse as it tried without success to stand up.

"Forget it, Ch'Thoon," said McCoy. "Your host has been dead too long."

The ink-black creature the Ch'Thoon referred to as their pet sprang into terrible action, growing taller and broader and sticking foot-long spikes out of its body as it advanced on McCoy.

Betty-12 slammed her fist through the face of the control panel, coming out with a thick power cable that sparked at the open tip with blue fire. With lightning speed she advanced on the creature, plunging the heavy cable into the heart of the black horror.

The creature screamed with rage as the electricity arced through it, its body shifting shape furiously before it lost cohesion and slumped into a tar-like puddle of goo on the floor.

McCoy watched as the ship's current finished off the creature. "Now, where was I? Oh yes."

He turned back to the wall and fired, pulling the blaster downward in a fast arc as he held the trigger, the beam lancing through the silvery circuit and cutting it off from the power supply without cutting very deeply into the wall. The metallic lines dimmed and faded, and the engine room filled with an almost deafening hum as everything shut down at once.

"*Nooooooo!!!!!*" the corpse screamed. Finally, with considerable effort, it got to its rotting feet. "You fools. You have doomed us all!"

The light, the very air around and behind the corpse of Lieutenant Tracer, warped. It stepped toward them, a blast pistol suddenly in its withered, leathery hand. It squeezed the trigger, but the blaster beam, pulled by the energy-hungry singularity, bent back toward the dead thing that ambled toward them, hitting it in the chest.

The corpse screamed, but not from pain. It was more a shout of surprise, echoed by a million alien voices. The blaster beam seared through the shrunken chest and narrowed to a thin point and disappeared behind the corpse. The thing that had once been Lt. Tracer disintegrated, shreds swallowed by the black hole behind it.

Dropping the now-dead power cable, Betty-12 turned to her commanding officer. "How did you know that would happen?"

McCoy gave his copilot a sly grin and a shrug as he holstered his blaster. "I didn't. I just figured that those circuits Tracer and the others scrawled in here had to have something to do with the black hole they penned in here."

"You took a huge gamble."

"So did you. I'm assuming that was enough current to fry your circuits."

Now it was Betty-12's turn to shrug, an expression that was strange coming from a robot. "The engines are offline. Shall we see where we ended up?"

McCoy nodded, and they ran from the engine room, pausing just long enough to glance back at the singularity containment area as it was rent and pulled into an invisible point and vanished.

Then the lights flickered and went out.

The battle for the *Star Lance* was getting more heated by the second, and Commander Verne did not like it.

He paced the deck of the command center, banging dents in the control consoles with his metallic right arm.

"Sir," said the communications officer, "the Orgum-Ree are demanding the immediate surrender of the *Star Lance*."

"Robes of the Emperor!" Verne shouted. "They can see it's gone!"

"They think we did something with it," said the officer.

"That's ridiculous," said Voroshilov. "If we had it, we wouldn't be here."

"Try telling them that," said Verne. He glanced at the viewport. The *Star Lance* had vanished again, and they were risking an interstellar war over a ghost.

Then a rainbow flash of light appeared, and the characteristic null space distortion belched forth the largest ship Verne had ever seen. It was long and thin, with heavy damage visible all along its hull.

The fighting stopped, all sides surprised by this new contender emerging in the middle of their battle zone. Black Birds and pirate ships kicked their thrusters into overdrive to get out of the ship's path. It listed wildly.

"That is the *Lance*," said Voroshilov.

"Get me readings, people," ordered Verne.

"There's some energy fluctuations coming from the engines, Commander," said the tactical officer. "X-rays, Hawking radiation. The rest of the ship is dead."

"Life readings?"

"Just one. And one robot. And they're coming this way."

"Yes!" said Verne, pounding his real left fist into his artificial right hand. "I knew Mars and Betty—err, that is, Captain McCoy and Lt. Betty-12—were still alive. Get them on the radio."

"He's calling us." The communications officer flipped a switch and the command center was filled with thruster noise and static.

"This is Black Bird Five to the Black Hole."

"This is Commander Verne. We read you, McCoy. What is going on?"

"Long story. There's a black hole onboard the *Star Lance*, tearing the ship apart."

"That explains the X-rays and Hawking radiation," someone said.

"You heard the man," said Verne. "Everyone pull back. This fight is over. Send out a priority message, all channels. I want the Orgum-Ree *and* the pirates to know. Recall the Black Birds."

Tactical zoomed in on the *Star Lance*. A Black Bird emerged from it, looking like a fast-moving fly against the looming bulk of the larger vessel. Seconds later the large bulge at the rear of the vessel imploded.

Even the Orgum-Ree could not deny that what McCoy said was

true. Section by section the *Star Lance* was pulled into a single point, its molecules superheating, giving off X-rays and Hawking radiation. Within minutes, the *Star Lance* was no more.

Without another word, the Orgum-Ree ships skipped into null space as one by one the space pirate vessels blinked out.

"We're still tracking the black hole, sir," said tactical. "It's shrinking. It won't hold together much longer."

"That's a good thing," said Verne. He glanced at Voroshilov.

"Black hole?"

Voroshilov grumbled low in his throat, but said nothing.

After having their injuries repaired, Mars McCoy and Betty-12 spent uncomfortable hours in a Black Hole conference room being debriefed by Voroshilov, Verne, and Navy brass. Confidentiality agreements were initialed and signed in triplicate, and they told everything about what happened onboard and what they had learned of the fate of the *Star Lance's* crew.

The Navy brass were especially interested in the fate of Science Officer Tracer and the Ch'Thoon, about which McCoy figured the Navy knew more than they let on. Eventually satisfied, the Navy brass let them leave— but not until they'd sworn an additional oath of secrecy.

When the meeting was over, Verne ordered McCoy and Betty-12 not to tell anyone what had happened aboard the *Star Lance*, though he promised McCoy the drinks tonight at the bar were on him if they could go through the story for him one more time.

McCoy and Betty-12 walked away from the meeting together, their journey taking them past a window cut into the skin of the asteroid. Betty-12 paused to look out at the stars.

"What is it?"

"I am thinking about the Ch'Thoon. Do you think they are still out there somewhere?"

McCoy shrugged. "What happens on the inside of a black hole? Was that every last Ch'Thoon inside Tracer's body? We'll probably never know."

"They seemed so smug, so full of themselves. Like many humans I've met."

McCoy laughed. "I've met a few braggarts myself. Maybe we're not as different from the Ch'Thoon as they wanted us to believe."

"Perhaps."

McCoy stared at his copilot, her dark hair spilling down her shoulders, her face limned in starlight. Did they have to make her so beautiful? He put his left hand on the small of her back.

"What are you doing?"

McCoy's hand shrank back, falling to his side. "I . . ." he trailed off.

"You saved my life today."

"You would have done the same for me," she said, moving away from the viewport and continuing down the corridor.

"Yeah."

"Besides," said Betty-12 evenly. "If something happened to you, there would have been a lot of paperwork."

McCoy laughed, then quickly stifled it. "I can never tell when you're joking. We have to work on that."

THE END

BLAME IT ON VAN

*T*his story is all Van Plexico's fault. If not for him, I would have never heard of Mars McCoy, let alone write a story for this second volume of his adventures. And writing this story was an absolute blast, if you'll pardon the all-too-obvious pun, and it was an experience and an opportunity I wouldn't have missed for all the worlds.

The reason I say this story is all Van's fault is because he's the one who introduced me to the wonderful group of pulp creators and aficionados at the Pulp Factory and Mars McCoy's publisher, Airship 27 Productions. I had been reading a lot of H.P. Lovecraft and Robert E. Howard at the time, and I started wondering if anyone was publishing this kind of stuff these days, as I wanted to try my hand at some stories told in these old styles. I knew Van from Dragon*Con, and thought he might know of someone, so I shot him an email. He told me about the Pulp Factory and got me an invite, and next thing I know I'm volunteering to write a space story about a Flash Gordon/Buck Rogers sort of character.

What really got me going on this character was the story bible that Ron Fortier and Van came up with. There are enough alien races, minor characters, and space pirates to fill a hundred volumes of Mars McCoy's adventures. I found several characters that I thought would be fun to play around with and include in my tale, but I couldn't come up with a suitable story that would work with most of them.

As for the genesis of my story, I do as I often try to do, especially with pulp stories, and start with the title. I think it was Harlan Ellison who wrote somewhere that your title is like the power source for your plot, and can actually suggest a good portion of the plot to you. This is probably why his best stories always have such wonderfully demented titles. Anyway, as I was thinking about the plot of my story, the title sprang suddenly into my mind: "Mars McCoy and the Curse of the Star Lance." And I immediately knew what it was going to be about: an experimental Navy ship, with an experimental drive and experimental weapons reverse engineered from a long-dead alien civilization, highly classified, that gets lost on its maiden voyage. I knew that when this ship resurfaced, everyone from the Navy to the space pirates would be after this thing. I also knew that everyone who encountered the Lance in deep space would meet with some tragic end, causing legends of a curse to spring up around the doomed vessel. The stuff about the long dead super race the Ch'thoon and the Lance's black hole power source came later on as I was writing the story.

This is the first story I wrote for Airship 27, though it's not the first to be published, and it's still my favorite. It hearkens back to the good old days of the space pulps, while giving readers a lot of modern characters and ideas to explore. I hope everyone enjoys this story as well as the others in the two volumes and make up this series. If you did, please give us a review on Amazon.com and ask Ron Fortier and Rob Davis of Airship 27 to do more of these anthologies.

JAMES PALMER is an author, editor, short story writer, and copywriter, but not necessarily in the order. He has written articles, interviews, reviews, columns, and poetry for *Strange Horizons*, *RevolutionSF*, *Blood Blade and Thruster: The Magazine of Speculative Fiction and Satire*, *The Internet Review of Science Fiction*, *Tangent Online*, *Continuum SF* and *SciFaikuest*. He also wrote the introduction to the White Rocket Books reprint of Edgar Rice Burroughs' *The Warlord of Mars*. James has had stories published in the anthologies *Van Allen Plexico Presents: Gideon Cain* and *Blackthorn: Thunder on Mars*. He is also a regular contributor to the Pro Se Productions magazine *Fantasy and Fear*. He is also the editor, with Jim Beard, of the anthology *Monster Earth*, published under his new iimprint Mechanoid Press. A recovering comic book addict, James lives in Northeast Georgia with his wife and daughter, and is currently hard at work on several projects. For more tales of his literary exploits, visit www.jamespalmerbooks.com.

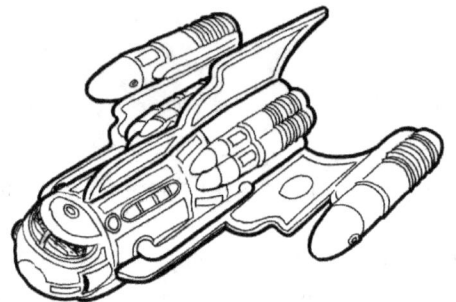

Mars McCoy and the Chaos Horde

by Van Allen Plexico

(The Present)

"**W**ar!" screamed Captain Jaxon at the top of his robotic lungs. "War has come to the Fringe Worlds, and you boys know what that means!"

One of his robotic pirate crewmen leapt up atop the navigational control panel and waved his metal arms wildly.

"Plunder, Cap'n!"

"Maybe so, maybe so," Jaxon agreed, sounding ambivalent. "But we do quite well on that score already."

A cheer from his "men" affirmed this.

"What else does it mean?"

"War profiteering," another crew-robot chimed in, his voice sounding like a recording played back a bit too fast.

Jaxon winced at the voice, then shrugged his metal shoulders.

"A good chance, yes. Helping out the various sides in the conflict by expediting the shipments of armaments—merely playing our *humanitarian* part, of course."

The robotic crew of pirates all chortled at the term "humanitarian." The sound was one of a dozen alarm clocks all going off at once.

Jaxon let the bridge crew settle down, then turned to glare at them with his burning-red eyes.

"But better than plunder—better than exploitation and profiteering—"

The crew sat still for a moment, their processors whirring, glancing from one to the other with looks of confusion and puzzlement. Then one of the communications robots tentatively raised a multi-segmented silver arm.

"This is no schoolhouse," Jaxon bellowed. "Tell me the answer!"

"The Space Patrol will intervene?" the robot asked cautiously.

Captain Jaxon's red eyes flared dramatically.

"Precisely!"

He whacked the communications robot on the back in friendly fashion. Bolts and gears sprayed out across the floor and smoke began to issue from the robot's orifices.

"The Space Patrol. Yes."

The seven-foot-tall pirate captain strode to the center of his flagship's bridge and rested his segmented arms against his dull gray sides with a resounding clank. His two fiery eyes peered up at the viewscreen that filled the forward portion of the chamber, and he nodded his smooth, oval-shaped head in satisfaction.

"And when the Space Patrol ventures into my territory," he said in a low, mechanical growl, "they will find they have fallen directly into my trap."

The robots all chortled at this and nodded with glee, save the one who had correctly answered the question—he had by now collapsed in a limp and smoldering heap on the floor of the ship, prompting a maintenance bot to roll out and drag his carcass away.

A few moments later, as the pirate captain mulled over his plans and the crew indulged in a little unscheduled lubrication, one of the scanner officers jumped from his seat, his antennae raising and lowering in rapid fashion. He whirled about and signaled frantically to Jaxon.

"Captain! Captain! A null-space distortion just ahead! Something is—"

The blackness of space just beyond their ship twisted and spiraled with rainbow colors momentarily. Through the opening streaked a most familiar shape.

"—coming this way."

Jaxon took in the sight, his eyes widening in surprise.

"I cannot be this lucky," he rumbled. "Oh, I cannot be this lucky!"

"Space Patrol ship off the forward bow," shouted the helmsman, somewhat belatedly. "Their null-engines are off line but their blaster-cannons are hot," he added.

The sleek form of a Black Bird spacecraft filled the screen. Jaxon studied its markings carefully.

"Black Bird Five. Well, well."

"Incoming transmission, Captain!"

"Put it on screen."

Static washed across the viewer for a moment, replaced by the smiling face of a man apparently in his late twenties or early thirties, with bright green eyes and wavy red hair.

"I thought I might find you here, JX-1," the man said with a wink.

"Mars McCoy. How pleasant to see you once again," the pirate captain replied. "And it's 'Jaxon,' as you well know. I have long since evolved beyond my original robotic designation."

"'Evolved?' You're a one-machine poster boy for the hazards of combining human and alien technology!"

A low growl issued from Jaxon's speakers.

"Enjoy your bravado while you can, McCoy," the pirate growled at him. "For you have foolishly placed yourself directly into my hands. Reducing you to random trace molecules is something I have long awaited with great anticipation."

"Stuff it, you big windbag," came the voice of Lt. Betty-12, the beautiful brunette who also happened to be both Mars's second in command and a robot, herself. "You don't think we'd be stupid enough to simply walk defenseless into your custody, do you?"

"Ah, Lt. Betty. As feisty as ever, I see." He spread his nubby metal hands wide. "But your argument seems to have no merit—for that is precisely what you have done, is it not?"

He gestured with one hand and the communications officer to his right punched in a quick series of signals on his console. Moments later, five spirals of light—the null-space jump effect—appeared all around Black Bird Five.

"You see, Captain McCoy, while you might conceivably make this a 'fair fight' just between the two of us, it turns out that I am not alone here. Not alone at all."

Five ragged pirate vessels had materialized, their gun ports open and their blaster-cannons energized.

"I'm sure it goes without saying that if you activate your null-engines, you will be vaporized," Jaxon added.

On the screen, Mars continued to smile.

Seconds ticked by, and no one moved, no one spoke. The tension ran high.

The pirate continued to stand there, studying the screen, waiting for the human captain to break down in tears—to beg for mercy, to offer anything in his possession for the chance for escape.

Instead, Mars continued to smile.

Finally Jaxon couldn't take it any longer. He raised both gray arms high and bellowed, "What? What is it? You are beaten! Why do you smile that infuriating smile, McCoy?"

Mars laughed.

"Because I'm thinking of how nice it would be to finally arrest you and run you in," he told the pirate. "But I suppose I'm going to have to let you go."

Jaxon's blazing red eyes blinked in surprise.

"Let me go? Let ME go?!"

Mars nodded.

"It would only be fair," the Ranger replied, "since you'll be providing me with some critical intelligence in a few moments, and I'll owe you something in return."

Jaxon gazed back at his nemesis in utter amazement.

"Is that so?"

"You don't owe him anything, Captain," came the voice of Betty-12 from the copilot's seat. "We should run him in anyway."

Both Jaxon and Mars ignored her this time.

"Jaxon," Mars said then, growing serious, "there are bigger things afoot than merely your little pirate operations out here. So I'm willing to look the other way—this time—if you'll be reasonable and cooperate and answer a few questions for me."

Jaxon laughed then—a curious sound, reverberating up from the depths of his wide gray torso and crackling out of the speaker set into his oval-shaped head.

"Mars, you must be smoking that Denarian pipe-weed you confiscated from me last month!"

He swept his big, rugged hand in a wide arc.

"You are currently locked in the sights of more than a dozen blast-cannons! I have you dead to rights! By all the worlds of the Empire and the holy throne of the Emperor, why would I want to answer any of your questions, much less let you go afterward?!"

On the screen, Mars shrugged.

"Maybe because of this?"

He motioned to Betty-12. She sent a signal.

The robot at the tactical station emitted a high-pitched shriek.

Jaxon whirled on him, crimson eyes boring in.

"What?"

"I—I—I suggest you switch the viewscreen to tactical display, Captain!"

"Do it!"

The image of the smiling McCoy vanished, replaced by a layout of the local area of space. A representation of Black Bird Five blinked at the center. Jaxon's six pirate ships surrounded it.

And now one single gigantic blip hovered to one side of the pirate fleet, along with numerous smaller objects.

Jaxon gawked.

"Is that—is that—"

"A Galactic Navy battleship, Captain," the tactical robot replied, his voice sounding an octave or two too high.

"Battleship?" Jaxon repeated, incredulous.

"Battleship," came the voice of Mars McCoy over the audio channel. "And I think you said something before about 'dead to rights.'"

"All seventy blast-cannons are locked on the pirate vessels, Commodore McCoy," came a crackling voice from another speaker aboard Black Bird Five.

Jaxon heard it, and his red eyes widened slightly. If half-alien mechanical pirate robots could be said to gulp, Jaxon gulped.

The pirate crew all eyed one another nervously, then turned their attention to their leader, waiting.

Jaxon eyed the big battleship floating on either side of his little fleet, considered his alternatives, and nodded his metallic head.

"So, Mars," the pirate said, his voice much less belligerent now, much warmer, and taking on an almost conciliatory tone. "Mars, my boy. I believe you had some questions for me, then?"

Mars, his face on the screen once more, was still smiling.

"And I'm hoping you'll have a few answers, Jaxon."

"Most assuredly."

Then Jaxon paused.

"Did that man just call you 'Commodore McCoy?'"

Mars's smile faded. Jaxon thought he detected the traces of what the humans called "pain" crossing over the captain's face.

"That—is a long story," Mars McCoy replied.

(Three weeks past.)

Three weeks earlier: Captain Marshall "Mars" McCoy stood with his back to a sheer rock cliff, a horde of vicious, slavering alien creatures pressing in toward him.

"I wish I hadn't called you here, Mars," choked the wounded man to his left. "I think I've led us both to our deaths."

"Don't give up hope yet, Flint," McCoy replied, his green eyes flickering from the power level indicator of his blaster pistol to the ranks of demonic beings shuffling ever closer. "There has to be a way out of this."

"Um, yeah," said Captain Flint Rogers, uncertainty heavy in his voice. He sat against a small boulder, his broken right leg stretched out in front of him. His jacket was off and lay across his lap, holding his gun's few remaining power cells. "Well, if you have a card to play, buddy, I think this may be the time."

Leveling his pistol at the nearest of the attackers, Mars unleashed a devastating blast, the powerful beam shredding three of the horrific forms, leaving behind scant remains. The advancing horde hesitated only for an instant. Then they filled in the ranks from behind and, single-mindedly, began to press forward again.

"That's not gonna get it," Rogers growled as he fired his own weapon at the bizarre creatures. "Our cells will run dry before we make a serious dent in this army."

Mars squinted out at the ranks arrayed against him and his fellow Ranger. More than seven feet tall, each of the creatures appeared more or less like all the others: vaguely humanoid in form and grayish in color, with multiple red eyes peering out from beneath folds of ectoplasm-like flesh. They smelled awful. And the sound they made—a low, rising moan, echoing throughout their shambling ranks—was enough to turn a normal man's hair white as snow.

But these were not normal men.

We are Rangers, Mars told himself firmly. *We are both captains in the Space Patrol, and facing strange menaces such as these, on planets far from home—that's simply part of the job.*

"Suck it up, Flint," he growled. "As long as we have shots remaining, we take 'em!"

Rogers glanced at his friend and colleague in surprise, saw the grim determination and courage so clearly etched on the man's face, and nodded. He picked out the closest target and disintegrated it.

Meanwhile, Mars took the opportunity to click open his comm link and signal to his ship once again.

"Betty! Come in! Are you there?"

Still no reply.

"I'm glad you sent her back to the ship," Rogers was saying as he continued to blast away. "Maybe she can escape, and get word back to the Black Hole about these things. And about...what happened to us."

Mars said nothing. He aimed his pistol carefully—though, at this point, surrounded on three sides as they were, such pinpoint precision was scarcely required—fired, and signaled the ship again.

"Black Bird Five. McCoy calling Black Bird Five. Betty, are you there?"

The disgusting creatures were nearly upon them now, their long, clawlike fingers reaching, reaching…

Mars fired and fired, his blaster growing nearly too hot to handle. Rogers did likewise. The monstrous forms surged forward, their eyes fiery, their stench overwhelmingly oppressive—

—and then they stopped suddenly, whirling about.

Mars realized then that the valley had been filled for the past couple of seconds with a roaring sound. Before he could even think of what it might be, a louder shriek echoed from the distance, and a group of the creatures off to one side of the horde disappeared. The others wailed much louder now and shuffled away from McCoy and Rogers.

"Something's getting to 'em," Rogers shouted, attempting to get to his feet despite his injury. "Something has 'em spooked!"

"I think you're right," Mars agreed, holding his fire and conserving his final shots.

The strange beings were in full retreat now, as with a shriek another group of them disintegrated off to the left. Just then, the source of their consternation became apparent: The sleek, gleaming form of Black Bird Five leapt into view above the rear lines of the creatures. Its twin blast-cannons erupted again, annihilating whole swathes of the enemy ranks.

"Wahoo!" shouted Rogers. "It's the cavalry!"

Mars grinned at the sight as well, knowing Betty was at the controls of his ship.

The remaining monsters broke and fled in every direction, and seconds later they were all gone, as if they'd never been there.

Rogers struggled to stand on his good leg as the Space Patrol ship settled to the ground nearby.

"That'll teach 'em," he shouted, waving his blaster pistol in the air. "Don't mess with the Patrol!"

But Mars's face was grim, his mood anything but celebratory.

"They vanished," he was muttering. "They simply vanished."

"Darned right they did," Rogers agreed, nodding. "And pretty quickly, too."

"Too quickly," Mars said. "And I mean it literally—they vanished. Into thin air."

"What? How can that be?"

"I don't know, Flint." Mars shook his head. "Not that anything else has made much sense on this planet."

Rogers, wrapping an arm over Mars's shoulder for support, thought about this for a moment, then shrugged.

"Well, take a victory for what it is," he said. "We can work out the technical details later. Or, better yet, the big-brains back at the Black Hole can, while we down a few pints of Galaxian."

"Yeah, sure," Mars said, helping his friend to the opening hatch of the ship. But he couldn't help wondering exactly what had happened, and the frown never quite disappeared from his face.

Two hours later, Rogers's injuries had been field-treated and the most critical damage to his own ship had been at least temporarily repaired. Now he was back in Black Bird Thirteen while Mars had joined his lieutenant, Betty-12, aboard Five.

"It was the strangest thing," Mars said to her as he strapped into his pilot's seat. "When I first found Flint, he was shouting about being attacked, but I couldn't see anything near him. But then, as I grew more and more worried about him, I could suddenly see what he was talking about—monstrous things, coming right out of the ground, all around us."

Betty turned, her long, lustrous dark hair flowing to her shoulders. She regarded her captain pensively for several seconds in silence.

"I know that look," Mars said when he could take her puzzled expression no longer. "What is it?"

"I—I hesitated to say anything, Captain," she began tentatively, "because I was concerned that I was malfunctioning in some way. But—"

Mars waited patiently.

"But I couldn't…"

Mars's eyes widened. He pointed to her.

"You couldn't see them, either, could you?"

Betty sighed.

"Not at first, no. Not for a long time. When I got back here, I heard you calling, but I was busy with the scanners, the analyzers, trying to locate a target. And I couldn't find one."

Mars bit his lip, thinking hard.

"But…clearly you saw them eventually, though. Right? Because you shot a bunch of them and scared the rest away."

"Yes." She smiled at him then, a warm and reassuring smile. "I saw them. And…it is good to know that you could not detect them at first, either," she added with relief. "Perhaps I was not malfunctioning."

"I have a feeling you were functioning just fine," he replied, patting her hand. "But let me ask you—when was it that you were suddenly able to see the creatures?"

She thought about that for a moment; Mars suspected she was replaying the entire incident back in her mechanical memory.

"After your last call for help," she said finally. "I could see them and target them after your final call for help. Before that, I was very concerned... but that time, you sounded as if you were about to give up hope, and I was..."

"You were *worried* about me. Fearful. About Flint and me."

Betty hesitated, then nodded. "Yes. To the degree that I am capable of experiencing that emotion, you are right." She looked up at him. "Do you think that's significant somehow?"

Mars mulled it all over for a moment.

"Let's just say I'm seeing some interesting patterns developing," he said to her.

Neither spoke for a few seconds, as Mars bounced ideas around in his head. Then, deciding to stow away his many suspicions for the moment, he keyed the comm and called over to the other spacecraft.

"Five to Thirteen—you good to go, Flint?"

"Absolutely," Rogers replied, his voice revealing a much more upbeat mood now.

"How's your lieutenant?"

"Old 59833LM is resting comfortably, as best as I can tell," he said.

"Okay. I'm firing up the main engines now."

"Whenever you're ready. Our systems are up and Thirteen's navigation is slaved to Black Bird Five. So I'll just sit back and enjoy the ride. Take us home."

Grinning, Mars launched his sleek patrol ship into the dim sky of Artinax-2, then hurled it into the void, Rogers's vessel following along obediently in his wake.

They had scarcely passed from Artinax's atmosphere when the null-radio beeped. Betty examined the readout on its small screen and frowned.

"A coded message from base," she told Mars. "From Commander Verne himself."

He perked up.

"Yeah? So, what is it?"

"Something big, apparently," she said, working through the top-secret military codes. "We've been recalled to base, effective immediately—though it's not stated why. But—Mars—it's Code Orange."

"Code Orange?" Mars considered that. He swallowed with some difficulty. "Betty, when was the last time we received a Code Orange transmission?"

She did not hesitate.

"Never. We have never received one."

Mars nodded.

"I didn't think so."

He punched in the null-engines.

"I think we ought to get back home."

Black Birds Five and Thirteen swept into null-space, their course set for the current secret location of the Black Hole.

Some minutes later, Betty looked up at McCoy again, her face still showing as much concern as it had since they'd first come to Artinax-2.

"What do you think those creatures were, Captain? And, perhaps more importantly, do you think we will encounter them again?"

Mars had no reply for his lieutenant, but deep inside he had a strong suspicion that their troubles with the savage aliens had only just begun.

A few hours earlier and two hundred light-years distant, the man called Deimos stood in a cold cavern beneath the surface of a desolated, long-abandoned world.

Come on, come on, he thought. *You people move fast enough when you have reason to.*

By all appearances Deimos was somewhere in his mid-twenties. His long, lank brown hair framed a narrow face, with pale brown eyes that peered out into the gloom. Pulling off the heavy gloves he'd worn on the journey down, he flexed his stiff fingers, waiting impatiently for his erstwhile allies to arrive behind him.

Some seconds later, those same allies began to file into the dank underground chamber. The emissaries of the Cabal—the Adversaries of All Mankind—nodded respectfully to him as they led their charges through the doorway.

The first to enter, the Shadowmen, were disturbing enough in their appearance. Though they wore long, black, tattered robes and hoods, a pale and blotchy white skin was just visible in the darkness underneath—skin covered here and there in bizarre, mechanical augmentations.

The creatures they brought in with them, however—the Berserkers, they were called—truly made Deimos's skin crawl.

Huge, muscular, and virtually free of intelligence, the Berserkers perpetually howled in rage or agony or some awful combination of the two. Their sounds vibrated in Deimos's ears as he watched their grotesque, bulky forms squeeze one after another through the narrow opening. The chains with which their masters held them in thrall rattled menacingly as they took up station around the perimeter of the circular room.

Watching the bizarre procession, Deimos scratched at his two days' growth of beard and pulled his long coat more tightly around himself, feeling a sudden chill in the air.

A chill. Cold. It's cold in here—too cold. He frowned, realizing what that might mean. *Not good*, he thought. *Not this soon.*

Surreptitiously, he slipped a hand into a pocket of his coat and withdrew a tiny device made up mostly of thin metal wires, then held it concealed behind his back.

Once the Shadowmen had their Berserkers positioned properly to guard the room, they moved aside to allow a second set of their order to enter. These new Shadowmen, almost identical to the first, were accompanied by pale, hunched, gangly figures, led in as though they were blind. In fact, they were; their heads and upper faces—including their eyes—were completely covered with dull metal helmets fastened tightly in place. From what Deimos could see, each of these latest arrivals looked exactly like the others.

Of course they do, Deimos thought. *They're Psi-Clones. Lobotomized psychics with little free will...but with a great deal of raw, telepathic power. Good to have around, so long as they're kept docile and under the Shadowmen's control.* Involuntarily he shuddered again. *Is there anything else that better demonstrates the differences between the Empire of Man and the Cabal Worlds in their approach to the uses of powers and abilities?*

Deimos put such academic thoughts aside and approached the lead Shadowman carefully, exhibiting a practiced deference and obeisance toward the strange, black-clad figure. The Shadowmen were not much for conversation, Deimos knew, but they at least could communicate directly—unlike the other two Cabal types.

"This has to be the right chamber," he told the Cabal agent in a soft voice. "We're very close now."

"Yes," the Shadowman hissed in reply, pulling back his hood. Tiny augmetic lights flashed in patterns along his mottled, bare skull. "Yes, we feel it as well. If you have led us to what we seek, your reward will be... vast."

Deimos suppressed a grin.

"I do not doubt that."

The Shadowman nodded once, then shuffled forward, stopping as he reached the far wall of the stone chamber. His clawlike hand reached out and felt along the surface, drawing back suddenly as his fingertips brushed over a patch of ice.

"Yes… Here…"

An instrument of some sort was suddenly in his hand. He directed it at the stone wall before him and depressed a switch. A hum filled the room as a bright green beam sliced out into the stonework.

Once the Shadowman had traced out a rectangle the shape of a doorway along the blank stone wall, he put his device away and gestured sharply. In response, two of the others brought their charges forward: two Berserkers, who at the Shadowmen's orders reached out and sank their blunt fingers into the stonework.

Groans emanating from the throats of the loathsome brutes, the Berserkers at last succeeded in pulling the stones apart. With a crash the wall collapsed, bricks tumbling in both directions and piling at their feet. Dust swirled, momentarily choking Deimos, who fanned it away and stepped back, even as he tried to peer through the murk into the newly-revealed cavern beyond.

The Berserkers retreated as the leader of the Shadowmen glided through the new opening.

"Yes," he hissed. "Yes!"

Deimos glanced around nervously, his fingers fondling the wire device he held concealed, then followed.

The new chamber was smaller and appeared much older, like some ancient crypt that had been sealed off from the world for ages. Odd patches of moss and mold grew here and there on the gray stones, with ice crystals forming across much of the surface area. But it was what lay at the center of the room that grabbed Deimos's attention the most.

There, on an elevated platform seemingly carved from a single gigantic red gem, sat an unadorned black iron box.

The Shadowman stood next to the platform, leaning over it, the claws that were his hands reaching out to the box, making obscene caressing gestures but not quite touching it.

"At last," the loathsome Cabal agent whispered, more to himself than to anyone else present. "At last!" He reached closer, his fingers closing around the box.

Deimos frowned.

"I don't know if I'd—"

The Shadowman's fingers brushed the box's surface.

Deimos quickly slipped the wire device he'd been carrying over his head, where it fit like a shower cap, tendrils hanging down past his ears on either side.

The black box on the platform instantly covered over with a layer of ice. Up the walls of the chamber on every side the ice formed, even as the temperature in the room dropped dramatically. A blue flame, coming from nowhere, appeared to dance within the room, flickering madly across the walls and floor and every other surface.

Deimos could see the Shadowman's breath freezing in the air before him as he gasped and stumbled back from the platform.

"Wha—no, no, this cannot be," the Cabal agent murmured, his face betraying severe shock and confusion.

The sounds of the Berserkers behind them rose to a frenzy of howls. The other Shadowmen started forward, then stumbled about in confusion, as though they'd lost their senses.

And the Psi-Clones, those powerful telepaths brought by the Cabal to this room in part to defend against just such a contingency, struggled to erect barriers against the powerful telepathic assault they all faced, but found themselves vastly outclassed. They, too, shambled about, groaning, their hands clutching at the heavy helmets that covered most of their heads. Shrieks and moans came from all the figures present—all save Deimos, who now wore the wire device tightly upon his head.

Deimos stepped to one side of the room and watched.

The other Shadowmen grasped for their leader and started for the doorway, but before they'd taken three steps the force of the attack grew too great. They shrieked and dropped to their knees.

The Berserkers were stumbling in circles, clutching their misshapen heads and howling. Their chains no longer held, they ran en masse out of the adjoining chamber and back out toward the planet's surface. Deimos watched them go, unconcerned—the surface was a wasteland, and the Berserkers could scarcely find the spacecraft they'd all arrived in, much less operate it.

The shrieking of the Psi-Clones, meanwhile, had risen to a nearly intolerable level. Deimos had a pretty good idea of what was happening— they had never faced a psychic force so great as this, and it was carving through their defensive screens as if they were not even there. Before Deimos could draw his pistol and put them out of their misery, however, the heads of the Psi-Clones exploded with a sickening pop inside their helmets. The lifeless bodies slumped to the cold stone floor, dark blood oozing out.

Deimos wrinkled his nose at this, then stepped quickly forward. He removed a silvery sack from his pocket, opened and upended it, and placed it down over the box. With a deft move, he had the box inside the bag, which he then tied closed.

It's not as heavy as I expected. Interesting.

Then he headed for the door.

Before he could exit, however, one of the Shadowmen clutched at his coat, stopping him.

"You…you *knew*… *knew* this would happen."

Deimos shrugged.

"I wasn't certain, but I had a pretty good idea, yeah."

He tapped the wire device that covered his head.

"Always good to be prepared, anyway."

The Shadowman scowled at him through his pain and confusion.

"The Cabal will find you—find the box. And you will pay. A thousand times over, you will pay."

"We'll see," Deimos replied. He drew his blaster and fired it point-blank into the Shadowman's head and torso. The loathsome figure collapsed at his feet.

The ice was melting now; with the box contained in the shielded bag, the temperature had risen a few degrees back toward normal.

With the psychic onslaught blunted, the other Shadowmen were beginning to recover. Deimos whirled and shot each of them in turn.

"Not a bad day's business," he remarked to himself, "though my day is far from over yet."

Then, gazing about in satisfaction, he clutched the box under one arm and exited the chamber, beginning the long climb back up to the surface.

Two weeks later, Mars McCoy strode purposefully through the winding corridors of the Black Hole, the asteroid base of the Space Patrol. Instead of whistling his usual jaunty tune, however, he moved in an unaccustomed and almost grim silence. Everyone he passed, from the other captains and lieutenants to the base's support staff, smiled and nodded to him as he passed. He returned their greetings perfunctorily, but did not feel terribly

"He...fired point blank into the Shadowman's head..."

cheerful at the moment. The bizarre enemy he and Flint Rogers had encountered on Artinax-2 still concerned him greatly.

Commander Verne has too much else to worry about to be overly focused on this situation, he thought to himself. *I understand that. But something is going on out there. The sooner I can get him to fully realize that, the quicker I can feel better about it.*

Rounding the corner into the command section of the asteroid base, McCoy ran headlong into Lt. Antonio Calderon, who had been coming the other way. The two men nearly fell, then extricated themselves from one another and managed to laugh.

"Sorry about that, Captain," Calderon said.

"My fault," Mars replied, straightening his light blue tunic and gun belt. He smiled at his old friend. "I'm a bit...distracted at the moment."

Calderon frowned.

"Something wrong, Mars?"

Just under six feet tall and sporting a dark mustache to match his short, black hair, Antonio Calderon had been a part of the Space Patrol for as long as Mars could remember. Entering the organization as a teenager, he'd quickly climbed through the ranks—and just as quickly plummeted back down, time and again. This was, Mars knew, mostly due to Calderon's hot temper continuously getting him into trouble with his various superiors. They could never quite toss him out of the service, however—Tony Calderon was simply too good, too talented a pilot and a Ranger, for that.

Unfortunately for him, his rank never quite matched his experience and his accomplishments, which explained why he currently served as lieutenant aboard James El Rey's ship, Black Bird Six.

"I'm...not entirely sure yet," Mars responded to his friend with a shrug. "But what are you doing lurking in the hallway?"

Calderon started to reply, then hesitated. He looked around, then back at Mars.

"Well—do you have a second?"

The big redhead glanced at his chronometer.

"A couple, actually. But not much more than that. I'm due for a meeting with Commander Verne shortly."

Calderon appeared surprised.

"You too?"

Mars frowned.

"Both of us? This must be a bigger meeting than I thought. I wonder what's afoot?"

"We'll find out soon enough," Calderon said. He checked his own chron, then waved Mars along behind him as he started down a side passage. "But this is what I wanted you to see."

"What?"

Calderon pointed to a big, transparent observation blister mounted into the wall just ahead.

"If I know the Navy—and I do—then they'll be showing up on schedule— right about... *now*."

"Showing up?" Mars gave his friend a quizzical look. "Who will?"

Calderon simply pointed out the big, circular window, and Mars turned to see.

For several seconds, nothing changed. The stygian depths of space, so peaceful in appearance, seemed to almost stare back at him. *Didn't one of the old Earth philosophers say something about that once? If you stare too hard into the abyss, it stares back into you...?*

Mars dismissed this thought with an inward laugh. *Let's not get overly dramatic here*, he thought.

And yet it's not nearly as peaceful as it looks, out there. I've learned that lesson over and over, through hard experience.

For a few more seconds he simply stood there, contemplating the universe that lay before him, conscious that it was truly neither ally nor enemy, but simply there—the canvas upon which all their adventures in the past, and all to come, had been and would be written.

And then—

"Look at that!"

Calderon's cry brought Mars fully back to the present and he gazed out through the observation blister in surprise.

Outside the Black Hole, a swirl of light was beginning to form—a portal out of null-space.

A blonde-haired technician joined them at the observation window, leaning in to see.

"Right on time," she breathed.

Mars could only shake his head and laugh.

"Was I the only one who didn't know about this?" he asked.

"Apparently so," Calderon said, even as two security guards crowded into the tight space with them. Everyone gazed outside in awe.

The swirl of color faded momentarily, then flared out, popping like a soap bubble made of light. From its depths emerged a gigantic shape, at first almost to complex in appearance to absorb.

Mars blinked at it, surprised.

"Is that what I think it is?"

Nearly half a mile long, its central cylindrical form was comprised of a latticework of metal girders, with the habitable sections laid out in vast pods up and down its length. A forward command section projected from the front, massive engines roared at the back, and long spikes and spires protruded from the core through every open space. Running lights pulsed regularly along its length and its call numbers were illuminated down the side of the hull.

"A battleship!"

Calderon whistled in appreciation while Mars studied the ship's markings.

"The *Jakarta*," he breathed. "What's she doing way out here?"

"I don't think the show's over yet," Calderon said by way of reply. "Keep watching."

Sure enough, moments later a second shape, much like the first, roared through the null-space gateway.

"That's the *Spitzbergen*," Mars gasped. "Two! Two battleships—here!"

"Don't see sights like that every day, out here in the Fringe, do you, Captain?" the blonde technician asked with a smile. She turned back to take in the view, nearly pressing her nose up against the transparent blister.

As a wave of smaller support ships flooded out of null-space and took up station around the two gargantuan vessels, Calderon glanced back at Mars and nodded.

"Just shows what can happen when you don't read the boss's memos," he said with a wink.

Mars nodded absently to his friend, took one last look, and turned to leave.

"I wonder who's in charge of all that?" he said aloud as he went.

Hurrying to get to the conference room on time, Mars ran headlong into a stocky, bull-necked man rounding the corner from the opposite direction. The two sprawled across the floor. Back on his feet in an instant, Mars got a clear look at who he'd run into. He felt his stomach sink at the realization.

"Lieutenant Commander Voroshilov. Well. Welcome back to the Black

Hole. Sir."

The other man wore a Navy dress uniform, but had the air and the appearance of a brawler rather than an officer. He sported close-cropped blond hair and a nose that looked to have been punched one time too many for its own good. Sprawled now on the deck, he gazed up at Mars and his eyes narrowed.

"McCoy. I should have known."

Mars extended a hand but Voroshilov ignored it and pulled himself to his feet.

"So you aren't just dangerous at the helm of a Black Bird—you're also a menace within your own base," the Navy man growled.

Mars suppressed a retort, deciding that discretion was the better part of valor—at least, when dealing with as big a jerk as Voroshilov.

"I apologize, sir," he said politely. "I'm afraid there's a meeting in a few moments, and—"

"Of course there's a meeting! That is why I am here, obviously."

Mars nodded, his curiosity over this big meeting only growing, if even Voroshilov had been summoned back to the Black Hole to attend it. "Of course," he said.

Voroshilov glared at Mars for a long moment, then straightened his uniform once more and began to move past him.

"I hope your stay aboard the Black Hole is a pleasant one," Mars said, following that sentence up mentally with *and a brief one.*

Voroshilov stopped, turned, and looked back at him with a burning fury growing in his eyes—it was enough to make Mars wonder if the man were psychic.

"It grows more unpleasant by the moment," the older man grumbled. He seemed to consider for a few seconds, then leaned in and pinned Mars against the bulkhead, his mass offsetting Mars's greater height.

"I have not forgotten, McCoy. I shall never forget. What you did—what you cost me. The Space Patrol may have sided with you in the official inquiry, but I know—and *you* know—of your guilt." He breathed in and exhaled slowly. "There is blood between us, and there always will be... until the day that we come to some sort of reckoning."

He kept Mars pinned there a second longer, then stood back, still glaring.

"So do not seek to befriend me or to smooth over our past. You waste your time and mine."

Mars said nothing, merely watching the man as he walked away.

Then, before he rounded the next corner, Voroshilov called back one last comment, colored with a touch of irony—he knew something Mars did not, as of yet.

"And we may be seeing more of one another in the days ahead than you realize."

With that, he was gone—at least, for the moment.

Mars shook his head, wrestling with anger, disappointment, and a sense of guilt he honestly believed he should not be feeling.

"That guy's an idiot," came the voice of Tony Calderon from the other direction.

Mars looked up and nodded to him.

"But a high-ranking idiot," he replied.

Calderon shrugged.

"I was hanging back—but if things had gotten ugly, I was ready to jump in for you."

Mars waved him off.

"No, no." He flashed a half-smile at his friend. "Idiots will be idiots, no matter what we do. No need to make things any worse."

Calderon appeared to be considering this deeply, as if he'd never thought about it before.

"Ehh," he finally said. "Sometimes there's a need, I think."

Minutes later, Mars and Calderon had filed into the conference room adjacent to Commander Verne's suite, with Mars's co-pilot, Betty-12, hot on their heels. The Commander himself stood at one end of the room, along with certain other members of the Patrol that Mars had not expected to be seeing here.

"El Rey, too?" he whispered to Calderon, nodding toward the captain of Black Bird Six.

"I know you're thrilled he's involved," Calderon replied, under his breath.

The tall, slender Captain James El Rey cast his steel-gray eyes about the room, met Mars's gaze, nodded almost imperceptibly, and moved to stand behind a chair on the other side of the big table.

A few minutes passed before door opened again and several more individuals entered. First came the stocky form of Voroshilov, followed immediately by three others. The first two were a man and a woman; both roughly middle-aged, they were clad in immaculate naval dress uniforms. Mars didn't recognize either of them, but guessed they were the captains of the two battleships that had just arrived. The third was an older man in full dress Ranger attire. At his appearance, both Mars's and Calderon's eyes widened and the two men exchanged meaningful glances. They refrained from comment for the moment, however, anxious to find out just what this could all mean.

Everyone took a seat. Things happened quickly then.

Commander Verne stood and looked the assemblage over once, quickly. In his usual brusque manner, he came right to the point.

"I know you're all wondering what the game is. What we're all doing here. The fact is, very few outside of this room know the whole story—what's really going on."

He paused, as if laughing to himself.

"And I'm not convinced we do, to be honest."

Then his demeanor grew deadly serious again.

"It's war. War's brewing out on the Rim, people."

The Naval and Space Patrol officers gathered in the conference room glanced nervously at one another, puzzled expressions creeping across the faces of some of them.

"And we," Verne continued, "have to put a stop to it. Immediately. Before this entire sector is torn to pieces."

A murmur arose from the group. Verne stood there, silently, allowing them to absorb what he'd said.

Mars noticed Calderon eyeing him curiously, but the redheaded spaceman could only shrug by way of reply. Then he raised a hand and Verne nodded his way.

"Yes, Captain McCoy?"

"Commander—I'm not sure I understand. Exactly *who* is at war?"

This time the higher-ranking officers in the room eyed one another knowingly, and one or two of them emitted a grim chuckle.

"Everyone," came Verne's reply.

The meeting wrapped up in record time, at least from Mars's perspective. Commander Verne introduced the two Navy captains as Ben Maruwari and Lakshmi Prasad, of the *Jakarta* and *Spitzbergen*, respectively. And the combined Space Patrol/Navy operation they would be participating in was officially dubbed "Task Force Obsidian."

A good name for it, Mars thought to himself. *Dark and murky and dangerous to the touch. But—if it's a combined operation, which of us of the Patrol will be going along?*

That was, in fact, the last bit of business Commander Verne needed to address. He paused, stroking his chin thoughtfully as if not fully convinced of what he had agreed to—*or, more likely, what's been foisted upon him,* Mars thought.

"While we are pleased to have the…*formidable* support of the Navy in this endeavor," the old war-horse began, "it should be understood by all concerned that this is primarily a Space Patrol operation. As such, its commander-in-chief will be a Space Patrol officer, serving with the temporary rank of Commodore."

Mars and Calderon exchanged knowing glances at that bit of information, and both of them shifted their gazes at once to the older, silvery-haired, dignified-looking man seated to Verne's right. At Verne's introduction, the man stood.

"Congratulations, Commodore Crabbe."

The newly-minted commodore smiled tightly, nodding to Verne and to the Navy officers seated across the table. Raymond Crabbe was a decorated hero of numerous Space Patrol missions, and had been enjoying a sort of semi-retirement of late, serving as a military advisor back home and embarking on various fundraising and goodwill tours. But everyone who knew him—and Mars and Calderon certainly counted themselves among that number—figured that the old man was anxious to see action again.

"I wonder how many arms he twisted and favors he called in to—"

Mars's glare caused Calderon to cut his whispered comment off in mid-sentence, though not before it had attracted Crabbe's unwelcome attention.

Before the Commodore could speak, however, Verne made one last introduction.

"Our new Commodore will take up his station aboard the *Spitzbergen*, while the rest of you will serve in supporting roles in your own Black Bird ships."

"Good," whispered Calderon, only to encounter another of Mars's *shut up* looks.

The Commander turned back to the assembled Naval and Space Patrol officers and opened his mouth to speak—

—and the room exploded in light.

"What in the—?"

Calderon slapped a hand over his eyes even as Mars gritted his teeth and peered into the glare. Betty quickly ordered her optical units to adjust to the sudden change, and exhibited no external reaction at all.

A wave of vibrant, oscillating colors washed over the walls, over the conference table, and over everyone present. The blinding flare of light seemed to Mars to have its point of origin somewhere off to his right, just behind the two Naval captains. As he squinted mightily, shading his eyes with his hand, a shape formed within the light.

"Guards!" called the Commander, hammering on the alert button near his place at the table. But no corresponding wail sounded from the walls of the station—only a still, deathly silence.

Mars was up now, fists balled, ready for danger. So were Calderon and El Rey.

Then the light diminished and the darker shape within it solidified into a humanoid form.

"What is this?" demanded El Rey. "Are we being invaded?"

As the light dimmed further, the being within it grew much more distinct. Male in appearance, his skin was a vivid, metallic blue and his eyes—lacking pupils—were entirely gold. He wore odd robes of white and blue. His head was smooth, as though he had never possessed any sort of hair at all.

Mars rubbed at his eyes, struggling to comprehend what he was seeing. A name came to him then, as from some long-lost memory.

"Monaik?"

The unusual being glanced at Mars for the merest instant. During that brief moment, he appeared to nod ever so slightly.

"Is that—is that a Faash'tan?" Calderon whispered. "Do you know him, Mars?"

"I—I'm not sure…"

The strange figure stood unmoving for a long moment, as the tension in the room ran high. He cast his strange, golden gaze at each of them in turn. And then, finally, he spoke, in words that seemed to echo as if from a great distance.

"This, then, is where it begins," he said. "Where the great events that are to come for you all truly find their origins. In your foolish, foolish decision to pursue this course of action."

The Rangers and Naval officers looked at one another in utter confusion.

"What—what are you talking about?" demanded Commander Verne. "Who are you? How did you get in here—past our screens and defenses?"

The strange being looked at him for the merest second, then turned his gaze to Betty-12.

"The mechanical woman. So interesting."

He moved closer to her.

"Do not be discouraged by others. Your hopes—your *dreams*—are within reach."

Betty's expression did not change; within her complex, computerized mind, she was directing dozens of different sensor instruments at him— though none of them were returning any sort of useful information to her at the moment. Even so, the word *dreams* caught her by surprise and caused her to flinch.

"And one other thing: Though you represent the height of your civilization's technology, remember that there are times when a good boot heel can serve you well."

Betty-12 took this in but offered no reply.

The bizarre figure turned to Calderon.

"Ah, yes. Antonio Calderon. I remember so clearly."

And then he actually seemed to smile, though what he had below his golden eyes was not something that could properly be considered a mouth.

"When the time comes, you must be prepared to think for yourself."

Calderon frowned.

"I'm sorry—?"

"The brain, Mr. Calderon. Do your own thinking—do not let *it* think for you."

If anything, Tony appeared even more confused.

"See here, now," Commodore Crabbe barked, feeling that with his new position of authority he needed to say something. He drew himself up to his full height and jabbed a finger menacingly. "What do you mean by this—coming here and delivering your cryptic remarks that no one can understand?"

"Captain Crabbe," the strange figure said by way of reply, shifting his gaze in that direction now. "Or should I say Commodore Crabbe—a signal honor, for the short time you will bear it."

"Wha—?"

"You have served long, and enjoyed an illustrious career. It is for the best. Best that you are remembered this way."

Crabbe was glaring at the alien now.

"Where are the guards?" he demanded.

Verne had been pressing the alarm button the entire time, but nothing was happening. It was as if the room had been sealed off from the rest of the station—from the rest of the universe.

The alien turned his attention back to the Rangers now, and stopped when he faced Captain El Rey.

"Ah. You. Well. What can I tell you? There is probably no hope."

El Rey gaped at him, nonplussed.

The alien raised a hand as if to fend off any retort. "No, no hope. I would have to go back much further in time to make any real difference with you." He appeared to shrug. "But you will arrive late, in any case. Your contributions will be of middling value at best."

El Rey started to speak but the strange being had already turned away. Now he focused his attention directly on Mars.

"Ah—Marshall McCoy. There you are."

Mars's initial expression of hostility and concern had lapsed into an odd bemusement once he'd determined to his own satisfaction that the alien was of no immediate danger to the station. Now he nodded and replied, "Here I am, yes."

The strange being bowed deeply—something that puzzled and disconcerted the higher-ranking officials present.

"It is a pleasure, and an honor, to meet you at last. We actually have met some dozen times before now—*before* being a relative term, of course—but only in my timeline. For you, this is the first, I believe—yes?"

Mars tried to process that, and decided that he more or less grasped its meaning. He nodded.

"The first, yes. I've never encountered you before."

The alien appeared to laugh.

"Ah, yes. There had to be a first time, after all. But first for you and first for me are not the same things."

He waved a slender arm, as if shooing away an insect.

"In any case, I tell you now as I always have told you—as I always *will* tell you: You will succeed, if you trust your instincts and remain true to yourself. Your friends are strong and will help you through what is to come—though you are right to distrust two of them. And one thing more, which will surely become clearer to you in the days to come: Though you eclipse your moons, they are an ever-present danger—and they are *two in one.*"

Mars seemed to be mulling the words over for a few seconds, even as the others in the room were reduced to merely watching and waiting.

"You can't possibly elaborate on that a bit, can you?" he asked at last.

"No. I am afraid that is all I may tell you. Even that may have been too much. Beyond that, I cannot say."

He shrugged; a gesture somehow both appropriate and outlandish for someone of his appearance.

"There are, it would appear, rules—even for one such as me."

Mars considered this, too, and nodded.

"And now," the alien said, as if all were now clear to everyone, "I bid you all a fond farewell—until our next encounter."

He paused.

"The others—those not directly involved in this—perhaps it would be better if they did not remember."

He gestured vaguely with one slender hand.

"There. Done."

Then he smiled once more at Mars.

"Farewell, Great One."

The light flared up once again, nearly blinding everyone present. And then it faded and vanished entirely.

Mars waited, watching the others, unsure of what he had just witnessed and heard, but with something of an idea as to what he should expect next.

Indeed, a few seconds later, with the light now gone and the alien gone with it, the others in the room blinked and rubbed at their eyes and then looked at one another in confusion.

"Did—did something just happen?" asked Commodore Crabbe, sounding disoriented.

Commander Verne looked down—down to where his hand hovered above the alert button. He frowned and moved it away quickly, wondering why he had been about to press it. "What was I saying?" he asked on one in particular.

Calderon, meanwhile, was looking directly at Mars.

"I still remember," he whispered. "And you called him by name. Monaik."

Mars nodded.

"We'll talk about it later."

Calderon frowned but nodded.

"Yes, we will," Betty added.

"To your ships, then," the Commander was saying, now back on track.

"The light flared up once again..."

"The task force embarks in one hour!"

Pulling Calderon and Betty along with him, Mars hurried out of the conference room.

El Rey's narrowing, knowing eyes followed him the entire time.

The hellish void of null-space surrounded the tiny, two-man flyer as it shot toward its destination.

At the controls, the man who currently knew himself only as Deimos kept one of his brown eyes on the forward windows and the other on the silvery sack that lay in the co-pilot's seat—the sack containing the strange, black iron box. In the more than two weeks since he'd taken the box from that cold, dead planet, he'd found he could not long look away from it. Sweat trailed down his face and neck, though whether due to the temperature aboard the ship, to some alien influence leaking through the shielded bag, or simply to his own anxiety, he could not say.

"Not far to go now," he whispered to himself. "Hold it together a little longer and everything will be just fine. That box will be in the hands of the man who truly wants it—who knows how best to use it—and I will be richer than I ever could have imagined."

Deimos replayed all that had happened on the abandoned world over and over again in his mind. While he regretted potentially making the Cabal his enemies, he doubted anyone in their order would ever discover what had happened back on that abandoned wasteland of a world. And by the time they ever pieced it all together, he would be safe and sound on the far side of the galaxy, with a different name and face, and a whole battalion of security guards to protect him.

Not that he had any real qualms about working with the Adversary—or, to be honest, *using* them. The Cabal agents had possessed resources and equipment and influence to help him locate that forgotten world and to dig down seemingly through miles of sealed-off sub-surface crypts until they'd finally found the chamber they'd been seeking for so long. But he'd never had the slightest intentions of actually allowing them to keep the box, once it was found. Deimos laughed at the mere thought of such a thing.

It had all been just as the forbidden alien texts had claimed. The box had been there—and the thing inside the box. And now it belonged to Deimos.

Well, it belonged to him for at least a little while longer, until the transaction could be completed. But then life would be good indeed. Quite good—

His head slumped forward, banging into the console, and lay there, still. Two long seconds passed, and then he snapped back up again. But now, his face was different—changed somehow. The differences were subtle but very real. His eyes flashed left and right, taking everything in, as if seeing the ship for the first time.

His hazel eyes. The eyes of Phobos.

"What—where am—?"

Then those frantic, burning eyes focused on the co-pilot's seat, and settled upon the silvery sack.

"No. No!"

Tenuously Phobos reached over with one hand, until his fingers lightly brushed the woven metallic surface of the container.

"It's in there. It's here!"

He snatched his hand back as though the bag might have bitten his fingers off.

"How? Why—why do I have it? The Cabal should—"

And then, as if some lost memory had come back in a flash, Phobos understood what had happened. Understood all of it.

"Ohhh. Oh, you fool. You imbecile! What have you done to us?"

Eyeing the sack now as if it contained all the evils of the world—and to him, it did—Phobos moved his hands across the ship's controls. Fear washed over him—fear in virtually palpable waves.

"Back. Have to go back. Have to give it to them—to the Cabal. They—"

The thing in the box responded to the fear—the overwhelming fear unleashed in tangible form by a natural telepath. It latched onto that fear, feeding upon it, growing stronger and stronger.

Throughout null-space the waves of fear radiated as it broadcast from some powerful communications transmitter. Across all the territory of the Fringe Worlds the telepathic signal washed. Meanwhile, the bizarre and scarcely-understood properties of null space itself magnified the psychic force and redirected it back in towards the man in the tiny ship. Phobos felt as if his mind, his body, and indeed the entire universe were shimmering, wavering, about to drop entirely out of phase with reality.

"No!" he cried, flailing about blindly.

His hands slapped at the ship's controls and deactivated the null-engine. Instantly, the tiny ship spun about and dropped out of null-space.

Phobos lurched forward, his forehead striking the console again.

The ship came to a near-halt, floating along serenely in space.

The figure at the ship's controls lay still.

Nearly twenty minutes passed.

The figure stirred.

It was Deimos who sat up.

"Ohh," he groaned, rubbing at his forehead. Then he gazed out the ship's forward windows. The stars twinkled coldly before him. A spiraling nebula filled the left side of his field of view and trailed lazily along behind the ship. Nothing moved.

"Wha—back in real space? Why—what happened?"

He leaned forward, one hand rubbing at his bruised forehead as the other manipulated the ship's controls.

"Dropped from null-space that long ago? But—what could have caused that?"

He frantically whirled to look at the co-pilot's seat.

The silvery sack remained where it had been all along, with the shape of the iron box outlined in the way that it lay.

Deimos breathed in and out twice, relief spilling over him.

"Must have blacked out," he muttered finally. "Could have been worse—could have woken up inside a star."

Then he began the laborious process of locating his position in space and plotting a course to where he'd been going before. Not a hard job for him—for someone who had completed Ranger training with the Space Patrol.

"The Sargasso… Have to get to the Sargasso…"

Things were okay. The operation had not been affected. All was as it had been.

Meanwhile, behind his brown eyes, phantom hazel orbs flickered frantically as the soundless voice of Phobos screamed.

INTRUDER ALERT!! INTRUDER ALERT!!

The alarm claxons resounded throughout the corridors of the Black Hole, sending Rangers and support personnel alike running for their action stations—some frantically, others with the measured cool that comes from a lifetime of service on the frontier.

Mars McCoy was halfway to his quarters, having sent Calderon and Betty to finish packing, when the alert sounded. A radio link to the command center was situated on the wall nearby and Mars ran up to it, slapping the activation switch. Even as he did so, he brought his surging emotions tightly under control, and when he spoke, it was with a remarkably calm, detached coolness.

"This is McCoy. What's happening?"

The voice of none other than Commander Verne came back instantly.

"We're being attacked, Mars. Invaded!"

Mars's shock was palpable—never in all its history had the Space Patrol's asteroid base been located, much less attacked, by any of the Rangers' many foes. So what could possibly be happening? Had an enemy force at last spotted the constantly-moving Black Hole and launched an assault?

Mars knew that the answers to his questions would come soon enough, presuming the station survived whatever was happening. So he set such thoughts aside and instead simply asked, "Where?"

Seconds later, he was racing for the long central corridor that led out towards the Black Hole's most exterior decks.

"What've we got?" he demanded as he rounded the last corner and encountered a squad of five other Rangers crouching behind a hastily-erected barricade. Even as he spoke, one of the men popped up and fired a volley of blaster shots into a murky darkness that appeared to have filled the hallway.

"A whole crowd of 'em, sir," a fresh-faced young lieutenant answered over the clattering report of another Ranger firing his pistol in the same direction. "All clumped down that way. It's hard to see 'em now, but they're there."

Mars started to ask exactly who—or what—it was that had invaded the station. But then the smell hit him. A smell so pungent—and so memorable—that he didn't have to pose the question aloud.

"It's those...*things*...we fought before," he muttered. "How is that possible?"

"Sir?"

Mars glanced over at the questioning young officer and shook his head. His mind was working over the possibilities, but as of yet he felt completely stumped.

A familiar voice echoed down the corridor. Mars looked up to see Calderon bounding towards him.

"What's going on, Mars?"

The screeching wail of one of the creatures reverberated throughout the corridor at that moment, and Calderon stopped short, his eyes wide and his normally tanned face growing pale.

"What in the name of all that's holy was *that?!*"

"Something I was hoping I wouldn't have to deal with again any time soon," Mars replied sharply. He motioned to the Rangers—all lieutenants, he saw with a glance—who were manning the barricade. "Take charge here, Tony. Hold the line. Don't let those things up into the main levels if you can help it."

"Got it," Calderon stated firmly, unholstering his blaster. "What are you going to do?"

"I'm not exactly sure yet," Mars replied. "But I'm working on it."

Calderon gave him a grim smile, then turned and opened fire into the murk. Vivid streaks of energy flashed down the corridor, disappearing from view in the darkness. Perhaps in reaction, the creatures wailed and moaned more loudly.

Mars ran in the opposite direction, heading for the command deck, passing startled technicians and Rangers as he went. Having spent so much of his relatively young life aboard the Black Hole, he knew it like the back of his hand, and took a couple of shortcuts that wouldn't have occurred to most other residents of the station. Seconds later he bounded up the steps leading to the command center three at a time and passed through the oval entryway.

Commander Verne stood at the center of the broad, circular room, surrounded on all sides by technicians and support staff at their various stations. A wide arc of display screens hung from the ceiling, their images flickering madly, sending garish, dappled colors across everyone present.

"How did those monsters get on board?" Mars asked without preamble.

"We don't know yet," the older man replied, his lined face grim. "We haven't been able to locate any non-Ranger spacecraft outside the Black Hole, or any attached to its surface."

"Cloaking technology of some sort?"

"Perhaps, perhaps," Verne said, frowning. "In any case, a veritable army of them are on board now." He jabbed a finger at a nearby scanner display. "And you've seen them before, haven't you?"

Mars nodded solemnly.

Operating at a different set of wavelengths from the human eye, the station's interior scanners were able to penetrate the murk and thus revealed a horde of the very same creatures Mars and his companions had encountered and fought mere hours earlier—and light years away. The same pale, ectoplasmic flesh; the same array of burning, red eyes; the same keening moan issuing from whatever they used for throats. The horrific monsters shambled through the corridors of the station, smashing equipment left and right and sending the Patrol's personnel scrambling for safety.

"It *is* them," he growled. "I knew it just from the smell, but…"

"I thought so."

"How can that be?" Mars wondered aloud, his green eyes wide with surprise. "Could they have…*followed* us back here? Or tagged along somehow?"

Verne glanced at him worriedly, not liking the sound of that.

"Commander," crackled Calderon's voice across the link, "we're not having much luck with these things. Our shots just bounce off them—or get absorbed by them. I don't know what else to do here. We're falling back to the next bulkhead."

"Understood, Lieutenant," Verne responded. "Try to hold the line as best you can."

"Will do, sir."

In the background, Mars could hear the whine and shriek of blasters firing away, along with the horrifying noise that arose from the horde.

"Blasters don't do much good against those things—as Tony is finding out the hard way, right now," he muttered. "If only we knew how they got here…"

Verne had returned his attention to the creatures on the monitor, watching as they continued to press forward, smashing everything in their path.

"I don't know where they came from or how they got on board, Captain, but first things first—we need to deal with them before they wreck any more of the station."

Mars took a deep breath, setting the unanswered questions that nagged at him aside, then nodded once.

"Understood, sir."

He moved his muscular frame to an unoccupied tech station and punched buttons rapidly. In response, the display flickered through a variety of station layout diagrams, one after the other.

"No, no, that's not it…"

Verne came up behind him, a puzzled look on his face.

"I assumed, Captain, that you would assemble a fire team and go—"

Verne's voice trailed off as he looked over Mars's shoulder and saw the array of schematics flashing by on the monitor.

"Mars—what—?"

The station diagrams clicked past in a blur until Mars found what he was looking for and froze the screen. A chill ran along his spine.

"If they continue along that path, sir," Mars explained, tapping the glass of the monitor, "they'll reach the main engines and the reactors."

Mars could hear a growl low in the older officer's throat. "They'll blow us all to kingdom come!"

Mars traced the path the creatures were taking with his finger, until he came to a Y-shaped intersection. Narrowing his eyes thoughtfully, he traced along the upper course. Seeing what he saw there, a plan began to form in his razor-sharp mind.

He pointed at the upper corridor—a long, straight hallway that curved along the very edge of the station, just opposite the outer hull.

"There."

Verne looked at Mars, blinked, then looked at the display.

"There what?"

"Have Calderon herd them in there, sir. Into that corridor. See if he can get them all in there."

Verne nodded slowly.

"All right, all right, but—why?"

"Because if we can't zap 'em," Mars replied, already dashing for the exit, "maybe we can get rid of them another way."

"Mars, this is crazy," came the voice of Antonio Calderon over Mars's hand-held comm link. "We've barricaded the corridor outside the primary reactor but they're still coming—and we can't push 'em back!"

"Just keep hammering away at them, Tony," Mars replied. "Slow 'em down as best you can."

"They've smashed their way through three bulkheads already," Calderon exclaimed. "I'm running out of ideas down here!"

Mars finished pulling the boots of his spacesuit on, fastening them securely to the rest of the outfit, then donned his gloves and reached for his helmet. "I know, Tony—but you've got to herd them into that outer passageway."

"Right," Calderon said, not sounding at all confident at the moment. "Some reinforcements are arriving now with heavier ordnance. We'll see what we can do..."

Mars snapped on the suit's helmet and latched the airtight seal. Then he grasped the one remaining object on the bench in front of him: A shoulder-fired, heavy assault rocket launcher.

"This had better work," he whispered to himself as he hefted the weapon and looked it over, popping it open and making sure everything was in order. Satisfied, he snapped it back together and then moved as quickly as the suit would allow out of the armory and down the hallway to the nearest airlock.

By the time Mars had gotten himself into the airlock and sealed the inner hatch, Calderon's voice sounded again on the link.

"Okay, Mars—we're forcing them into that corridor now, like you wanted. It hasn't been what I'd call easy, but with enough firepower, I guess anything's possible."

"Get 'em all down there, Tony," Mars replied tersely, "and then get out of there and seal the bulkheads behind you! You read me? *Seal the bulkheads!*"

"Yeah, yeah..."

Commander Verne's voice crackled over the link just as Mars was opening the outer hatch.

"Captain, I think I know what you have in mind, and I know it won't do any good to order you not to do it. So I'll simply say, 'Good luck.'"

"Thank you, sir," Mars replied. The outer hatch out of the way now, he shoved himself out into space.

The stars filled Mars's view, sending that same sense of awe flooding through him that it always did. This time, though, he shoved such thoughts aside and concentrated on the business at hand. Activating the small jets on his suit, he spun around until the massive, dark bulk of the Black Hole was all he could see.

An asteroid that had been hollowed out and restructured by the Space Patrol for use as their main base, the Black Hole wasn't terribly pretty from the outside. In point of fact, it looked like any other asteroid—just another big, gray rock spinning through space. That, along with its constant relocation to various spots along the Fringe, meant that the Patrol's enemies could never locate it, never lay siege to it.

Until now, anyway, it appeared.

Mars angled around the curved, craggy surface until he came to what he was sure was the same portion of the station's exterior that he'd seen on the schematic diagram. He didn't possess photographic memory but he'd made very sure to acquaint himself with the look of this location, fearing the consequences if he chose the wrong spot.

Squinting at the rocky mass, he could visualize the position of the long corridor a few feet beneath the surface, running just so—from one end to the other of this portion of the asteroid.

First he used his jet pack to put some distance between himself and the station. The hiss of the little rockets came to him through the suit, clicking on and off as he reached what he hoped was the proper range. Stopping his momentum, he re-oriented himself, seeing the dark form of the Black Hole slide before him once again. Then, nodding purposefully inside his helmet, he hefted his weapon onto his shoulder and pointed it toward the station.

"Tony, what's the word down there? Where are the creatures now?"

A pause, then Calderon's voice crackled back, the thickness of the station's rocky hull distorting the signal somewhat.

"They're all in the corridor you wanted them in, Mars—but don't ask me how we managed it. And I don't think they're gonna stay for long— they're already starting to batter their way through the wall here."

"Okay, Tony, good work. Just get out of there. Get through the hatch and seal it. Now!"

"I'm gone, pal. I just hope you know what you're doing."

"Yeah, me too," Mars whispered to himself.

The rocket launcher in place on his shoulder, he clicked off the safety and popped the trigger mechanism into place. Then he lined up the sights.

"I never thought I'd be firing on my own home," he whispered to himself. "Here goes nothing…"

His gloved thumb pressed down on the firing button.

Fire erupted behind him as the rocket streaked out of its tube and lanced toward the station's surface in a blinding glare. It impacted with a fantastic explosion, followed by a bigger blast as the rocky hull gave way and the atmosphere behind it erupted out.

The shock of the blast, once it reached him through the evacuating air and debris, was such that Mars found himself buffeted to the side. He fought to re-orient himself as quickly as possible, his sharp eyes flickering across the newly-created space junk as it whizzed past him.

"Where are they…where are they…?"

He triggered his jets once more, backing away in order to better see the rapidly expanding cloud of debris. He searched through it with increasing anxiety for any signs of the invaders.

Did I hit the wrong part of the station? The wrong corridor? Where are they?

After a few seconds, most of the debris had tumbled away from the station. Mars had never once seen any signs of the creatures amidst the results of his blast.

"Tony, this is Mars. I'm not seeing anything. What do you have in there? Did I hit the wrong spot?"

"No way, pal," Calderon responded instantly. "You hit the right deck—it was a perfect shot. That was right where they were conglomerated, I guarantee it."

Inside his helmet, Mars chewed his lip. He hesitated to put his friend in the path of danger, but knew Calderon would insist on doing what needed doing. So...

"Tony, I'm going to jet in closer from this direction. You approach from the inside. Let's see if we can triangulate on them—figure out where they've gone off to."

Calderon's response was instantaneous.

"No problem, Cap'n. On my way now."

Twenty minutes of careful searching later, both men had to admit that the creatures that had invaded the station were nowhere to be found. Scans revealed nothing of their presence amid the debris field that had been created when Mars had blasted the hull. And searches all throughout the interior of the ship likewise gave no signs of their presence.

"I don't get it," Calderon growled as he helped Mars out of his spacesuit. "How could they just disappear like that?"

"It's not the first time," Mars replied, pulling the bulky spacewalk boots off his feet and storing them away in a locker along with the rest of the equipment. "I should have expected as much, given what we saw back on Artinax-2." He shook his head grimly. "They don't like to leave prisoners behind. Though how they do it—I have no idea."

Just then the wall communicator buzzed and Tony smacked it with his fist.

"Calderon here."

The gruff voice of Commander Verne crackled over the link.

"Lieutenant, is Captain McCoy with you?"

"I'm here, sir."

"I'm sure you boys have lots to talk about, with regard to our uninvited guests—and by that you understand that I mean the creatures, not the Navy."

Mars and Calderon exchanged wry grins.

"But we're on the clock, and that clock is ticking. You'll have plenty of time to discuss your theories in transit. In other words—Task Force Obsidian is still on, and it launches in twenty minutes!"

The two Rangers' expressions changed from smiles to surprise—the old man wasn't letting a little thing like an invasion of their headquarters by monsters push him off track!

"Understood, Commander," Mars replied with crisp precision. "We're on our way to the hangar level now."

"Good hunting, gentlemen!"

"So, Commodore Crabbe once captained Black Bird One?" asked Betty-12 as she and the two male Rangers hurried for their ships. She had caught up with them en route to the hangar deck after they'd made a quick swing by their quarters to pick up fresh uniforms and other supplies.

"Years ago, yeah," Mars replied. "But they've been trotting him around like a show horse for the last few years, using him as a living recruiting poster and fundraiser for the Patrol."

"The scuttlebutt has been that he hasn't entirely hated that posting," Calderon said with a shrug. "Fine dining, fancy parties, and—"

Mars was frowning at him.

"The man's accomplished too much in his career to write him off that way now. Let's give the new Commodore the chance to show he still has it, before we trash him like that."

"Sorry, Mars," Calderon said, looking chagrined.

"Poor Flint," Betty added. "I'm certain he would like to join us for this mission. If only he hadn't broken his leg."

"They've nearly gotten him fixed up already," Calderon noted, huffing and puffing and beginning to fall behind the athletic Mars and the robotic Betty-12. "But there are no guarantees the Commander would have chosen him or his ship for the mission, even if he were okay."

"I'll give him a call after we've gotten underway," Mars stated flatly. "Cheer him up as best I can."

Arriving at the hangar complex, the three Rangers encountered several of their comrades already preparing to board their vessels.

"So, three Black Birds, then?" Calderon noted, looking over the ships and crews.

"You're quite the observant one, aren't you, Lieutenant?" sniped back Captain El Rey, looking none too happy about the situation. He was loading stores into a side hatch of Black Bird Six. "And shouldn't you be doing this, while I prep the flight plan?"

Calderon gave Mars a quick and hidden look of annoyance before hurrying over to his captain's side, where he began loading boxes into the ship.

With a half-laugh, half-sigh, Mars turned and strode toward his own ship, Black Bird Five, parked just across the hangar, Betty alongside him as always. They had made it about halfway when a tall, willowy figure suddenly moved out of the shadows and stepped in front of them.

"Oh! Jeez, No-Rah, I wish you wouldn't do that," Mars exclaimed.

"My apologies, Captain," the Vayren Ranger replied with a slight bow. He pulled the hood back from his head and smiled—it was an expression that might have chilled anyone not familiar with the Vayren race. "Occasionally," he went on, "I forget how—*unearthly*, shall we say—my appearance can seem to your kind."

Mars regarded his fellow captain's deathly pale skin and the round goggles covering his large eyes. He merely shook his head with a smile.

"So you're coming along on this trip, too, eh?"

"Indeed," No-Rah said, gesturing toward his own ship, Black Bird Seven, where it rested to the right of Mars's vessel. Its hull shone as if recently polished, and the emblem of a silver star in a white circle stood out on the ship's black fuselage. "Although I must admit, I do find myself lacking in a co-pilot at the moment."

Mars frowned, as did Betty-12 a second later.

"Lt. Thern is on leave at the moment. It seems he had no idea a galactic conflict was about to erupt in his absence."

Mars grinned at his friend's dry comments.

"Well, you have to have somebody with you," he said. "And we're awfully short on time. Any ideas about—"

Captain No-Rah was already nodding behind Mars, toward the lifts. Mars turned and saw that the doors had just opened and an odd pair of figures had emerged. As they approached, one with a clear degree of timidity and the other with a noticeable limp, Mars's expression changed from puzzlement to a clear understanding—and rejection.

"No. No way."

"Aw, come on, Mars—I'm fine," Flint Rogers asserted strongly, waving away the other captain's objections. "Fit as a fiddle. Whatever that is. Ready to go!"

"You have a broken leg," Mars pointed out.

"You have a broken leg," Betty echoed beside them, concern apparent on her face.

"It's nearly healed already," Flint replied. "The docs have all kinds of fancy equipment—they set it and accelerated the healing process—it's already back to normal. Mostly."

"Mostly," Mars repeated.

Mars and Betty both scrutinized Rogers closely while No-Rah merely stepped back, awaiting the conclusion of their strange, alien negotiations. He had long since ceased trying to follow such matters.

Meanwhile, the other figure who had come with Rogers and helped him across the hangar stood back and waited, as well. He carried a travel bag under one arm and appeared to be a human male in his mid-thirties, with curly, black hair and pale blue eyes. Of course, as with most things in the Space Patrol, appearances could be deceiving.

Mars turned to this new arrival—an unusual presence on the hangar deck—and nodded to him.

"Can we help you with something, Dr. Bosco? Because we're just about to launch."

Bosco looked quickly from Mars to Rogers and then back to Mars again.

"I—um—I—that is—"

Mars waited patiently.

"I wish to go on the mission," he finished at last, having seemingly summoned up an unexpected reserve of courage.

Mars smiled politely.

"I appreciate the offer, Doctor, and your willingness to be involved, but I'm not sure we will be needing a xenobiologist on this operation. Not even a robotic one such as yourself."

"Yeah—no offense, Doc," Rogers interjected, "but unless you can reload a blast-pistol with one hand while firing with the other, I don't think we'll have much use for you."

Mars shot the junior captain a look.

"Flint, it hasn't been determined yet if we'll be needing *you* on this mission."

Rogers clammed up quickly.

Mars turned back to the dark-headed doctor.

"So unless there's something I don't—"

"You will likely be encountering hostile alien races," Dr. Bosco stated firmly.

"Yes, that's probably true," Mars replied. "And that's a big reason why you shouldn't be—"

"Including perhaps the hostile alien race that wiped out my world," he continued, running right over Mars's words.

"I don't know, but I—"

Mars paused in his response, thought about it for a moment, and then glanced at the others around them. Calderon shrugged; Rogers seemed surprised but gave a sort of half-nod; Betty actually nodded firmly; and No-Rah remained aloof and detached as ever.

Mars looked back at Bosco and met as firm and determined a glare from the man as he'd ever encountered in his life. Almost despite himself, he said, "Okay, that's fine. You can fly on our ship for now. Stow your belongings on Black Bird Five and buckle up."

Without another word, Dr. Bosco hurried over to the ship and stowed his travel bag away. As he finished and turned around, Betty-12 came up to him and nodded once. He seemed at first to shy away from her look, but then straightened and nodded back.

"You are welcome on our ship," she stated flatly, emotionlessly.

"Thank you," he replied. Perhaps as an afterthought, he added, "It will be good to spend an extended voyage with one of my own kind."

If Betty heard this or agreed with it, she gave no indication. Instead she merely continued with her task of prepping the ship for launch.

After a moment, a seemingly crestfallen Dr. Bosco shuffled through the hatch and disappeared inside.

"Time to go," Rogers was saying as he limped toward No-Rah's Black Bird Seven. "No more time to argue."

Mars sighed and nodded.

"Okay, Flint—but take it easy. Stick to co-piloting and do what No-Rah tells you."

"You are welcome on our ship."

"Not a problem," the cocky young Ranger replied with a blindingly bright grin. "I haven't been a captain long enough to forget all the tricks of the co-piloting trade, unlike you old guys."

Mars laughed and, throwing Flint a salute, hurried for his own ship, while the slender form of No-Rah approached Nine.

"I assume, then, that your labyrinthine and incomprehensible human negotiations are concluded, and that you will indeed be serving as my co-pilot for this operation."

Flint couldn't help smiling at his new captain, as the wraithlike figure glided up into the ship.

"That's right, Cap'n," he replied. *And this,* he thought to himself, *should make for one heck of an interesting trip...*

Five minutes later, Black Birds Five, Six, and Seven blasted out of the hangar deck of the Black Hole station and zoomed out into the darkness, there to rendezvous with the two enormous battleships that awaited them.

Moments after that, with a null-space gateway opened by the lead ship, Task Force Obsidian roared off into the unknown.

The sea of wrecked starships stretched for thousands of miles in every direction.

Great cylinders and cubes and curving pods of a million designs twirled past. Severed electrical cables and sparkling crystals tumbled here and there, occasionally bumping into one another and slightly changing the paths of their never-ending dance. Blackened hulks the size of major cities collided with pieces of singleships and escape pods. There was no order to be found in the swirling currents of the spaceship graveyard; and yet that somehow seemed to represent a sort of bizarre order itself, lending strange symmetry and form to the chaos.

Deimos peered out at the tableau before him in awe. No one could gaze upon such a sight without feeling some semblance of shock and amazement at the sheer number of wrecked craft clumped together in this area that humans referred to as the "Sargasso of Space."

Some of the ships were of human origin; not many, though, as humanity had not traveled among the stars long enough to contribute greatly to the vast collection of galactic detritus. A careful and knowledgeable observer would also discern ships from the Orgum Ree, Barabanaborgugi, Caspas,

Trenago, Trions, Verib, and even a few belonging to the Vayren—all the starfaring races that made up the Galactic Alliance appeared to have at least one representative in the sea of wreckage.

Digging deeper into the ocean of refuse would turn up ancient starships originally constructed by alien races no longer known to the galaxy, worn nearly smooth by the unending millennia through which they had collided with one another. At the heart of the Sargasso floated strange and bizarre vehicles—if vehicles they were—never seen by any race that currently traversed the spaceways, their pilots and passengers long-since mummified or gone to dust.

Occasionally a brave and adventurous explorer would attempt to navigate his or her way deep into the Sargasso in search of the elusive "alien super-tech" that might bring a fortune to its lucky discoverer. Rarely did such adventurers ever emerge again. When they did, most babbled on about sights no mortal soul was meant to see. And thus did the dark center of the sea remain a mystery, even in this age of easy interstellar travel.

As he always did when passing near the Sargasso, Deimos spared a moment to consider what might be found—what priceless wonders gained—by the individual who managed to penetrate to the heart of the starship graveyard and bring back wondrous alien technology. But he did not dwell on such thoughts. He dared not. His was another mission, another set of priorities.

He had the Box in his possession, and he meant to rid himself of it— and fill his bank account with great wealth—at the Sargasso. And then to get out of there with all possible haste, in order to survive and to enjoy the fruits of his labor in more pleasant climes, far from this dark corner of the galaxy.

Yet for all that the great sea of hulks appeared utterly devoid of life, Deimos knew this was not true. In fact, he wondered just how many sets of eyes—human or otherwise—were scrutinizing him at this very moment, studying his ship's markings and attempting to determine just who he was and why he was here—and what he might possess of value. Dozens of eyes? Hundreds? The thought made him shiver, but he put it aside and got on with the business that had brought him here.

Pausing just beyond the outer periphery of the cloud of wrecks, he sat back in his seat and recited the mnemonic devices that, if all went according to plan, should cause him to recall the proper string of digits…
Yes.

The numbers and letters emerging from behind their hypnotic blocks and forming clearly in his mind, Deimos keyed them into his ship's communications array. Then he set the dial to the proper channel and waited.

After a few moments, a faint burst of static sounded from the cabin speakers. Deimos frowned and waited a few more seconds for the second burst, identical to the first. And, right on schedule, came a third squawk.

Nodding in satisfaction, he manipulated his ship's controls and spun about until the static burst had become louder and more distinct. Then, slowly and with great care, he moved his ship into the Sargasso, following the path of the broadcast.

On the surface, the act of actually entering the sea of wreckage appeared suicidal. Ships much, much larger than Deimos's own tumbled all about. Any one of them spelled instant and certain death should it strike him. In fact, his ship looked to be the smallest one for quite some distance. And yet, after only a few seconds of travel into the Sea, it became obvious that more was at work here than random chance. None of the wrecks came close to hitting him. They fell past in every direction, all around, but left a clear path, almost tunnel-like, down the center of the Sea.

Deeper and deeper he plunged into the swirling swarms of hulks and rubble, with many near-misses but no actual impacts along the way.

After a short while it became obvious to him that he was no longer in danger—at least, not from the swirling swarm of hulks. Setting his ship on autopilot, he relaxed into his seat and waited, allowing his mind to roam freely over the events of the past few days.

Originally there had been no hurry to get to the rendezvous with the buyer. They had arranged in advance a fairly broad window of time in which to meet here. But as Deimos had traveled along the straightest path to the Sargasso, he had begun to encounter disturbing signs—signs of a major conflict brewing here in the Fringe. Just who was fighting who had never become entirely clear to him, but beyond any doubt, a war was coming—if it hadn't arrived already.

After a while his ruminations were interrupted by a *ping* coming from his console. He looked up and saw that the tunnel of clear space through which he'd been traveling was ending. He had apparently reached its terminus, and now a massive cluster of wreckage loomed directly ahead.

Quickly he switched off the autopilot and brought his vessel to a halt.

"What in the—?"

He peered out at the slowly spinning structure, an amalgamation of bits and pieces of countless alien ships, all cobbled together into a gargantuan Frankenstein's monster of space. Every color of the rainbow shone along the surface of the conglomeration, with some parts appearing relatively new and others seeming to be many, many millennia old and worn away to dull smoothness. At first glance, it looked to be just another random clustering of hulks and debris, albeit a particularly large one. Closer inspection, however, revealed the work of a conscious design—a plan.

"Ohh," he whispered then. "Right."

It was a base—a space station. And one as well-hidden and protected as any in the galaxy.

Even as Deimos realized just what it was he was seeing, a wide panel on the station's exterior slid slowly open. From the revealed hangar bay shot a trio of fighter ships. Deimos squinted at them, studying them carefully even as they closed in on him.

"I guess they take whatever they can get," he muttered.

Indeed, the three ships were nothing alike. Each must have begun its career here as salvage from some earlier battle or accident. Repaired in visibly haphazard fashion—yet still clearly very deadly—these fighters now served the masters of this base. Deimos didn't need to see the crude markings on their sides to know who that was—whom they belonged to.

"The pirates."

The fighters circled around his ship as the pilots scrutinized him carefully. Then one of them pulled close enough for him to see inside its canopy, and the pilot there—a ragged looking sort—motioned sharply for Deimos to follow.

Dutifully he trailed the three ships into the hangar bay, the door panel sliding closed again behind them.

Moments later, his ship securely resting on a wide empty space, he studied the environmental scanner. Gravity and air—neither quite up to human standards, but probably the closest this strange amalgamation of alien technology would allow. Shrugging, he popped open the canopy, retrieved the silvery bag from the other seat, and started to climb out. Meanwhile, the three fighter ships also landed in a triangle formation, surrounding him.

Within moments, he found himself surrounded by a veritable battalion of pirates.

In appearance, the crowd pretty much ran the gamut from the most aristocratic, well-dressed dandy to the most flea-bitten scum. Some wore heavy coats of red or blue—understandable, given the deep chill in the air that Deimos had become aware of—while others stood like savages, nearly naked but for their intense body modifications and perhaps a loincloth or two. Some appraised him coolly, others all but salivated, disconcerting him to a degree.

Ignoring this as best he could, he smiled and nodded politely to them. "Gentlemen."

Half the pirates sneered, the other half growled, and all together they gave Deimos a distinct impression that they might well decide to simply kill him then and there and sift through his belongings at their leisure.

But both he and they knew that they worked for the man known as Kargan. And Kargan was one of the most powerful and influential of the pirate lords. These were Kargan's men, through and through. They didn't dare oppose his will—didn't dare take some precipitous action that would jeopardize one of his operations.

Or so he fervently hoped.

Unfortunately for Deimos, it took scarcely two minutes of walking through the motley station before the pirates sprang their trap.

They had just rounded a tight corner and Deimos had lost sight of half the group for a moment when the lights suddenly went out.

Deimos turned about slowly, his eyes flickering this way and that, seeing nothing.

"Wait, now—I have a deal," he called out desperately. "A deal with Captain Kargan. He won't like you interfering with it—he won't like you holding up the process, gentlemen!"

"He won't care," a raspy voice growled in reply, "if he never hears about it. If he never knows you were here."

From the depths of the darkness all around him, Deimos could hear the ring of daggers pulled from their sheaths, the clatter of the boots on the metal deck as the pirates closed in.

Task Force Obsidian emerged from null-space and flashed out into the normal universe once more. And, just like that, the war was upon them.

Bursts of weapons fire and violent explosions rocked the entire fleet. Alarms wailed as Navy techs and crewmembers rushed to battle stations, while the Commodore and the captains demanded information.

Black Bird Five shot past the two big battleships and curved around for a look, the other two Ranger ships just behind it. At the controls, Mars peered through the cockpit windows and frowned.

"It's the Orgum-Ree," came Flint Rogers's voice over the null-radio, filled with excitement. "I knew it!"

"Orgum-Ree? Where are you seeing them?" Calderon replied, a tinge of nervousness in his voice. "I don't see any. But I see some Baraban ships, and they're fighting—what, the Trenago?"

Mars blinked at this unexpected news, then flashed his keen eyes across the starscape again, as numerous ships of all shapes and sizes swarmed past, weapons blazing away.

"Why would the Baraban be fighting the Trenago?" asked Betty-12, beside him. "Neither race has ever expressed much in the way of militarism, and certainly not toward one another. Indeed—"

Rogers's voice over the null-radio interrupted her: "Now I'm seeing Caspa ships. Caspas! Are you kidding me?"

"Insanity," came the flat voice of No-Rah, summing things up in his usual, succinct manner.

Mars shook his head. "What's going on here?"

Dr. Bosco came up from the passenger area and leaned down to see out better. He exchanged a very puzzled look with Mars.

"No, Flint," Calderon was saying, "it's not the Caspas—it's the Trions!"

"Yeah, yeah, I see them too, now. Jeez—I think just about every race in the galaxy is represented in this battle. What in the—?"

"Enough," came the sharp voice of Captain El Rey in Black Bird Six. "Cut the chatter and form up on the battleships."

Mars felt a bit of resentment in the pit of his stomach over El Rey issuing orders in such a fashion, but he bit his tongue before he could say anything he'd regret. Besides, he reasoned, El Rey had a point—they needed to settle down and find out what was going on here. And they needed to do so fast, before the damage to interstellar peace grew too great to repair—if it hadn't reached that point already.

The three Black Birds swooped back out of the thick of the carnage, somehow managing to avoid being blasted by random fire along the way, and settled into position around the massive, cylindrical forms of the *Jakarta* and the *Spitzbergen*.

"Captain McCoy," radioed Commodore Crabbe once they'd reformed the task force, "I'm assuming you are seeing what we here are seeing. Can you determine any pattern or logic to this conflict?"

"None whatsoever, Commodore," Mars replied, still gazing in shock at the carnage just ahead. "It's a brawl—a melee."

There was a pause as Crabbe spoke with someone else away from the microphone. Then, "That's indeed how we see it. We are hailing the various parties on all frequencies, but have yet to receive a single response. Thus we are about to attempt to get their attention through… other means. Stand by for quick action, Captain."

"Aye, sir," Mars replied, before glancing over at Betty-12. "Brace yourself," he told her. "I have a feeling I know what those 'other means' might be."

Indeed, before the words had all left his mouth, bright flashes of light flared out from both the *Jakarta* and the *Spitzbergen*. The big ships had opened up with full volleys of blast-cannon fire, momentarily turning the eternal night of deep space into high noon.

The carefully-aimed shots struck no ships, but certainly came close enough to many of them. Under ordinary circumstances, any sane ship's captain would have frozen his vessel in its tracks and hauled-to for boarding, given such a message. But these were hardly ordinary circumstances.

"They're ignoring us—ignoring the battleships," Flint gasped over the radio. "You have to be kidding me!"

Another volley of blast-cannon fire erupted out of the big ships, this time actually striking—and vaporizing—two smaller vessels along the way.

"Still nothing." Mars watched in astonishment. "They just don't care."

"They only appear to be concerned with destroying one another," replied No-Rah.

"Further," added Betty from the co-pilot's seat, "I have studied the patterns of their attacks upon one another, and they seem to be completely random."

Mars frowned at that, glancing over at her.

"You mean—?"

"It is purest chaos," came the voice of No-Rah.

"Exactly," El Rey added. "There are no 'sides' in this conflict. They're all shooting at each other. All of them. It's every man—or being—for itself!"

The voice of the Commodore crackled across the line again.

"We're not getting anywhere with this—we're only endangering our own ships. Pull back. Pull away. We'll let 'em fight it out and see what comes of it."

Mars started to object to this. The thought of allowing such senseless, wholesale carnage left him sick to his stomach. Yet if even the devastating fire of a Navy battleship couldn't so much as get the attention of the warring parties…

"Understood, Commodore," he replied, as did the other Rangers.

Within moments, Black Birds Five, Six and Seven had joined the battleships on the periphery of the battle. Mars and the other captains and crews reluctantly sat back, only able to watch the dance of death and destruction occurring before them; unable to affect it in any way short of actually destroying the warring ships themselves.

Minutes after that, only a handful of ships remained in combat, the rest having destroyed one another.

And then:

"Captain," Betty said suddenly, pointing through the clear canopy towards the scene of battle far beyond. "They have stopped shooting."

Mars sat up. He leaned forward and peered out into space.

The firing had indeed stopped.

"How many ships are left?" It was difficult to tell, given the extent of wreckage spread across the sector.

Betty performed a quick calculation.

"Twelve ships still functional and moving, Captain."

"What could have made them stop?" asked Dr. Bosco, leaning forward into the command section of the Black Bird.

"What made them start in the first place?" Mars replied. "We figure that out, maybe we'll figure out the other answer, too."

"The *Spitzbergen* is hailing all surviving ships now," Betty reported, a comm device clutched to one ear. "The alien captains are responding now. They—" She frowned. "They sound confused. Every one of them. As if they are just waking up from some nightmare. They don't know what they're doing here, or why they were fighting."

Mars frowned deeply.

"I don't like where this is headed," he growled to no one in particular.

"Mind control?" Bosco speculated. "Something is forcing war upon this sector—by remote control?"

"I don't like it at all," Mars repeated.

"Yes, Commodore," Betty-12 was saying, and Mars looked up at her in anticipation.

"We're ordered to dock with the flagship. The Commodore wants to talk with you. In person."

Swallowed up in absolute, stygian blackness, Deimos cast about with both hands—even as he felt other, rougher hands clutching at him from every direction.

"Hey! Back off," he shouted, reaching for his own hidden blaster—but it was already gone.

And in the next second, he felt the silvery bag torn from his grasp.

"NO!"

He whirled around, reaching, reaching—but no one was there. Footsteps clattered about. He cried out again.

The lights came back on, brighter than before.

Deimos blinked in the glare.

"Give me back that bag," he demanded, rubbing at his dazzled eyes.

Deep, resonant laughter echoed down at him from above.

"I knew they would take it," came a heavy, British-accented voice. "They are nothing if not predictable. In fact, often times, I believe that is *all* they are."

The pirates were shuffling back into the room now, most of them looking chagrined and sullen.

"You don't know we wasn't gonna give it to you, Captain," one of the older pirates grumbled.

"Of course I know you weren't, Mr. Muller," the voice replied. "But you want no part of this thing. I can assure you, you would have regretted keeping it. Though no more than you will regret taking it," he added—and a gleaming sword flashed out from the shadows. Muller's head dropped to the deck and rolled past Deimos, even as his body collapsed on the spot, spurting blood.

"Sorry about the trouble," the deep voice boomed again.

"That's no problem," Deimos was saying, even as he spotted the silvery sack in the dead man's clutches. He made to grab for it—

"Ah, ah," came the voice, followed instantly by another of the pirates appearing from nowhere and grabbing the sack before Deimos could reach it. Deftly the pirate tossed the sack up into the air, in the direction of the ceiling.

As the sack reached the top of its arc, a tall, dark-bearded figure in black stepped out onto what Deimos saw was a balcony that loomed out over the room he was in. That figure snatched the silvery sack from the air and held it in his outstretched arm, studying it.

"And here it is," he growled in satisfaction. "Well. So many have sought it, so much has been offered for it—and here it sits, in my hands."

Deimos smiled up at him—and at the tall, slender pirate wearing a black eye patch who stood next to him—even while keeping one eye on the other pirates that he knew lurked in the shadows all around him.

"Glad to have another satisfied customer," Deimos replied with a nod.

"So we ain't gonna kill him, then, Captain Kargan?" came the ragged voice of the one-eyed pirate who stood next to him. His voice carried distinct disappointment.

"Bullock, please. We are a civilized society here, are we not?"

Rough laughter from all around greeted this query, none of it making Deimos feel better about things.

"I know you're all very busy here, what with plundering and counting your treasure and so on, and I don't want to take up any more of you gentlemen's time," Deimos said. "So if you'll just pay me what we agreed on, I'll make myself scarce and—"

"And why in the Seven Hells of the Galaxy would we be wanting to do that?"

Kargan stepped up to the balcony's edge and leered down at Deimos.

"What I have here is what I like to call an 'advantageous bargaining position.' And finding myself in such a position, I see no reason why I shouldn't exploit it." He stroked at his curly, dark beard with one hand as he leaned against the rail with the other. "So let us say I am making a revised offer for the services you have provided."

Deimos felt a sick feeling in his abdomen.

"A revised offer?"

"Yes. In exchange for the contents of this sack, I will grant you one thing even more precious to you than money: your life."

Anger swelled up through Deimos.

"Do you know what I've gone through to secure that item and bring it here to you?"

"Do you know what you will go through if you don't accept my generous offer?" Kargan countered cheerfully.

Deimos felt his heart racing, the blood pounding in his ears.

"You—you—"

He choked, fell forward; his hands splayed out on the cold metal deck, holding him up.

"What's the matter with you?" Kargan demanded, before beginning to issue orders to the pirates to seize him.

Still on his hands and knees, Deimos looked up suddenly—but the face that stared balefully up at Captain Kargan was no longer that of the man who had been there before. Now the features were twisted with fury and bitterness. The mouth was pulled back in a teeth-baring grimace. And the eyes—the eyes were no longer brown but hazel.

"What is the meaning of—" Kargan began, before Phobos leapt over the railing and onto the balcony beside him.

The Captain's scream slowed the reaction time of his men for just a moment. By the time any of them were moving again, Phobos had the big man out over the drop, held up by a clawlike hand clutching his thick collar.

"No—no, I—you—"

The lieutenant, Bullock, started forward suddenly.

"You won't hurt the Cap'n," he growled. "You ain't stupid enough for that."

The man who now knew himself as Phobos hurled the captain down the twelve foot drop to the hard metal deck. The big pirate impacted with a sickening crunch and lay sprawled and unmoving.

With a cry, Bullock and the other pirates rushed forward.

Phobos leapt off the balcony directly into their midst.

The fight was as short as it was brutal.

Phobos moved faster than the eye could follow, his body flowing from one martial arts move to the next. He smashed the nose and broke the arms of the first pirate, then whirled and took the legs out from under the next.

Daggers flashed towards him in the hands of two attackers, but he performed a seemingly impossible move that dropped him below one blade and to the side of the other. Grasping the wrists of both shocked attackers at once, he pulled them together with violent force, impaling each on the other's blade.

Leaping into the air before three more could converge on him, Phobos twisted and spun, his hands shooting down and making contact with the heads of two of the men. Before either of them knew what had happened, he'd clashed their heads together, then landed behind the third. Grasping him around the neck from behind, Phobos shoved a knee into the man's spine, causing a horrific cracking sound that left the pirate prostrate on the floor.

All of this had transpired in a scant five seconds. Phobos stood at the center of a pile of bodies, his head snapping this way and that, looking for more foes. None were to be found. The few he had not incapacitated had fled into the depths of the base.

Stepping over and through the bodies, Phobos loomed over the broken form of Captain Kargan. The pirate leader's arms and legs lay twisted at sharp angles and blood oozed from a dozen locations. Next to him lay the body of Lt. Bullock, and Phobos could not tell if he was alive or dead—not that he cared.

Inexplicably, through bloody lips, the captain was softly laughing.

"You think… your fancy moves… will save you here?" he gasped, his breathing coming in rough and shallow gasps.

Phobos realized then that the silvery sack was nowhere to be seen. He leaned down and grasped Kargan by the throat, hoisting his massive form up off the floor.

"Where is the item I brought? Answer quickly—for it must be destroyed! Destroyed or returned to the ancient vault from which it came—hidden away forever!"

"Destroyed? But you yourself brought it here—"

Phobos increased the pressure of his left hand on the pirate's throat, causing the big man to choke and gasp, blood spraying from his mouth.

"You fool," Kargan slurred. "I've called the reserves—all of my men! They'll be here… in seconds. And they will put you out the airlock…after they've had their fun, of course."

Even as he leaned in to reply, Phobos knew the man had spoken the truth: the sounds of boots—dozens of them, fast approaching—resounded from the deck.

"You'll be dead soon enough," Kargan gasped. "So what harm in giving you one last glimpse of your prize?"

He managed to reach out with one of his broken arms, and the silver sack dangled down from his fingers.

"I don't know precisely what this is, or what it is for," Kargan growled, his old bravado returning to him, "but I have buyers who will pay me dearly for it—dearly enough to repair any temporary physical damage you may have caused me. That and much more!"

The boots were much closer now. At any moment Phobos would be surrounded by a hundred bloodthirsty pirates. A thousand.

Phobos's hazel eyes glared into those of the captain for a long second. Then he began to laugh, and those hazel eyes became brown once again.

Kargan's face contorted in puzzlement.

"You are a lunatic! You are about to be torn to pieces—after being slowly roasted over a fusion reactor! And yet you laugh!"

By way of reply, the man who was now Deimos merely reached out and

"…causing the big man to choke and gasp…"

snatched the silver bag from the captain's hand. He pulled the item inside it out.

Kargan stared at it.

"Wait—by the galaxy—that cannot be what I think it is—?!"

The pirate army had arrived: a slavering, bloodthirsty lot that quickly formed a ring around Deimos and Kargan. Deimos ignored them all. He knew that those men would have other things to worry about—other things to occupy them—very shortly.

And indeed the Box did just as he had expected.

Waves of psychic energy lashed out all around. The temperature in the station dropped forty degrees in a mere instant and continued to drop. Ice formed along all the metal surfaces.

Uncomprehending, the pirates looked around themselves, searching for answers. What they found instead was utter terror.

Hideous, chaotic shapes were forming all around them. Somewhat manlike, the creatures were each over seven feet tall, with clusters of blood-red eyes peering out from an area that could only vaguely be called a head.

A massive stench rolled through the chamber.

The shapes lurched forward as one, a low keening moan sounding from inhuman throats as they moved.

Some of the pirates reached for weapons, others sought to flee. Neither action made any difference.

As the horrifying, nearly formless protoplasmic creatures shambled from the shadows and reached out to drag their bewildered and dumbstruck victims away, Deimos leaned in close to Kargan's bloody face, looking past the wild, terrified expression and commanding the doomed man's attention one last time.

"Your buyer. The one who would pay so dearly for the item. Who?"

"No—no, I cannot—"

On the floor next to them, Lt. Bullock had come back to his senses just in time to hear the conversation from the start. He was about to move—to attack the bizarre man again—but then he thought better of it, and he waited. And he listened.

"Who was the buyer? *Who?*"

A stinking, gelatinous hand reached out and scraped along Kargan's face. The pirate lord grimaced at the repulsive, burning touch.

"I—no—it—it is the Governor—Baron Serling, the Governor of Gothika. Now—make them go away! Make them—"

The pirate captain's horrific scream echoed throughout the miles of corridors that filled the motley station.

The razor-sharp tip of the rapier flashed just in front of Lt. Calderon's nose and he stopped short, nearly stumbling backwards, automatically bringing both hands up in defensive posture.

"Yikes!"

"Tony!"

Mars stopped his blindingly-fast motions and brought the rapier down to his hip in a resting posture, then leapt forward to catch his friend before the man could fall over.

"I didn't see you come in!"

"Yeah, well—I should've known better than to bother you while you're swinging that pig-sticker."

Mars set the ornate, meter-long weapon down and smiled.

"I don't get that many chances to practice while on patrol," he said. "I like to stay sharp."

"I would say 'sharp' is the key word, alright—and I don't want to find out just how sharp!"

Mars smiled more broadly as he picked up a small towel and wiped his face and hands.

"So," Calderon began, changing the subject to the reason for his having sought Mars out in the first place. "How did things go with the Commodore?"

"Fine, fine... I think," Mars replied, his smile fading a bit. "They took aboard three of the alien ships. Ostensibly to provide medical assistance and for repairs. While they were aboard, though, the Commodore and his aides had a... *conversation* with the captains."

"You mean they interrogated them?"

Mars winced.

"Something like that could violate all kinds of interstellar treaties, Tony. Let's stick with, 'they had a conversation' with them."

Calderon smiled a wry smile.

"Right. So—did they learn anything?"

"Not much, to be honest. But here's the thing—apparently, the last place each of the ships visited—all independent of one another—before ending up in the battle here... was the Sargasso."

Calderon's eyes widened a tad. He took this news in with interest, stroking his chin.

"And they think there's some kind of connection…?"

"It's all we have, so far," Mars replied. "The Commodore is really grasping at straws. He's trying to make sense of what's happening out here in the Fringe."

"I know how he feels," Tony said. "It's all so strange—all the different alien races fighting one another, not to mention those weird creatures that keep popping up…"

"Right."

Mars dropped the towel into a receptacle and pulled his uniform top back on.

"That's why Crabbe's sending me out on a scouting mission."

"Scouting mission?"

Mars nodded. He led Calderon out of the gymnasium area and together they strolled down one of the cylindrical corridors that ran the length of the huge battleship. The curving walls were transparent for long stretches, revealing a majestic view of the depths of space just beyond, alien stars and suns twinkling in the black void.

"Just BB5," Mars continued. "Just Betty and me on this trip. And the Doctor."

Tony considered this.

"You don't want some backup?"

Mars shrugged.

"With everything that's going on, Crabbe doesn't want to risk more than one ship for this."

"Where are you going? Oh—of course—"

Mars glanced at him with what could almost be called nervousness, then returned his gaze to the sparkling tableau outside the ship.

"Yep, you guessed it. Same place the alien ships went. The Sargasso. The graveyard of space."

Mars and Calderon rounded the final turn and reached the battleship's hangar bay. In the distance they could see the *Spitzbergen's* deck crew working to ready Black Bird Five for flight. Standing on the open boarding ramp was Betty-12, a comm pad held in one hand as she went through pre-flight procedures.

Before the two Rangers could pass through the hatch and into the bay, however, a man stepped out from the shadows and blocked them.

"Captain McCoy. I was hoping to catch you here."

Mars sized up the squat, blunt-nosed, powerful-looking figure who faced him.

"Voroshilov."

"That's Lt. Commander to you, Captain."

"Of course, of course. Lt. Commander." Mars smiled an easy smile. "What can I do for you?"

"You can escort me aboard your ship, Captain."

Mars blinked, glanced at an equally puzzled-looking Calderon, and returned his gaze to Voroshilov.

"How's that again?"

Now Voroshilov was smiling.

"The Commodore has authorized my inclusion on your mission. The Navy would like a representative—another set of eyes, shall we say—aboard your ship."

Mars was frowning.

"I don't think—"

"What you do or do not think is not relevant, Captain. You have your orders, and from the Commodore himself. Check with him, if you must—if you think I'm lying to you."

Mars glanced at Calderon again. The second-in-command of Black Bird Six merely shrugged.

"What are you doing here?" Voroshilov suddenly demanded of the other man. "You are not a part of our mission. Its details and parameters should not be shared with you."

Calderon reddened and started to reply, but then Mars moved swiftly between the two.

"I would appreciate your treating Lt. Calderon—and all the other Rangers—with a bit more respect," he growled at Voroshilov. Then, before the shorter man could reply, he turned to Calderon. "Take off, Tony."

"But—"

"Don't make me order you, Lieutenant."

Calderon was frowning deeply, peering around Mars's shoulder at the stocky Navy man.

"Aye, Captain," he said, sketching Mars a salute and sending one last glaring look at Voroshilov. With that, he strode away down the corridor.

"Thank you for that, Captain. I'm sure you helped us all avoid an unnecessary...unpleasantness."

"Get this straight, Lt. Commander," Mars shot back. "I don't like you. I don't want you aboard my ship. But orders are orders, so off we go. Try not to get in the way."

With that, Mars began to walk toward his ship.

Now it was Voroshilov's turn to redden.

"Perhaps you were unaware of something, Captain," he called after Mars, not having moved a step.

"And what would that be?" Mars said, not slowing or looking back.

"I have been granted broad, discretionary powers by the Navy High Command."

Mars froze in his tracks. He turned back, his brow furrowed beneath his short red hair.

"And what sort of powers would those be?"

Now Voroshilov's expression softened. He walked up alongside Mars and laughed softly.

"If, at my sole discretion, I determine that the hostilities within the Fringe constitute a grave threat to galactic security, I can recommend the strongest possible actions on the part of the Navy."

Mars did not like the sound of that at all.

"What sort of actions?"

"Military actions. Pre-emptive actions. Actions that would surely end any risk of the conflict spilling over into the more…civilized regions of the galaxy."

"Do you plan on getting any more specific than that?"

"I am referring, Captain," Voroshilov replied with obvious relish, "to the carpet bombing of all the Fringe Worlds involved in the conflict."

Mars took this in, his face a mask of utter shock.

"You cannot be serious."

"Oh, indeed I am most serious, Captain." He smiled more broadly. "If in my judgment the conflict among the Fringe Worlds cannot be resolved or otherwise contained by Task Force Obsidian, I am authorized to call for the complete and utter annihilation of the worlds involved in the actions."

Now he was the one who strolled away, headed for Mars's ship.

"In other words, Captain—if you and the Commodore and your friends cannot get these alien barbarians and their governments to settle down and get back in line, we of the Navy will bomb them all back into the Stone Age."

Deimos's body dutifully and obediently went through the motions required to pilot his ship toward the planet Gothika, but his mind was lost in thought—and in confusion.

Of the past hours and days he possessed only the slightest memories, and none of them made any sense. Vaguely he recalled the Sargasso of Space. In fragmented images scattered here and there throughout his consciousness, he remembered meeting the pirates, and even talking with Captain Kargan. And somewhere in there—a betrayal. A violent encounter with Kargan and his men. But beyond that... nothing.

And then, he'd awoken here, aboard his ship once more, as if the entire thing had been a very vivid and powerful dream—and one that had slipped into obscurity as soon as he awoke.

But none of it made any sense. Because if he'd been to the Sargasso— if he'd met with Kargan—then why had the silver bag been clutched in a near death-grip in his left hand when he'd come to? Wasn't Kargan supposed to buy it from him?

Perhaps even more disturbingly, he could no longer find the thin, web-like metal device that protected his mind from the box's psychic emanations. Finding a replacement for that—particularly since he still possessed the box—had become a priority, but he had no idea where, out on the Fringe, he might find another.

All he knew for certain was that he had to get to the planet Gothika and meet with the governor there. How he knew this, he had no idea—had Kargan told him?—but it was the single clearest thought still vibrating through his skull—and that made it very welcome and very reliable, considering most every other thought in his head was dull, fragmented, and obscure.

And so he set course for Gothika and sat back, trying to sleep. Of course, as almost always, any truly restful sleep eluded him. Sometimes he believed he would never sleep again.

"It's this box," he whispered to himself. "I have to get rid of it. And soon."

On he flew, his ship on autopilot, his eyes closed. And thus he failed to notice on his display the small, sleek, dark-hulled warship that arrived at the Sargasso just after he had departed it.

The ship looked to be a grotesque cobbling together of parts from many different vessels of various vintages, covered over in a layer of black paint and with numerous strange nodules and protuberances projecting forth here and there. It unhesitatingly followed the pathway straight down through the wreckage as though its navigator knew precisely where he was going—because he did. Hours of torture and psychic probing of captured pirates in recent months had yielded this information and much more besides.

The dark, hellish vessel moored alongside the pirate base station and connected itself to the main airlock. Doors were forced open and booted feet stomped through and into the base. Swords and pistols rattled along the corridors. Soon after, those sounds were joined by the clank of chains and eerie, horrifying moaning.

With Deimos's departure from the base, the mysterious box going along with him, the chaos horde had vanished as suddenly as it had appeared. Surprisingly, several dozen of the pirates had survived their encounter with the ghastly creatures and had been in the process of celebrating their seeming triumph when this new crowd arrived. Their happiness proved to be short-lived.

Into the central chamber of the base burst howling, bloodthirsty Berserkers, their heavy chains stretching out behind them as they surged forward. The injured pirates fell first, swept up and dashed into the bulkheads, their heads and bodies shattered in an instant.

Those pirates able to run managed to flee some distance into the station's bowels before the second group of intruders entered the central chamber. Hunched, twisted, helmeted figures, these Psi-Clones unleashed their tremendous psychic powers upon the pirates, taking over their minds one by one and forcing them to halt in their tracks, turn about, and shuffle slowly back the way they'd come.

When at last a dozen or more of the surviving pirates were gathered together in the central chamber, absolute terror glazing their eyes and psychic energies locking their bodies rigid, the final group of intruders presented themselves. They were the masters of this horrific company— the Shadowmen. Tall, slender figures in black robes and hoods, they moved into the room with the quiet smoothness of mercury and took up positions around the perimeter.

As the pirates frothed at the mouth and lost control of their bowels, the leader of the Shadowmen approached them. His feet were not visible beneath the tattered dark robes, so that he appeared to be gliding on thin air. Drawing back his hood, he exposed deathly white flesh pierced in numerous places by wires and tubes and augmetic mechanics.

He looked at each of the pirates in turn, then glanced to one side and moved to the nearest bulkhead. His bony fingers reached out and he slid one taloned finger along the metal wall. The merest residue of almost-melted ice trailed behind his finger, and he studied it momentarily.

"Oh yes," he whispered at last. "It has been here. And recently."

As if in reply, the Berserkers howled and moaned for several seconds.

When the silence had returned—a silence increasingly like that of the tomb—the lead Shadowman moved closer to one of the pirates and leaned in close. His voice, when it came, was the merest whisper.

"The box. You have seen the box."

The pirate could scarcely meet his eyes, and his response was so wracked by trembling nerves that no one else in the room could hear it. "B-box, milord?"

"The box."

The pirate merely gazed back, his expression reflecting confusion and ignorance as well as fear.

The Shadowman's clawlike hand reached out and stroked along the pirate's cheek. This seemed to have a more dramatic effect on the man than would an actual physical blow; he recoiled, his teeth now chattering fiercely.

Red and blue lights flickered across the Shadowman's augmetic enhancements as he peered into the pirate's eyes. He held this stance for nearly a minute, as the man writhed in torment. Then finally the Shadowman exhaled sharply in disappointment—and turned to the next pirate, who instantly blanched and wet his breeches.

The Shadowman repeated his inquiry with each of the surviving pirates, and received the same response each time. Even with the Psi-Clones pressing hard at the men they still could tell him nothing, save that their captain had met with an individual who was offering to sell an item of some value—but that things had gone sour and the man had apparently escaped.

The Shadowman was considering this information when another of his brethren drew near and whispered a few words.

"So," he replied when the other had finished his report. "The Space Patrol—the accursed Rangers—involve themselves in this matter."

"They draw near even now, brother."

The leader pondered this news for a few more seconds, and then a plan came to him.

"Move our ship," he hissed. "Hide it."

"Yes, brother."

Gathering his fellows together, he issued quick and terse instructions.

And then, like ghosts, the agents of the Cabal slipped into the shadows and vanished.

Meanwhile, the pirate lieutenant, Bullock, cringed in the shadows himself, gripped by sheer terror and knowing the span of his life was very nearly spent. For he knew the answer to the question the Cabal agents were asking, and he knew it was but a matter of time before they found him and extracted that information from him—along with, in all likelihood, his sanity… and then his life.

The sea of wreckage stretched out before them in every direction.

"Unbelievable," Mars whispered softly, more to himself than to anyone else aboard.

For miles upon miles, up, down, left, right, and straight ahead, the blackness of space was almost entirely obscured by a field of debris. Spacecraft, pieces of spacecraft, clusters of multiple spacecraft stuck together, and a seemingly infinite number of wholly unidentifiable mechanical chunks and objects drifted in a chaotic swarm.

To call it a simple field of debris was to call the Sahara Desert a sandbox.

"It really is remarkable," Mars continued.

"By my calculations," Betty-12 interjected, "this phenomenon is caused by a conjunction of gravitational fields from three nearby stars. Coupled with the pull from the two large gas giant planets we can see to port, the result is a region of space into which any object falls and eventually becomes trapped…forever."

Dr. Bosco leaned in from the passenger area. "I hope that doesn't include us," he said.

"The object must have no self-propulsion capability," Betty explained patiently.

"Yes, I get that—I was attempting… humor."

"Ah. I understand." She glanced back at him. "Keep trying, Doctor."

Bosco gave her a half-smile but looked hurt.

Mars ignored their exchange and continued to gaze out at the sea of junk that filled their view.

"This galaxy offers some strange and unusual locales, but this one has to rank near the top of the list," he said.

"You have been here before, have you not, Captain?" asked Betty, only half turning to look at him, keeping one eye firmly on the slowly spinning debris just ahead and one hand securely on the ship's controls.

"Oh yes, a time or two," he replied, following some of the larger chunks with his eyes as he nodded. "But it's still an amazing sight."

"I would concur," said Dr. Bosco.

Voroshilov pushed his way forward, leaning down to peer out at the ocean of debris.

"Where exactly are we going? Not *into* that, surely."

"That's the trip you signed on for, Lt. Commander," Mars replied with a slight smile that he kept turned away from Voroshilov. "It's just a matter of finding a way in."

"I wish we had brought one of the battleships with us," Dr. Bosco remarked. "They could blast us a pathway right through all of this."

"I'm not sure that's true," Mars replied, his eyes shifting from the tactical display to the swirling panorama just ahead of them. "Some of those wrecks look to be even larger than a battleship. I doubt there's a ship in the Navy fleet that could survive very long in there."

"And yet here we sit, trying to find a way in," Bosco noted.

Mars couldn't suppress his smile this time.

"Yep," he nodded, "here we sit, trying to find a way in."

"A way in to where?" pressed Voroshilov. "All I see is junk."

"That's because you're not a Ranger," Betty pointed out.

"What's that supposed to mean?"

"She means that we Rangers keep tabs on what the various criminal organizations of each sector are up to, and—more importantly, in this case—where they like to hide out. And this—" He pointed out at the swirling morass of wreckage—"is a favorite hideout for several prominent pirate groups."

"They can go in there? Safely?"

"They can—and so can we, if we do this correctly."

"Do what?" Voroshilov demanded.

"...*This*," Mars replied. He seemed to be counting to himself, silently, for several seconds...and then he moved the Black Bird's controls forward in one smooth motion, rocketing the ship directly toward the Sargasso.

"What—what do you think you are doing?" Voroshilov nearly leapt from his own skin. "Captain! Captain McCoy! I demand that you—" His words, growing increasingly shrill by the second, trailed off into a near-shriek as the Black Bird reached the forward edge of the debris field. He flung his hands up over his face and cringed, bracing for the deadly impact.

Instead, the Black Bird slipped easily into the hidden hollow corridor and zipped along smoothly and safely.

Slowly Voroshilov opened his eyes and peered out from between his fingers. The first thing he saw was that the ship was still intact around him. The second thing he saw was the debris field flying past on all sides of them. The third thing he saw was his shipmates, all looking back at him and smiling.

Flushing a deep red, Voroshilov sputtered a few incoherent words, then turned on his heel and strode back into the passenger compartment.

Mars allowed himself a deep breath, his green eyes twinkling.

"I think that was well worth the trouble of having to bring him along," he whispered to Betty. The beautiful brunette only nodded once in reply.

Dr. Bosco was watching in utter fascination as the hulks spun here and there around them. Silently he performed a string of mathematical calculations in an effort to quantify what he was seeing, but eventually he gave up. Then he leaned in between the two Rangers and asked, "So—where exactly *are* we going?"

"The heart—the center of the Sea," Mars replied.

"There's a pirate base there," Betty-12 added. "We think they might know something."

Dr. Bosco nodded. He appeared to be lost in thought for a few moments. Then, "I can see we are in some sort of protected tunnel running through the debris field, but—Captain, if I may ask—how did you know where to fly in order to find it?"

Mars flashed his famous smile over his shoulder at Bosco.

"It was more Betty than me," he replied.

Dr. Bosco frowned.

"Betty? But—I don't follow."

"We've been here before," Mars explained. "Tracked a squadron of raiders here a year or so back. Betty worked out the formula for how they keep the debris moving—and where there is no debris. And she keeps it all—" He reached across and tapped his lieutenant on the temple. "—right up here."

Betty-12 merely shook her head in disdain.

"Did I make it too overly dramatic?" he asked her, after Dr. Bosco had moved back into the passenger compartment.

"No, no." She winked at him. "I just thought it was better when they didn't know how you'd done it."

Mars couldn't help but laugh.

A few minutes later, Black Bird Five arrived safely at the big, ramshackle pirate base station at the heart of the debris field.

"Tell them 'hello,'" Mars suggested. "And that we come in peace, and all that."

Betty worked the radio for more than a minute, her frustration growing.

"No one is answering," she announced finally.

"That's impossible," Mars stated flatly. "They always keep at least a token force here. Kargan and Rajali both use it as their main headquarters, and there are others, too." He frowned. "Somebody is bound to be here. Try again."

Betty's face expressed diffidence. She turned back to the radio. Meanwhile, Mars and Bosco stared out at the rusted station.

"You think they'll talk to you?" Bosco asked.

"They'll talk," Mars said. "They don't like we Rangers very much, but they are very skilled at knowing when to fight and when not—and whom to fight."

After several more minutes of failed attempts to communicate, Mars let his frustration show.

"This is ridiculous. Someone has to be there. Maybe they're having a communications failure."

"Or an environmental one," Bosco suggested.

"They could need help."

"They're pirates," Voroshilov growled from the rear. "Who cares if they all suffocate in the vacuum?"

"True," Mars replied, "except, of course, for the whole bit about why we came here in the first place—to ask questions, and to get some answers. Corpses don't say much."

Voroshilov did not reply.

"There's a docking port," Betty-12 pointed out. "Perhaps we should simply go in…?"

Mars followed with his eyes to where she was pointing, then nodded and directed the ship in a graceful arc that left it adjacent to the docking ring. A few deft maneuvers later, the sound of the automatic docking latches closing reverberated throughout the ship.

Mars and Betty gazed out through the viewport at the mottled hull of the station curving away into the distance. All around it swarmed the sea of derelict ships and debris.

"Let's get on with this," Voroshilov growled from the rear, his impatience oozing from every word. "We're not here to sightsee."

And with that, the spell was broken and the four-person crew of Black Bird Five went to work. Betty-12 set the ship's controls to standby, Mars shut the engines down, and Dr. Bosco prepared his various scanners and analyzers. Voroshilov checked the setting on his blaster and reholstered it.

The hatch slid smoothly open and the Rangers and company stepped through and into the pirate base.

Darkness greeted them.

Quickly Mars lit a variable-flashlight and directed it all around.

"Nice place they have here," Betty-12 noted, attempting sarcasm.

"I'm sure it serves their purposes quite well," Mars replied.

"Let's go, then," Voroshilov barked.

Mars suppressed a retort, nodded curtly, and started into the base, Betty-12 just behind him. Dr. Bosco frowned nervously and then followed. Voroshilov trudged along at the rear.

All around them, the variable-flashlight cast shadowy shapes on the mottled, rusty walls.

Some of those shapes looked back at them, and the shadows began to move.

The two-man flyer settled gently onto the rough cobblestone courtyard, its propulsion system wailing as its engines cycled down. The canopy popped and slid open, revealing the disheveled form of the pilot within. His long hair was dirty and tangled; his brown eyes bloodshot and ringed in dark circles. A long leather coat was wadded in a ball on the seat next to him. From underneath it could just be seen part of a silvery metallic cloth of some sort.

"Hello?" the man called out, gazing up at the stone ramparts high above him. He had not yet made any effort to climb out of the ship. "Anybody there?"

For a moment there was no indication that anyone had heard him. The vast, sprawling mansion that was really more like a medieval castle loomed above, dark and ominous. Then the massive wooden front door creaked open on its heavy iron hinges and two guards clad in navy blue dress uniforms emerged. They stepped quickly across the courtyard to the ship and took up positions on either side of it, weapons at the ready.

Giving up on the notion that either of the men planned to help him out of his ship, Deimos reached up with weary, shaking hands and grasped the edge of the cockpit, pulling himself free from his flight seat, then swung up onto the fuselage. Reaching back inside, he grasped his coat and lifted it out, first making sure its brown leather completely covered the silvery metal sack that lay underneath it.

"There you are at last," came a smooth, polished voice from the doorway as Deimos hopped down onto the cobblestones. "And only a little behind schedule."

The man who strode out into the courtyard was tall and lean, appearing to be in his fifties with salt and pepper hair and a neatly trimmed gray beard. His blue eyes and aquiline nose gave him a distinct appearance, along with the haughty way he carried himself. He wore a crisp, dark blue Imperial military uniform with shiny gold buttons but with no visible signs of rank.

"Governor Serling," Deimos said, bowing slightly. "I appreciate your willingness to meet with me."

"I prefer *Baron* Serling, actually," the man replied. "Your communication made it quite clear that you possess something I am most interested in. Why would I not meet with you?"

"Fair enough," Deimos replied with a half-grin.

"So you have it with you, then? I will admit I am extremely curious."

Deimos raised his wadded coat up in one hand and pulled it away with the other, revealing the shiny metallic sack that had been hidden underneath.

"Yeah, I have it."

The Baron's eyes lit up.

"Ah, yes. That must be it. May I see it?"

"In good time, Excellency."

Deimos stuffed the sack back within the folds of his coat.

"It's quite dangerous," he added. "Certain precautions have to be taken."

"Very well," the Baron replied half-heartedly, his eyes never leaving the prize.

"Before we get to that, though," Deimos continued, "there is the matter of payment. If you will recall, we only briefly discussed—"

Deimos broke off the sentence midway through, making a small, choking sound. The Baron, still focused entirely on the silvery bag now half hidden again under the coat, took the opportunity to interrupt.

"Of course, of course—have no fears on that score. All arrangements have been made with regard to your compensation, depending on just

"Hello? Anybody there?"

what it is you have, and—"

Now it was the Baron's turn to halt in mid-sentence, as he realized that Deimos was bent over double, coughing and shaking. The Baron took a half-step towards him, then thought better of it and took two steps back.

"Are—are you alright?"

The coughing continued for another few seconds before abruptly ending. He who had been Deimos straightened, his now hazel eyes glaring up at the Baron. This look, along with the almost palpable waves of fear that seemed to emanate from the man, drove the Baron to back away further, his hands raised between himself and his agent.

He who was now Phobos moved his gaze slowly from the Baron and his surroundings to the object bundled under his coat in his right hand. He gasped.

"Still with me? I still have it?"

He tore at the coat, pulling it away, revealing the silvery metallic bag, holding it high.

"And I was going to give it to you?"

The Baron frowned, unsure of what to make of this. His guards had come up behind him, weapons at the ready, but he signaled for them to wait. He found himself very curious as to how this strange and unexpected tableau would play out.

Phobos shook the silvery bag at the Baron.

"Do you have any idea what this is? What it is capable of?"

The look of dread etched across his narrow face deepened.

"Or what I've had to do to acquire it?"

The Baron merely waited, silent.

Before Phobos could speak further, he gasped and doubled over, choking again. The silver bag dropped from his hand and hit the cobblestone surface with a *thunk*.

In that instant the Baron moved forward and snatched the bag.

Phobos leapt up from his crouching position in a flash and knocked the bag out of the Baron's hands, then grasped the man about the throat, his fingers tightening instantly.

The guards moved into action scarcely a second later, grasping Phobos by either arm and wrestling him off their master, dragging him back, holding him firmly.

"What—what has come over you?" the Baron managed to choke out, shocked. Then, upon receiving no reply save a low whimpering sound: "Take him away! Lock him in a cell! I shall deal with him later."

Even as the Baron continued to choke and cough, the guards

manhandled a cringing Phobos through the doorway and into the depths of the castle.

Recovering, the Baron watched as they carried the man away. He shook his head in wonder at the sudden and inexplicable change that had come over him. Then he returned his full attention to the silver bag. He picked it up from the cobblestones and held it aloft.

"Could it possibly be…?"

Almost against his will, he pulled the bag open and reached inside. His fingertips brushed across the hard metal surface, very cold to the touch.

"Yes…"

Even as some portion of his brain cried out against the action, he couldn't help but draw the iron box out of the sack.

"Yes."

Ice formed on the cobblestones in a circle around him. His breath emerged in visible clouds of white.

"*Yes!*"

Waves of psychic energy washed at him, battered him. The waves expanded outward, ever outward, traveling beyond even the speed of light as they bounced back and forth across the null-space barrier. Within mere moments, the entire galactic sector was permeated.

How long the Baron stood there in his courtyard, arm outstretched, holding the bizarre iron box, not even his own guards could later say. But it was long enough. Long enough to bring about a cataclysm—perhaps only the first of many.

"This is no pirate base," Dr. Bosco gasped as he stared around in horror. "It's a slaughterhouse!"

Indeed, the description was apt: Bodies lay strewn all about the main corridor of the station, many in mangled and nearly unrecognizable states. Worst of all was the central hub, where numerous corridors came together in a nexus point. There it looked as if a herd of wild animals had run loose, goring and trampling everyone in sight. Blood coated the walls and body parts lay here and there. Betty-12 took all this in with wide-eyed amazement, while Dr. Bosco checked each victim in turn for any signs of life—and found none.

"They could have done it to each other," Voroshilov growled, his face twisted with repulsion. "They are pirates, after all. Or rather, *were.*"

"Somehow I doubt it," Mars McCoy replied. He had made his way carefully past the bodies and to the main computer console, and was now scanning through its data.

"Anything?" Bosco asked, coming up beside him.

"It's all been erased," Mars told him with a frown, "and recently, at that."

"Recently?" Betty-12 turned a full circle, her eyes moving from one dark corridor entrance to the next. "How recently?"

"It's hard to be sure, given the state of this equipment—outdated and poorly kept up," Mars muttered. "Within the past couple of hours, I think."

Betty and Bosco exchanged worried glances.

"Let's find what we can and get out of here," Voroshilov said, his hand straying repeatedly to the blast pistol at his side.

"For once, we're in agreement, Commander." Mars straightened from the console and turned.

At that moment, a flurry of movement from the shadows caught Betty's eye and she cried out. Mars whipped out his blast pistol and leveled it in one superbly swift motion.

"Help! Help me!"

From out of the darkness stumbled a long-haired man in ragged finery of blue and gold. Blood streaked down his face, partially discoloring a patch that covered one eye; the other eye was wild with fear and desperation.

"You're Rangers, right? Oh, thank the gods! You have to help me!"

"A stinking pirate," Voroshilov barked, backhanding the man and sending him crashing to his knees with a cry.

"Wait!"

Mars stepped between the two men and bent down, kneeling in front of the shaken man. Before Voroshilov could further react, Betty and Dr. Bosco stepped in; Betty helped steady the man while Dr. Bosco drew out a medical instrument and began to check the man's vital signs.

"Who did all this?" Mars demanded. "Who?"

"I—I don't know," the man replied, his voice shaking and his eyes darting here and there, never quite focusing on his would-be rescuers. He seemed not even to be aware that he was now sitting on the metal deck.

"You didn't see them?" Mars asked.

"No—no, I saw them, but—"

"Maybe he did it himself," Voroshilov stated.

"No! It wasn't me! I—I—"

The pirate's eyes cast down toward the blood-spattered floor.

"I hid."

"Ha! I knew it! A filthy coward of a pirate," growled Voroshilov.

Mars shot the Navy man a steely-eyed glance, then turned back to the pirate.

"What's your name?"

The man took a deep breath, then whispered, "Bullock."

"And Mr. Bullock, what exactly did you see? What happened here? Who killed these men?"

"It was…creatures. Ghastly, unimaginable creatures!"

Voroshilov took this in and started to laugh, but then Betty-12 gasped and asked, "Can you describe them?"

The pirate quickly described the appearance of the shambling horrors that had appeared, attacked, and disappeared with such bizarre suddenness. When he was finished, Betty and Mars nodded at one another.

"I think he's telling the truth," Mars stated. "We've encountered those things ourselves."

"But that's not all," the pirate added frantically. "After them came—the enemy! The Adversary!"

It was now Mars's turn to react with shock. "The Cabal? They came here?"

"Oh, no," Bosco murmured, involuntarily stepping back a couple of steps and looking around, eyes moving to the shadowy recesses.

Voroshilov had reddened and now he moved into a defensive crouch, his blast pistol at the ready.

"They—they tortured the others, but I managed to hide, and—"

"What did they want?"

Bullock seemed to gather his wits about him a bit at that point. He considered for a moment, then shrugged.

"They were looking for a box. I think it's the same one the Captain—Captain Kargan—was after."

Mars frowned.

"A box?"

"A little thing, only about this big." He motioned with his hands. "Kept in a silver sack. They were very determined to find it. But it's not here. It was, briefly, but not anymore." He shuddered. "Their Psi-Clones interrogated everyone still alive—except me, of course." He actually managed a nervous laugh then. "Which was a good thing for whoever actually has it."

"Why is that?"

"Because I know who has it and where he's gone."

Around them, the dark shadows moved. A red light flickered deep in the darkness.

Mars straightened. He glanced back at Betty, nodded, and then helped the pirate up onto his feet.

"That's the first good news we've heard in a while," he said. Then, to the pirate, "I think you should come with us."

A low, keening moan echoed from the depths of the station.

The group moved together in a tighter formation.

"I don't know what that was," Mars whispered, "and I don't really want to know." He indicated the pirate, Bullock, then pointed back toward their ship. "I think we have what we came for. Time to go!"

"I couldn't agree more," Dr. Bosco replied. Steadying Bullock with one arm, he joined in the procession as it marched quickly back along the bloody corridors.

The shadows detached from the walls and followed after them.

By the time Black Bird Five returned to Task Force Obsidian, the chaos horde had fallen upon them.

Minutes earlier, Dr. Bosco had been in his usual position, leaning into the cockpit from the passenger cabin. He was busy laying out all that he knew and all that he had learned from a very hurried bit of research in regards to a certain small metal box.

"It's ancient—that much is certain," he was telling the other Rangers. "It appears to date back to well before the arrival on the galactic scene of humans or most of the other major spacefaring races."

"But just what is it, exactly?" Mars asked, his eyes not leaving the forward windows as his hands smoothly manipulating the ship's controls.

"None of the sources I could access agreed on that," Bosco hesitantly replied. "The only thing they all agree on is that it is an object of great power—and greater danger. And," he added after a second's thought, "that it involves the manipulation of psychic energies."

Now Mars did glance back worriedly, first at Bosco and then at Betty, who was seated to his right.

"Great," he finally muttered. "A box that reads your mind."

"I fear it is capable of far worse than that, Captain," Bosco stated ruefully. "*Far* worse."

As the little ship dropped out of null-space, its skip-engines hot and roaring, Mars looked at the display in front of him and gasped.

Wave after wave of alien warships were assaulting the task force, with explosions blossoming all around. The two great battleships burned more brightly in spots than the stars behind them. Fighter ships and the other two Black Birds darted in and out of the melee, weapons firing continuously.

Mars frantically keyed the radio.

"Black Bird Five to *Spitzbergen*! Commodore Crabbe—do you read?"

Static at first, and then: "*Spitzbergen* here, Captain. Glad to have you back." Crabbe sounded rough around the edges and stressed in the extreme—not surprising, considering what was happening. "Able to lend us a hand?"

"Not a problem, sir," Mars barked back. "Bring the blast-cannons on line, Betty!"

And with that, Mars steered his ship into the heart of the battle.

As had been the case earlier, the attacking vessels were of many different points of origin and belonged to many different alien races. Betty-12 glanced up from the navigation controls long enough for her computer mind to quickly observe and catalogue at least five different navies represented.

"It really has become a general war among the Fringe Worlds," she commented, her voice betraying both surprise and dread.

"I'm starting to wonder if it's really that at all," Mars replied even as he deftly maneuvered the ship, triggering the blast-cannons and unleashing violent destruction on the task force's foes. On the receiving end, two small cruisers disintegrated at the caress of the devastating beams. Mars scarcely had the time to notice to which alien race the ships belonged; he was too busy veering the Black Bird out of harm's way and targeting his next opponent.

"What do you mean, Captain?" Dr. Bosco asked curiosity plain in his voice. "Surely it's obvious that virtually all the races of the Fringe Worlds have gone to war with one another. Pure chaos!"

"I'll agree with the chaos part," Mars replied, his eyes never flickering from the tableau before him, "but not about the war. I think something else is going on out here—something connected to the prize we're searching for."

Bosco seemed to consider this but said nothing in reply. Voroshilov, who was leaning forward next to him from the rear cabin, followed the conversation in silence.

The battle raged on for another four or five minutes, with the two big battleships holding their own but besieged from all directions by wave upon wave of smaller craft. The Black Birds did everything they could—Captains El Rey and No-Rah maneuvered Six and Seven, respectively, with a skill level that even Mars had to respect and appreciate, and their blast-cannons cleared the sky of dozens of foes.

Despite all that, however, the inevitable finally happened:

"Captain McCoy!" squealed the loudspeaker. "We have an emergency!"

"That was from the *Spitzbergen*," Betty announced.

Mars looked up and spotted the huge, lumbering ship ahead and to starboard, slightly above them in the z-axis. Flames roared from more than a dozen spots along the big vessel's four rotating hull segments, but none of the damage looked to be critical—at least, not yet.

"McCoy here, *Spitzbergen*. Go ahead."

"We've lost rear guns, and we detect four enemy fighters on approach." The voice of the comm. officer aboard *Spitzbergen* was frantic. "Can you help us?"

Rather than replying verbally, Mars deftly redirected the Black Bird's path and sent it hurtling at top speed toward the battleship.

Just before Black Bird Five reached the besieged warship, a blinding beam of energy lanced out from the other battleship—the *Jakarta*—and speared the trailing member of the four-ship attack squadron, instantly vaporizing it.

"We took out one of them for you, *Spitzbergen*," came the sound of *Jakarta's* comm. officer, "but the other three are now blocked by your hull."

"Not a problem," Mars barked, diving Black Bird Five down into the fray, passing through the very spot that, a second earlier, had been occupied by the gigantic blast beam.

The three remaining fighters were visible now, just ahead. Two looked to be Trions and the third a Trenago ship.

"Has to be something other than a war," Mars repeated to himself. "No way would any of these guys be fighting each other—much less attacking two Navy battleships!"

Even as he said those words, Mars lined up his sights on the first ship. In a flash, he'd squeezed the trigger and transformed the Trenago ship into a fiery ball of expanding gases.

Retargeting even before the first ship had exploded; Mars locked his Black Bird's blast cannons on one of the Trion ships and unleashed the fury. The ship came apart in a blazing blossom of flame and death.

He was turning his attention to the final target when he realized with a start that he was going to be too late. Even as his blast-cannons locked on, the Trion ship collided with the rear rotating section of the Navy battleship. The resulting explosion was as enormous as it was blinding.

Mars looked on in horror, unwilling to accept that he'd failed to destroy the last ship in time.

"Pull up, Mars! Pull up!"

Betty's cries from the co-pilot's seat brought Mars back to reality. He shoved the controls hard to port, causing Black Bird Five to angle away from the stricken vessel. Then he shoved the throttles forward and got away as fast as possible.

It was almost too late.

"Oh no," whispered Dr. Bosco.

The rear section of the *Spitzbergen* tore itself loose, its spin decouplers shredding under unthinkable levels of torque and shifting mass. Fuel cells ruptured and more explosions blossomed along the central shaft.

"She's going up!" cried Betty as all four passengers aboard Black Bird Five were hurled back into their seats from the acceleration.

Flames gutted out in every direction as the *Spitzbergen* exploded. The remaining three circular rotating sections tore themselves free even as flames gutted out through every newly-blasted opening.

The crew of the Black Bird could only look on in stunned silence as the huge vessel—the command ship of their expedition, the ship carrying Commodore Crabbe—came apart in an eruption of fuel and ammunition and oxygen.

Strangely enough, the battle seemed to fall apart to nothing after the *Spitzbergen* exploded. One by one, the remaining enemy ships departed or were destroyed. As before, captured enemy pilots appeared dazed and disoriented and, during interrogations, did not understand what they were being asked. Many of them were incredulous and claimed to be shocked when told what they had been doing even minutes earlier.

The *Jakarta* had sustained heavy damage but was not in imminent danger, with the engines intact and the hull solid enough. Thus it was that the *Jakarta's* captain requested the Rangers to join him on board, so that their current situation could be examined and their next course of action determined.

Once the three Black Birds had docked with the remaining battleship, the crews made their way to the command deck. All of the Rangers moved with a determined resolve, but each of them felt the loss of the *Spitzbergen* deep inside, like a kick to the gut.

"We can mourn our losses after the job is done," Mars told them along the way. "Because, if we fail, the *Spitzbergen* will be the least of our losses."

The Rangers emerged onto the *Jakarta's* bridge. Captain Ben Maruwari stood to one side, his dark hands nervously smoothing the wrinkles in his naval uniform.

"Why didn't you call us when this all started?" Mars asked him immediately as he approached. "We could have come straight back."

"I wanted to contact you, Captain," replied Maruwari nervously, his eyes darting from Mars to the cold deck below, "but the Commodore wouldn't allow it. He told me, 'Either we can defeat the enemy with our task force, or we cannot. But what difference can one more little Black Bird make if we can't?'"

Mars considered this and reluctantly nodded.

"And now I'm not exactly certain how to proceed," Maruwari said to the Rangers as they strode together onto the bridge. "Should we return to base or continue the mission? And who is in charge now?" He motioned out the big forward window at the still-burning wreckage of the *Spitzbergen*, where members of his crew were making one last effort to rescue any survivors. "Do we still *have* a task force at this point?"

Mars nodded to the man and made a placating gesture with one hand.

"We'll have answers soon enough."

"Indeed," said Captain El Rey, who had entered just behind Mars. "Lieutenant," the tall, slender Ranger barked to the communications officer stationed to his right, "contact Commander Verne back at the Black Hole. This entire project is his. He will make the call as to how—or if—it proceeds." He shot Mars a withering glance. "And who directs it now."

Moments later, the *Jakarta's* communications officer had a link to the Black Hole via null-radio.

"This is a great tragedy," Verne acknowledged in a grave voice once they'd described what had happened. "A black day for us all."

The others nodded solemnly.

After a few respectful moments, Verne cleared his throat and continued.

"It does sound as though you have been making progress—hot on the trail of some answers, at last."

"I believe so, sir—yes," Mars replied solemnly.

"Those who died aboard *Spitzbergen* were doing their duty to the very last, I have no doubt," Verne went on. "They all understood the risks that accompany serving in the Navy and in the Space Patrol. It would insult the memories of the many who sacrificed so much, if we were to end the mission now. It must continue," Verne stated firmly. "You must push forward and complete this business—and soon!"

The gathered Rangers all nodded in agreement.

"We're completely behind you on that, Commander," Mars said.

"But we need to know," El Rey added, "who's in charge of the task force now."

"Yes, yes," Verne groused, "that's true. You must have a new commodore."

He seemed to consider for a few seconds.

"This is a Space Patrol-led mission, as was intended from the start," the Commander pointed out at last. "The Navy is there in a support capacity only. Therefore, a Ranger should assume the position of commodore."

Captain El Rey smiled, straightened his uniform and started to speak.

"And so I hereby appoint Captain Marshall McCoy to the position of Commodore of Task Force Obsidian."

El Rey froze in mid-movement. He darkened. "But—"

Mars was shocked but managed to speak. "Thank you, Commander," he said. "It's an honor."

"And, Mars," Verne continued, his voice now very low and terse, "I meant what I said about wrapping this operation up quickly. It's all I can do to hold the Navy back—they're ready to carpet-bomb the entire Fringe and have done with it."

Mars glanced around somewhat nervously at the naval officers that surrounded him. "Understood, sir."

"I will expect periodic reports," Verne said then, loudly again. "Good luck, *Commodore*." And with that, he broke communication.

"Thanks," Mars replied, adding, "I think we're going to need it."

Captain Maruwari stepped forward, saluted, and shook Mars's hand. "Congratulations, Commodore. What are your orders?"

"Set course for Gothika."

The captain took this in, then nodded once. "As you wish." He turned to issue the orders to the navigator.

The otherwise immobile El Rey's steel-gray eyes had been burning into Mars's back this entire time. Now his expression hardened. Stepping forward and extending a hand, he shook Mars's firmly. His voice, when he finally managed to speak, was low and hard.

"Congratulations."

"Thanks."

El Rey paused, then: "Now don't screw this up."

"Three nights! For three nights you have been in my custody," the Baron shouted, "and for each of those nights I have been assailed by the most horrendous of nightmares! Nightmares so overwhelming, so...*real*... that restful sleep has eluded me!"

Through the bars of the cell, Deimos merely gazed back at the Baron impassively.

"You are doing this," the Baron went on. "You are causing it! You are doing something to me—something to disrupt my sleep! To meddle with my very sanity!"

Still Deimos said nothing. His pale brown eyes peered up at the gray-haired aristocrat with all the regard one might give an insect.

The Baron growled deep in his throat, then motioned for his guards to move forward, taking up position on either side.

"When you have become well acquainted with the accommodations of my dungeons, my friend, perhaps then you will reveal precisely what you are doing to—"

"It's not me, Excellency," Deimos replied, his voice slow, laconic. "Not me at all."

The Baron's eyes narrowed.

"Then what—?"

"It's the box."

"What? The box?"

"Yes. Or to be more precise, the thing in the box."

The Baron took this in, considering it for a few seconds.

"Impossible. The box is an ancient artifact. An object of power. That is why I coveted it—why I was paying Captain Kargan so handsomely to retrieve it for me. And," he added, "while I admit that you were treated poorly by the captain and deserved the payment..." He shrugged. "Had you simply handed it over to me when you arrived, you would now be a free man—and a wealthy one, as well."

"You are doing something to me…"

"I have no memories of that," Deimos replied. "I've told you that before. My last memory is of climbing out of my ship and greeting you. Things go black for me at that point. The next thing I knew, I woke up here. I assumed your men knocked me out so that you could avoid having to pay me what you owe. To be blunt—so that you could rob me."

"Of course not," the Baron barked back. "I would have paid you—but you attacked me!"

"I have no memory of that, Excellency."

"So you claim."

The Baron strode back and forth in front of the cell for a few moments, the guards standing to one side, waiting.

"You said the box is what is causing my nightmares?"

"Yes. I am certain of it."

"You seemed quite agitated about the box, just before you attacked me."

Deimos only sighed at that.

"The box is more than what you think. It is not just a lost object of power—another trophy for your collection. I am happy to hand it over to you—at the price we discussed before, plus a bit more to make up for my less than cordial treatment since my arrival—but you really should know exactly what it is you're dealing with in that box."

"How would you know this?"

"I have done much research on it. I had to, in order to locate it and prepare myself for any defenses I might encounter along the way."

"And you say you worked with the Cabal during that process—and then betrayed them."

Deimos's expression was flat, even. "Yes."

The Baron shook his head.

"I cannot imagine working with the Adversary. Why would you do so?"

"I needed their resources, their technology, to find the item."

"So why did you then betray them?"

"I'd found it."

The Baron smiled. "That simple, then?"

"Well, they aren't great conversationalists," Deimos added. "I thought Kargan would pay better—or his buyer would. And I also wouldn't have to worry about waking up one morning with a lobotomy and a chain around my neck."

The Baron's smile grew sharper. "You're so sure you've escaped that fate?"

Deimos wasn't certain how to take that, so he just snorted.

The Baron considered all of this, then nodded.

"And what have you learned? You claim to have such insights into the thing, so tell me: What precisely *is* the box?"

"The box is nothing—a container, a vessel. But what it contains..."

He paused, then regarded the Baron with an inquisitive expression.

"You haven't actually opened it yet? Peeked inside?"

"I—no, I haven't opened it. I—"

"And do you know *why* you haven't?"

"...No."

"Because it doesn't want you to."

"Doesn't—it doesn't *want*?"

"Exactly."

"How—how can it *want*?"

"Because it thinks. It thinks very powerful thoughts."

"It—it is alive? How can it possibly be alive? Just what are you saying?"

Deimos grinned.

"Your box contains a mind. A brain. An alien brain. Or..." He shrugged. "Or else perhaps a computer. A computer so ancient, so alien, so advanced, that there's scarcely any difference. But, in any case, it is a mind—and one that has been sleeping for a very, very long time."

His grin widened, the opposite of the look of horror now covering the Baron's face.

"But now... Now, it is awake. And it is not happy."

The Baron considered all this. Sweat ran down from his brow and he mopped at it absently with one hand.

"Can this be true?"

He glanced from Deimos to the guards, his eyes growing feverish. He feared he knew the answer to his next question already, but asked it anyway.

"But—it's safely in its box. It cannot move, I assume. How can it threaten anyone?"

"It is a telepathic mind. Incredibly powerful. Surely you've sensed this already, even if you didn't understand it."

"I—yes..."

"And I am of the impression now that it must... *feed*, from time to time, when it is awake."

"Feed?"

"Feed on the minds of others. You. Me. Your guards. Anyone within range."

The Baron took this in, swallowing slowly. Fear was growing stronger in the pit of his stomach. "And what exactly might its range be?"

"I have no idea. But I suspect, based on what I've seen thus far, it is quite vast."

The Baron recoiled once again.

"What—what can we do?"

Deimos grinned now.

"Why, my dear Baron, I should think the answer obvious."

He laughed—a laugh that sent chills down his captor's spine.

"We must feed it."

(The Present)

Captain Jaxon's robotic visage filled the screen aboard Black Bird Five. Outside in space, the robot pirate captain's little fleet was held at bay by the massive form of the battleship *Jakarta*, its many weapons trained on his five small ships.

"Again, congratulations on your field promotion, Commodore McCoy," Jaxon was saying—and if robot pirate captains could feel fear and anxiety, Jaxon looked to be feeling both those things at the moment. "And of course—given my sudden tactical disadvantage—I would be delighted to offer my dear old friend whatever information or advice you might be seeking from me."

"I don't need your advice, Jaxon," Mars growled back at him. "But information is precisely why I came looking for you in the first place."

"Certainly, my boy, certainly. What can I help you with?"

"Just hypothetically," Mars began, "I want you to assume there's an artifact of considerable value floating around out here in the Fringe."

"Hypothetically, yes," Jaxon replied, his electronic eyes twinkling. "Meaning this is only a word exercise, a thought puzzle."

"Okay, sure."

"And further meaning it will have nothing to do with all the talk I have heard recently of a most remarkable and unique artifact being sought by a number of interested parties among the Fringe Worlds."

Mars only glared at him.

"Of course, Cap—*Commodore*, of course. As you say. *Hypothetically.*

All right. What is your question?"

"Assuming such an item was found in this part of the galaxy—where would someone take it?"

"A fence, you mean?" Jaxon seemed almost to be relishing this conversation as much as Mars was hating it—probably in part because it allowed Jaxon to talk to the acclaimed Mars McCoy about his own area of expertise, and it made him valuable to Mars—something Jaxon secretly enjoyed, though he never would have admitted it.

"I don't know," Mars replied. "Maybe a fence... but what if it was even more valuable than that? Something so valuable and unique—and dangerous—that..."

"Ahh," Jaxon interjected. "I believe I follow you now. No, no, you're not talking about a fence. You're talking about someone so wealthy that he could sponsor whole expeditions to scour the backwaters of the galaxy for items he desires—items of power. Someone who would pay up front for such searchers, and then pay even more lavishly upon delivery."

"Okay—that sounds reasonable."

The robotic pirate held up a single gleaming metal finger. "Then I have one name for you. *Serling.*"

Mars's face did not waver.

"You mean Baron Serling, the Governor of—"

"Of Gothika, yes," Jaxon replied, his silvery robotic head nodding.

"But—"

Jaxon waved away what he anticipated to be Mars's instant objections.

"Yes, yes, my boy—I am fully aware that Serling is a nobleman, a high-ranking member of the Imperial elite. But he's also dirty, Commodore—dirtier than any pirate on my ship."

"Does that include you?"

"You wound me! Of course it includes me, Mars. I would kill you; same as any self-respecting pirate would—but you'd know it was coming! I make no secrets about it. This sort—Serling and his ilk—they pretend to nobility and honor—and then they stab you in the back. Baah. I have no use for any of them." He cackled a laugh. "Except as galley slaves, when I'm lucky enough to hijack one of their pleasure yachts."

Mars started to say something to that.

"I'm joking of course," Jaxon quickly asserted. "Of course I would never take a human into slavery. I'm an honest businessman."

"Of course," Mars said distractedly. His mind was awhirl with possibilities now.

"Yes, your esteemed Governor of Gothika is well-known among my associates for trading in strange and exotic...and *dangerous*... artifacts from the Fringe—and beyond. And here's a bonus for you, dear boy. It is equally well-known among the...*cognoscenti* of the Fringe Worlds that Baron Serling often works with one of my competitors: Captain Kargan of the Sargasso."

"Kargan?" Mars seemed skeptical. "Even assuming that's true—why would you rat out a brother buccaneer like Kargan?"

"Kargan? Bah," Jaxon spit in electronic tones. "I have no love or loyalty for him. He gives pirating a bad name. He's put me on the short end of enough deals that I don't mind selling him out—him or that governor."

Lt. Commander Voroshilov's voice broke into the line. "I don't like this, Captain," he said. "I've had some dealings with the Baron in the past, and have never found any reason not to trust him—certainly no reason to believe the things this—this *thing* says about him."

"This *thing*? Ahh, Lt. Commander Voroshilov, you wound me."

If Voroshilov was surprised to hear that Jaxon knew his name or recognized his voice, he didn't show it. Instead, he continued, "This is a mere pirate. How could we trust his word over that of a planetary governor—a hereditary Imperial baron?"

Mars said nothing, waiting, weighing what he was hearing.

On the screen, Jaxon appeared to shrug.

"I only give the information I was asked to provide. Whether you believe it—and what you do with it afterward—is entirely up to you."

Mars nodded.

"Thank you for your cooperation, Captain Jaxon. I'm sure we can bypass the usual inspections and allow you to get on with your...perfectly legitimate trading operations today."

Jaxon's robotic face seemed somehow to be smiling.

"Ahh, my boy, you are a good soul. I wish you well in your mission, my old friend, and hope that you don't get yourself killed on this fool's errand."

"You do?"

"Of course. It would deny me the pleasure of killing you myself!"

And with that, Jaxon severed the connection. Seconds later, his little armada of pirate ships had vanished into null-space.

"You folks were all listening in, right?" asked Mars.

"I had them all tied in," replied Betty from the co-pilot's seat.

"Yeah, I'm here, Mars," came the voice of Lt. Calderon over the radio from aboard Black Bird Six. "There's the confirmation you were looking for, right? Now both that one-eyed pirate you fished out of the Sargasso *and* Jaxon have implicated Baron Serling."

"It does seem pretty persuasive at this point," Mars agreed, rubbing his chin in thought.

"This is garbage," Voroshilov barked from aboard the *Jakarta*. "You're actually trusting the word of a couple of pirates over the reputation of an Imperial noble!"

"The nobleman is still human," came the smooth tones of Captain No-Rah from aboard Black Bird Seven. "Regardless of their stations in life, any could be tempted by great wealth and power."

"Even a baron," said Betty.

"Power corrupts, as they say," added Calderon.

"Look—I'm not concerned with Serling's title or nobility or what have you," Captain El Rey added in. "But slapping cuffs on an Imperial Baron without any real proof…"

"We don't have to run in, guns blazing, and arrest the man instantly," said Flint Rogers from Black Bird Seven. "We can just, y'know…investigate a bit first."

"That makes sense," Calderon agreed.

"It's the strongest lead we have," Mars told them all. "We're going. But—we're being careful. Very careful. Careful for the Baron and his reputation…and careful for the lives of everyone in this task force." He sighed tiredly. "Or at least what's left of it."

"So—no one has told me yet. Precisely what job is the Baron hiring me to do?"

A tall, slender man had approached the commercial telepath just outside the castle and bowed formally to him. He wore a deep red robe with a hood that mostly covered his head and face.

"We're pleased to have you with us," the man purred. He made no effort to address the question he had been asked.

The telepath was a bit over five feet tall, with black hair and a golden complexion. He introduced himself as Mr. Wei.

"And you are?"

"My name is Deimos. I am a…special assistant to the Baron."

The telepath nodded. "And—again—what exactly will I be doing?"

"Oh, this and that," Deimos answered evasively, his brown eyes not quite meeting those of the telepath. "Your reputation precedes you, of course, and the Baron has great need of your services."

Still somewhat puzzled, Mr. Wei followed Deimos as he pushed open the huge wooden door and led the new arrival into the castle proper. The two men continued on across a broad, open entry room with a floor tiled in marble and walls decked in magnificent, gold-tasseled tapestries that depicted hunting scenes from what looked like old Earth. Sentries stood here and there, armed and dressed in immaculate, navy blue and white dress uniforms. None of them so much as looked in the direction of Deimos or Wei.

The two men reached the far wall, into which three large doors were set. Deimos ignored these and opened a smaller door off to one side, indicating that Wei should go through.

Mr. Wei passed through the doorway and found immediately that the steps led downward. The passage was dark, and he could find nothing in the way of a light switch or other illumination at hand. He turned back to Deimos, a confused look on his face.

"No, no, that's right—go ahead," Deimos reassured him. "I'm right behind you."

Wei shakily navigated the broad stone steps, darkness growing thicker and more impenetrable all around.

"Can we not have a light?"

"We're almost there," Deimos replied.

At the bottom of the stairs, Mr. Wei encountered another wooden door bound in metal. He ran his hands along its face carefully, as he could scarcely see it, then turned back again, growing increasingly agitated.

"What should I—"

The door creaked open inward.

Wei hesitated. He didn't like blindly traveling through this ancient castle, particularly when he was in the lead of the procession. But standing here in the dark stairwell didn't seem like much of a good idea, either. Inhaling deeply and sucking up his courage, he stepped through the doorway.

He was in a round chamber, approximately ten yards in diameter. Bare stone walls arched up into a sort of domed ceiling a dozen feet overhead. A pale blue light flickered from somewhere deeper inside, revealing a pedestal at the center of the room.

"Hello?" Wei called out. "Excuse me?"

He turned back. Deimos was gone.

Carefully at first, he reached back in that direction with his mental abilities.

Nothing.

But—he couldn't have gone far... Not in so short a time...

And yet Wei's telepathy could find no one in the immediate vicinity. Only the very slight buzz of the guards' thoughts as they stood in the entry room, high up at the top of the stairwell. It was as if Deimos had vanished from the world.

Enough of this, Wei thought angrily. He started in the direction of the doorway.

The door slammed closed.

He nearly jumped out of his skin.

"Hey!" he cried. "Hey, what do you think you're—"

A tingling sensation raced up his spine.

"Hello?"

He whirled back again, peering into the gloom, now illuminated more strongly by the sourceless, dancing blue light.

Again came the tingling, a row of pins and needles along his scalp.

I know that feeling, he thought. *Another telepath.*

"Stay back," he called into the gloom. "I can feel you—feel your presence."

He stepped quickly to the iron-bound door and pulled on it again. It did not budge; the thing was bolted tightly shut. He started to bang on it—to shout—but then he thought better of that.

Maybe this is a test. Maybe they want to see what I'm made of—how tough I am—before they hire me. Well, fine.

He considered his possible actions, alone there in the dark. Finally he turned back toward the center of the room, to where the pedestal stood. Slowly, gingerly, he approached it. That felt like the right thing to do; in fact, it seemed to him as if something—some voice—were calling him there, encouraging him to approach.

Now it seemed as if the blue flame that illuminated the room surged and fell rhythmically, as if in time to some huge, awful heartbeat—the heartbeat of the castle itself.

Wei stood before the pedestal. It was a white marble column about three feet high, with a flat disk of the same material for a top. He looked down at its surface. Something sat there.

A box. A small, rough, metal box.

Now the blue light pulsed very rapidly, as if keeping pace with his racing heartbeat.

His hand rose of its own volition. His fingers reached out, tentatively at first but with increasing determination. The tips brushed the surface of the box.

The temperature in the room dropped thirty degrees instantly. Forty. Ice formed along the walls and across the floor.

Wei drew back his hand in shock and surprise.

The blue flame flickered madly all around him—now even dancing within his own eyes. His mouth fell open, his jaw slack. His voice burbled nonsensically in his throat, dying there.

The thing in the box reached out with talons of mental force and raked them across his mind.

Wei wanted to scream but could not. He could not even remember why he should, now—or even who he was.

The ice grew thicker. The temperature plunged below zero.

The guards above heard the laughter then, but could not later have said if it belonged to Mr. Wei, or to the strange Deimos, or to someone—some*thing*—else entirely.

"I'm not happy about this arrangement, Deimos," said the Baron as he looked on in surprise and revulsion from a hidden room adjoining the round chamber. "But if it's the only way to keep that—that *thing* in there content… until I can make *use* of it…"

"It's hungry," Deimos replied, pulling back the hood of his robe to reveal a thin, silvery metal web that covered his head, blanketing his mind from telepathic probes. "It needs to feed. And telepaths—telepathic minds— are what it most desires." He shrugged. "It's a small enough price to pay. And soon, it will be strong enough to carry out your plans for you."

Whether Deimos himself actually believed what he was saying to the Baron, the older man accepted it with an uncomfortable nod—his eyes never leaving the grotesque scene playing out in the adjoining room.

Meanwhile, deep within Deimos's brown eyes, another set of eyes— hazel rather than brown, entirely different and yet precisely the same— danced and flickered. And a second scream, soundless but echoing endlessly across the mental plain, joined the first.

The remains of Task Force Obsidian hurtled through the void of null-space.

On the bridge of the *Jakarta*, Mars McCoy stood with his hands clasped behind his back, gazing through the huge viewing port at the hellish blackness surrounding the ship. Just to his right and a step down on the little stairway leading to the observation deck, Tony Calderon waited anxiously.

"You don't take well to long transits, do you, Lieutenant?" Mars called over to his old friend as several of the ship's crew looked on with amusement.

"Never have, Captain," Calderon responded with a half-smile.

"Must be tough being in an organization that's responsible for patrolling the entire length, width, and depth of the Fringe, then."

Calderon laughed. "I find a lot of time for crosswords and old novels," he replied.

Mars stood there a few more seconds longer, then abruptly turned and hopped down the steps, two at a time. Calderon, startled, hurried after him.

"What's going on, Mars?" Calderon asked once he'd managed to catch up to the rapidly striding Ranger. "I mean, aside from everything that's happened since we left the Black Hole."

"Since even before that," Mars corrected him.

"Well, yeah, true…"

Mars turned a corner and came to a lift. He punched the control and the doors opened. As he stepped inside, Calderon hurried in beside him.

"Hangar Deck?" the stocky man asked, hoping that would be the answer.

"Not just yet," Mars replied. "You and I have a couple of things to attend to, first."

Calderon was not sure he liked the sound of that, but he kept his mouth shut and punched the proper instructions into the door control. With a whoosh, the doors closed and the lift zipped them along the length of the huge battleship.

Unbeknownst to Mars and Calderon, a short distance from where they had just been standing, Betty-12 and Dr. Bosco were seated at a table in the Officer's Club. Betty had a glass of cocoa on the small table in front of her that she had not touched, though she was capable of processing it if need be. Bosco was pretending to drink from a glass of water, in his usual effort to fit in—though he never actually took a drink.

"I'd like to thank you for…for this," Bosco said tenuously, his eyes flickering up briefly at Betty before returning to the glass.

"For what?"

"For—for just sitting with me here…For having a drink with me…"

Betty turned and regarded the doctor full-on, her sparkling blue eyes seeming to take his measure in an instant.

"Doctor, you are an important colleague and a valuable member of our team."

"Thank you. But—beyond that—we have something in common, and—"

"And what might that be?" Betty asked him, her face utterly straight.

The robotic doctor hesitated, taken aback. He blinked at her, looked away, and then sought to gather himself.

"We are both…artificial entities," he said, choosing his terms carefully.

Betty's mouth twisted into a severe frown and she started to stand.

"No—wait! I'm—I'm sorry, Lieutenant. Please—"

Betty looked across at him, pursed her lips, considered for a moment, and sat back again. She gazed across the table at him warily.

"Lieutenant," he finally said, when his fear that she really would get up and leave overcame his fear of actually conversing with her, "I don't meant to broach topics that are uncomfortable for you…"

"Then why do you insist upon doing so?"

"I—" Bosco was taken aback by that, and thought for a moment. "It truth, I suppose it is because…" His voice trailed off, then came back, very soft. "Because I have no one else to talk with about it."

Betty looked at him again, this time seeing him as if for the first time. She glanced at her watch, looked around the club quickly, then turned her full attention on Bosco.

"Very well, Doctor," she said. "What would you like to talk about?"

Bosco swallowed nervously, his eyes reflecting a glimmer of hope and excitement.

"Actually," he said, "and if you do not mind me asking this—what do you seek out of this strange existence that we share?"

Betty glanced at him, still not entirely comfortable with the conversation or with the topic. "I wish to serve the Rangers, of course," she replied quickly. "To help in any way I can."

Bosco considered this answer, and seemed somehow disappointed by it.

"Have you no other hopes—no other dreams?"

Betty's mouth inched upward in a tiny hint of a smile.

"Dreams?" She started to rise once more. "Robots do not dream, Doctor."

Bosco licked his synthetic lips.

"...I do..."

Betty froze in place. Her eyes flickered towards him, then she turned to face him full-on, her expression reflecting great surprise. When her voice came, it was a mere whisper.

"You too?"

The Baron strode arrogantly into the great hall of his castle, his armed guards snapping to attention crisply on both sides. Down the long, navy blue carpet he stalked, his eyes facing forward and intense and his fists clenched at his sides.

"What is it?" he demanded as he reached the far end of the vast room and came to the communications console that filled the corner.

"A null-radio signal coming in, Baron," the specialist reported nervously.

"From whom?"

The specialist stared at the readout for a long moment, frowning. Then, "I'm not...entirely sure, sire. I first believed it to be a Naval signal, but now, I can detect no Naval protocol code in the carrier signal."

The Baron considered this for a moment. He knew of roughly a half-dozen highly placed agents within the Naval command structure who were on his payroll, sending him tidbits of information now and then. In the past, such inside knowledge had proven exceptionally valuable to him, allowing him to stay ahead of such developments as impending Imperial inspections and possible tax increases. He'd yet to have such a report prove entirely worthless.

"Put it through," he growled, staring at the screen.

The tech nodded and manipulated a series of dials and switches. Wavering lines danced across the screen, and then a voice crackled out over the speaker.

"Baron Serling. I trust you are well."

The Baron's eyes narrowed.

"Do I know you?"

"I will make this quick, for I have little time. Know that a Naval task force is on its way to you now, and will arrive within forty-eight hours. It is led by Marshall McCoy of the Space Patrol, and thus is somewhat outside of regular Naval control and restrictions."

The Baron's expression soured further, but he remained highly suspicious.

"Why should this concern me?" he demanded quickly. "Why should I of all people—a planetary governor—fear the glorious Imperial Navy?"

A pause and the static rose and fell rhythmically. Then, "Why, I'm certain you have no reason at all to fear such a task force entering your orbit, Baron. I am equally certain you have no problem whatsoever with the Patrol sending down Rangers to crawl about your various facilities, poking their noses in every nook and cranny."

The Baron felt his blood pressure rising but he remained silent. He did, however, consider what he was being told—he considered it very carefully.

"Just remember that you do have friends within the Navy—this is known to me. But the Rangers are another matter entirely. They will not be so...*understanding*...of your various activities. They will not be so accommodating with the little prerogatives that you and the rest of the Imperial nobility are inclined to indulge in from time to time."

"I...see," the Baron replied at last, his face now flushed a deep red. "Well. You have my thanks for this... friendly warning, Mr...?"

"Lt. Commander," the voice replied. "Lt. Commander Sergei Voroshilov."

"Thank you, Lt. Commander Voroshilov."

"My pleasure, Baron. I have no doubt that you would prefer not to be embarrassed by having the various—and quite understandable—activities that all nobles may engage in from time to time exposed. I am equally confident that you would never engage in the much more terrible crimes these ridiculous Rangers suspect you of."

"Indeed," the Baron muttered back. "Indeed."

Baron Serling thought about all he'd just heard, and a tiny tinge of fear took root for a moment in his stomach. Then he considered the amount of time he would have before this task force arrived, and he allowed a tiny smile to spread across his face.

"I'm certain," he said then, "that the Rangers will find me most accommodating—my hospitality matchless among the Fringe Worlds. Yes," he added, a touch of menace showing through his words, "I'm sure they will find me quite well prepared for their visit."

"I do not doubt it for a moment," Voroshilov tried to reply. But the Baron had already cut the connection and was stalking rapidly out of the chamber.

Mars McCoy and Tony Calderon emerged onto the main deck of the forward section of the vast, cylindrical battleship. There the main hangar bays for the fighter craft were located, along with storage compartments for fuel, ammunition, and other supplies for the *Jakarta's* complement of small attack and support ships. Additionally, certain other items and substances were kept in this location, as far away from the bridge, engines, and living quarters as possible. It was this latter fact that had drawn Mars there.

"So—you wouldn't want to give me even a hint as to what we're doing here, would you, Mars?" Calderon asked as they rounded a series of corners, nodding and saluting various busy naval personnel along the way.

Mars didn't reply. In silence he continued to lead Calderon along the winding corridors.

"But you do need me, though, right? I mean, I'm not just following you here for nothing."

"I need you," Mars replied, not even glancing back.

"Okay…"

Calderon nearly ran into Mars when the Captain rounded a corner and suddenly halted at a broad double-door that ended the hallway they'd been following. It only took Tony one quick look to determine exactly what this trip had been about.

The lettering on the door consisted of one word: ARMORY.

"Ahh…" Calderon said.

A moment later, after Mars had spoken with the Chief inside via intercom, the doors slid open and the two Rangers entered.

Tony looked around in awe, his eyes widening.

They were surrounded by shelves and crates and racks of every size and description. And each of those shelves and crates and racks was filled with items designed to deal great amounts of damage upon demand.

"Wow," Calderon whispered, taking it all in.

Mars was already striding boldly forward, examining the labels on the shelves and racks.

"And I thought our armory at the Black Hole was well-stocked," Tony breathed.

"It is," Mars replied, "for our purposes." He gestured around. "But this is, after all, a battleship. This is what these people do."

"Yeah, true."

With that, Mars grabbed an empty wheeled cart and positioned it behind him, then began to pull items from the shelves and study the markings on them. Some he dropped in the cart, others he returned to the shelves.

The Armory Sergeant, a middle-aged man with thinning hair and a heavy, brown mustache, approached the two Rangers. His face betrayed a growing sense of concern.

"Um, Captain, I—"

"That's actually 'Commodore,' at the moment, Sergeant," Mars interjected politely, never breaking his rhythm of pulling items.

The sergeant seemed to shrink back for a moment. Then he cast a glance at the growing pile of armaments in the cart—armaments for which he was responsible—and summoned up his courage to address Mars once more: "Do you really think, *Commodore*, that you'll be needing all this stuff?"

Mars paused and looked at the man.

"You recall what happened to our sister ship, the *Spitzbergen*, do you not, Sergeant?"

The shorter man appeared taken aback at that.

"Of course."

"If all goes well, we will be confronting those directly responsible very soon. And for that encounter, we will be needing guns." Mars looked down into the cart, at the pile of items he'd already collected. "Among other things."

The Sergeant considered this for a moment. Then he smiled a flat, tight smile and nodded.

"Take whatever you like, sir," he stated evenly.

Mars nodded once to him, eyes steely.

"Thank you, Sergeant."

The man wasn't finished. He climbed up a ladder set into one bulkhead, then stepped across to a somewhat hidden shelf and popped open a concealed bin tucked away there. "You might want to take a look at some of this stuff, too," he said, indicating another stash of armaments hidden away there. "I try to hold onto it for the really critical missions—and from what you've said, I figure this qualifies."

Mars climbed up alongside the sergeant and peered down into the storage bin. He smiled broadly. "You're a good man Sergeant."

Five minutes later, Mars and Calderon were wheeling their cart, now overflowing with a selection of weapons, ammunition, and other items, toward the hangar deck.

*"And I thought **our** armory…was well stocked."*

"One thing's certain, anyway," Calderon noted as they made their way past wide-eyed techs and midshipmen. "We may go down, but we'll go down shooting!" He glanced down at the mound of ordnance he was helping to push along. "And bombing and zapping and slicing and…"

"They're coming," Baron Serling growled before lighting a cigar and drawing deeply.

Deimos sat back in his chair, which was set off to one side of the Baron's library room.

"Who's coming?"

"The Navy—and the Space Patrol, as well," the Baron replied coolly. "Their leader is a Commodore McCoy. I did a bit of checking; he has something of a reputation as a straight arrow—incorruptible—even by Ranger standards."

Deimos considered this. A wry smile snaked across his features.

"Sounds like someone it would be fun to kill. Slowly."

"I hope it won't come to that," the Baron sighed. "If all goes as planned, he and his team will look things over, decide they're on a wild goose chase, and take their leave."

Deimos nodded, and the two of them sat in silence for several moments, smoking.

"But," Deimos said, finally breaking the tension, "if things should get complicated…"

The Baron considered that for a moment.

"Yes?"

"Well," Deimos continued, "your world here is out on the very edge of the Fringe, isn't it? Incidents occur quite frequently here. Deadly incidents."

"This is true," the Baron agreed, nodding slowly.

"In which case," Deimos concluded, "our Commodore McCoy and his team of Rangers might simply… disappear… before anyone *officially* noted their arrival on Gothika."

"The tragedy such a thing would be," the Baron chuckled, tapping his cigar on the ashtray edge. "To lose so fine an officer, along with his entire retinue…"

"Tragic," Deimos agreed. He reached to take another cigar himself—

and then he froze in mid-motion. For, within his head, the seemingly endless screaming that he endured at all times had grown louder and louder—and then had suddenly stopped altogether.

"*Him. McCoy. Him,*" came the voice of his other ego, then, echoing within his skull.

"Shut up," Deimos growled, clawing at his head. The Baron looked on, puzzlement at the man's behavior quickly becoming outright revulsion.

"Shut up. Shut up!"

"*Him. McCoy. We must give it to him. To him! McCoy!*"

"*Silence!*" shouted Deimos, bringing up his fist and smacking it hard to the side of his skull. But this had no effect. For the voice within his head had become a scream, awful and endless, drowning out everything else.

Black Bird Five swept down from orbit into the lower atmosphere of the planet Gothika, its engines blazing and its occupants scanning the landscape below them for signs of trouble.

"There's the castle," Dr. Bosco noted, though he scarcely needed to say a word. The Baron's sprawling, gray stone complex covered acres of the rugged terrain of Gothika. All around its squat structure gaped the great mining pits that had been roughly gouged deep into the soil, eradicating all plant life and exposing layer upon layer of the world's interior to view.

"Not the prettiest place we've been," observed Mars.

Betty regarded the catastrophic environmental damage and merely frowned her disapproval.

Mars considered the ugly scars pockmarking the surface below and had to remind himself again that this man Serling and his ancestors had been planetary barons of Gothika long before being granted the political title of governor by the Empire. The source of the wealth upon which that family had based its power was apparent. Indeed, Mars wondered if the planet could possibly have many resources left to exploit, given the way it had been so ruthlessly strip-mined.

Standing here and there amid the open pits, Mars saw next, were what looked to be people—unmoving men clad in yellow and black. But instinctively Mars understood that the scale was all wrong. From this altitude, those "people" would have to be several hundred feet tall, at least. He rubbed at his eyes and looked again.

Machines. Mining-Titans. Of course.

The giant, human-shaped constructs loomed over the ruined surface, their arms doubling as shovels and drills, their heads actually control cabs that could accommodate a work crew of up to a half-dozen men. An array of industrial lasers and rugged gripping claws adorned the shoulders and lower arms.

Looking on past the Mining-Titans, Mars located the castle's courtyard and maneuvered around until Black Bird Five was on a direct course.

"We'll set down there," he indicated to Betty, who nodded and took over the controls. Then, into the radio mike, "Black Birds Six and Seven—everything looks okay from here. Follow us in."

Captains El Rey and No-Rah replied in the affirmative.

"I've been doing a little background research on the Baron," Calderon added over the connection. "I don't much care for him, based on what I've seen so far."

"I'm sure you're his kind of guy, too," El Rey snapped back. "Now clear the line, Lieutenant."

"We're not here to make friends," Mars stated flatly to the other crews and to his own. "But then again, we do need to be as polite as possible—to follow protocol, at least until he reveals that he's as involved in all of this as we suspect. So let's just handle this one by the book."

The others voiced their agreement and Mars cut the link. All three Ranger ships zoomed down towards the castle of the Baron.

Mars could see a large, reinforced iron door opening as Black Bird Five settled to the cobblestone surface of the castle's courtyard. Seconds later, as the blast of wind from the ship's engines subsided, three uniformed guards emerged through the doorway and took up positions surrounding the ship. Just behind them came a tall, slender man who appeared to be in his fifties, wearing an elaborate, dark blue dress uniform with gold buttons. Blue eyes peered out from a narrow face that also bore an aquiline nose and short, gray beard.

"That's him, right?" Mars asked Betty-12 as he switched off the engines. "The Governor?"

Betty blinked one, twice, accessing her data records.

"Yes," she replied, "though he prefers the hereditary title of Baron."

"I'm sure he does," Mars muttered, observing the stiff and haughty way the man carried himself. "All right—everything looks on the up and up so far, so let's leave the heavy ordnance on board—for now."

"An excellent suggestion," said Dr. Bosco, casting a disapproving glance at the sealed case that took up much of the passenger area—a case containing many of the items Mars and Calderon had requisitioned from the *Jakarta* earlier.

Betty unlocked the hatch and Mars hopped out nimbly, his boots smacking the rough cobblestone surface. He allowed a warm smile of greeting to spread over his face as he approached the Baron. Betty-12 and Dr. Bosco climbed out and followed him.

"Welcome to Gothika, Captain McCoy."

"Thank you, Governor."

"Erm—that's *Baron*, if you don't mind."

"Certainly," Mars corrected himself. "Baron Serling. And," he added with a chuckle, "it's currently *Commodore* McCoy, since we're setting things formally straight."

The Baron frowned at him for a moment, then allowed a slight smile to appear.

"Ah, yes. Quite right. Congratulations on your temporary appointment."

"Thank you," Mars replied, silently noting the verbal emphasis the man had placed on the word *temporary*.

After Betty-12 and Dr. Bosco had been introduced as well, the Baron gestured towards the door leading into the castle.

"If you will all come this way? I have ordered a state dinner in honor of your presence." An objection began to form on Mars's lips, but the man cut him off. "You'll have to indulge me in this, Commodore—it is not often that I receive visitors of such particular eminence, here in our remote corner of the Fringe."

Mars nodded and bowed. "Certainly, sir. We are honored. Ah—but we do have two more ships coming down with us…"

The Baron turned and looked up into the sky, where Mars was directing his attention. Black Birds Six was swooping down on final approach.

"Yes, yes, that is fine," he stated stiffly. "We have more than enough room at the table for your associates. They will be shown in when they have landed. Now—if you would be so kind…?"

The Rangers followed the Baron and several of his guards through the open doorway and along several winding and oddly dark corridors deeper into the castle. At last they reached a broad, high-ceilinged hall with deep red and dark blue curtains bound by golden ropes hanging here and there. Elaborate tapestries covered two of the walls and a long, oaken table with many chairs dominated the center. It was all like something out of a Medieval fortress—and lit from above by a massive ringed chandelier that depended from a rope that looped through a pulley attached by a chain to the ceiling, then ran back down to be tied off against the far wall. A fire burned in a fireplace at one end of the long room, with two rapiers crossed on the wall above it.

"So—let us get down to it," the Baron said, once they'd all taken seats in luxurious, richly upholstered chairs and been served beverages. "What brings you out to this dull and uneventful corner of the galaxy?"

"I'm hoping it will continue to be dull and uneventful, Baron," Mars replied. "Unfortunately, trouble may be on the way."

Before the Baron could respond to this, Captain El Rey and Lt. Calderon were shown into the hall and seated themselves next to Mars's crew. The Baron greeted them both before returning his attention to Mars.

"Now then—as you were saying, Commodore. Trouble on the way?"

"War, Baron. War engulfing the Fringe Worlds."

"War?" The Baron considered this, then gestured grandly around himself, as if trying to indicate the entire surface of his world with the sweep of his arm. "There is no war on my world."

"One is coming," Mars replied coldly. "And coming maybe sooner than you think."

"Oh, so?" The Baron's eyes widened in mock surprise. "And have you brought this war with you, then?"

Seated next to Mars, Calderon took this in and felt his blood pressure escalate. He leaned in towards Mars and muttered, "What's he trying to say, Mars?"

"Mars!" The Baron's mouth turned upward in a broad smile. "You are called Mars!" He laughed aloud. "So appropriate—Mars, the bringer of war!"

As if on cue, the first building strains of Holst's *The Planets* filled the hall.

"And yet I am to understand that you are here to *avert* a war? The irony is vast, wouldn't you say, Commodore?"

Mars frowned at Calderon first, then turned to regard the gray-haired nobleman.

"Very theatrical, Baron. And not the first time I've heard that line—though I must admit, it's the first time it's actually been accompanied by the music."

The older man laughed. "I must confess, I did a bit of research on you before you arrived. Your nickname—and your methods—are quite well known, it seems." He smiled again, but the smile had grown flatter, colder.

"I welcome you to my world, and to my home, but I feel it only just to warn you." At that, he cast his gaze particularly toward Calderon. "I will tolerate no violence, no extra-legal activities, while you are here."

Calderon's face darkened. "Just what's that supposed to—?"

Mars raised a hand. "We understand," he replied.

The Baron stood.

"Excellent. Then perhaps you will all join me for dinner."

He indicated the massive table with a sweeping gesture. At Mars's nod, the Rangers stood and moved to their seats there. Echoing through the hall, Holst's famous "Mars" music built to a surging climax.

The guards, standing in a semicircle around Deimos, glanced at one another nervously, unsure of how to react.

The man had walked confidently, almost arrogantly, up to them moments earlier, where they were stationed in a darkened corridor deep in the castle. Behind them stood the door to the sealed room that held the mysterious metal box. The guards knew to keep any intruders away; but since Deimos himself had delivered the box to the Baron, they were not clear on precisely how they should react to his presence.

And then, quite suddenly, before he could say a word, Deimos had dropped to his knees before them and begun to scream.

One of the guards bent down and laid a hand on Deimos's shoulder, his expression one of puzzlement.

"Sir—are you alright? Can we do anything?"

The screaming—an incoherent wail—went on for several more seconds, the guards growing more troubled all the while. Then the dark-haired head snapped up, and the eyes that glared feverishly up at the guard were not the eyes of the man who had first approached. These eyes were hazel, not brown, and they were filled with an inchoate rage—a brimming madness.

The guard stumbled back a step in shock—but not fast enough.

The hand—the hand of Phobos—shot up and grasped the guard about the throat, flinging him into the two others who stood to his left. Before all three of them had hit the ground, Phobos had pivoted about in a single, unbroken move and chopped the fourth guard in the neck. The man went down soundlessly.

As the first three guards struggled to rise once more, the fifth and final one rushed forward, grabbing for his pistol. Phobos ducked low, kicked out in a spinning move, and took the man's legs out from under him. Two quick and savage blows and the man did not move again.

Now Phobos turned back to face the other three. They had seen him in action and were wary this time, hanging back, uncertain. One reached for a radio at his belt.

Phobos lunged into them, dragging the entire group to the floor. Tightly controlled blows connected with vulnerable points in a flurry of action. A mere instant later, the three guards lay unconscious.

Phobos stood, brushed himself off, and regarded the heavy iron door that stood between him and his objective. Reaching down to the leader of the guards, he took a ring of keys from the man's belt and studied each of them. Twenty seconds later, the door was open and Phobos had vanished inside the chamber.

Captain No-Rah and Acting Lt. Flint Rogers climbed out of Black Bird Seven and nodded to the guards who met them at the door to the castle.

"Last to the party, it looks like," Flint observed as he gestured towards the other two Black Birds already parked nearby. "Hope Mars leaves some of the dessert for me. I'm starving."

"We are not here to socialize or to indulge in gluttony, Lieutenant," No-Rah admonished his colleague in his ghostly, hollow voice. "The Fringe— the galaxy itself—stands poised on the knife-edge of catastrophic war. Remember our mission."

"Oh, I'm remembering the mission, all right—never doubt it," Flint replied, slightly annoyed. "But I won't be in much position to help matters if I've starved to death."

No-Rah gave him a dismissive glance and then started forward, following the guards into the castle. Flint came along behind him.

Deeper along the winding, dark corridors they traveled, No-Rah's unwavering attention seemingly locked on the men in front of him while Flint swiveled his head from side to side, studying everything, looking for any suspicious activities while simultaneously seeking to memorize the path they were following, in case trouble came up later.

"Nice place—really cheerful and uplifting," Flint noted sarcastically to the guards as they rounded yet another corner and he stared ahead at the next in a seemingly never-ending succession of dark hallways.

And then the darkness was shattered by a scream.

The whole procession halted in its tracks. The guards drew their pistols and looked around anxiously while Flint crouched and tensed for action. No-Rah, of course, appeared to float in his ethereal way off to one side, his goggled eyes as inscrutable as ever.

A second passed; another. Flint could feel his heart beating hard within his chest. He opened his mouth to make a comment to No-Rah—

—and a door just ahead and to the right burst open, a lone figure charging out through it. The man wore a long coat and his lanky, brown hair was a tangled mess. His hazel eyes, when they turned to meet those of the Rangers, seemed to burn with eldritch fire. In his extended right hand he held a small metal box.

In an instant he had taken in the scene and recognized the uniforms the two Rangers wore. Then, "The box!" he screamed. "They have the box!"

No-Rah and Flint glanced at each other in puzzlement.

"Deimos brought it to the Baron! Foolish, foolish Deimos! But I have taken it! Liberated it! And—"

Before he could continue, the chief of the guards aimed and fired. Phobos dropped and spun about faster than the eye could follow, dodging the blast. And then, before anyone else could move, Phobos had disappeared once more into the dark labyrinth of corridors.

The party stood unmoving for a long second. No-Rah and Flint Rogers considered what they had heard, as did the Baron's guards. Then both Rangers went for their guns, but the guards had theirs out already and leveled them.

"What are you doing?" Flint demanded. "We're Rangers of the Space Patrol! We're here with the Navy, too! You can't just—"

The chief guard held up a hand, stopping Flint in mid-tirade.

"Our apologies for this…inconvenience, gentlemen," he stated flatly as his fellows disarmed the two Rangers. "But—because of what you have just witnessed, and until I have conferred with the Baron—I believe the two of you must be taken into… well, let us call it 'protective custody.'"

Flint started to object once more, but then saw no real purpose in it. Sullenly, angrily, he allowed the guards to hustle him down the corridor.

High above, a spiraling portal skewed open in the heavens and a bizarre spacecraft emerged from null-space with a blast of its engines. Its guns tracked relentlessly back and forth as its maneuvering thrusters settled it quickly and smoothly into Gothika orbit. Grotesque and deadly in appearance, the ship's surface was black and pockmarked with dozens of odd projections.

In the dark ship's main cabin, the leader of the Shadowmen sat in the command seat and watched the tactical screen carefully. Meanwhile, in the rear of the passenger cabin, three Psi-Clones began to howl.

"It is here," came the gravelly voice of the Shadowman in the rear as he handled the heavy chains that served as leashes to the Psi-Clones. "The box. They can feel it quite plainly."

The leader nodded once. His hideous, pale, clawlike hand gestured toward the tactical station.

"The Rangers are here as well, yes? You detect their ships?"

"Ships, yes, replied the Shadowman who occupied the tactical station. "And more than just their usual Black Birds."

This interested the leader. "Indeed?"

"Three of those pitiful vessels are parked on the planet's surface—at the Baron's castle," the tactical officer replied. But..." He leaned over a scope, his hood flaring. "...There is also a Navy battleship in geosynchronous orbit above the castle."

The leader's partially hidden eyes widened somewhat.

"A battleship?"

He sat back, taking this news in. Clearly, it represented both great danger—and great opportunity.

At last he nodded, his ragged black hood bouncing up and down twice.

"Signal the fleet. I want them here now. Tell them to destroy the battleship first, then follow us to the Baron—and to our prize." He motioned to the helmsman with his hideous appendage. "Take us down."

Back in the dining hall, Mars had only taken a few bites of the admittedly excellent fare being served by the Baron's kitchen staff when he glanced over at the empty chairs opposite him and realized with a start that No-Rah and Rogers had not yet appeared.

Wake up, Mars! How did you miss that?

He started to raise the matter with the Baron, then thought twice about it and decided to hold off, at least for the moment. Something didn't seem right here—hadn't seemed right from the moment they'd landed.

He caught Calderon's eye and nodded almost subliminally toward the empty seats.

Calderon nodded back—he'd noticed.

Mars thought for a moment, but before he could decide on the best course of action, Calderon cleared his throat and stood.

"Sorry, all—um, Baron, could you point me towards the nearest restroom?"

The Baron's face betrayed his displeasure, but nonetheless he gestured for one of his retainers, who stepped forward and indicated the proper direction to Calderon.

"Thanks—I'll be quick. Don't drink all the Shiraz before I'm back!"

The other Rangers continued to eat in silence for a few minutes. Still the crew of Black Bird Seven did not appear, and then Mars realized that Calderon had not come back, either.

When Mars at last pointed out the Lieutenant's failure to return, the Baron reacted in a perplexed manner.

"Should I have one of my men—?"

"No, no need to go to any trouble just yet," Mars interjected. "He probably found something to distract him. Leave it to Calderon…"

Mars maintained this somewhat jocular air on the surface, as best he could—but inside he'd grown very concerned and very suspicious. He resolved that if none of them arrived within the next minute or two, he was going to take action. He would—

With a scramble of boots on stone, Calderon burst back into the hall. He was out of breath and sweating from his dash down the long corridor, and two of the Baron's guards raced up behind him as he halted at the table.

"Mars! Black Bird Seven—it's parked outside! And it's empty!"

"What?"

Mars rose to his feet, followed by El Rey and the others. The Commodore regarded their host with a wary expression.

"What's become of my other men, Baron?"

The older man rose as well, his face now dark and deeply lined with a growing anger and outrage.

"I'm certain I have no idea, Commodore," he replied in a controlled, icy tone.

"Then we'll search for them," Mars shot back, before issuing quick orders to the others.

"Now, see here," the Baron all-but-shouted. "Before you go ransacking my home, perhaps you should see if they have simply gotten lost—wandered off, or gotten into something they shouldn't have."

"These are Rangers of the Space Patrol," Mars replied angrily. "They don't just 'wander.' Something's not right here."

Before the Baron could object further, Mars had brushed past him and started down the corridor from which Calderon had emerged. But then came an echoing cry from off in the distance, almost inaudible through the stone walls of the castle.

The Rangers glanced at one another, then drew their blast pistols as one and started forward.

Mars took four steps and stopped, remembering his new command duties. He gestured for the others to go on and investigate while he drew out his com link and keyed it to the frequency of the battleship in high orbit.

"Commodore McCoy to *Jakarta*. Come in please."

Only rough static emanated from the link.

After a second attempt yielded no better results, Mars cursed and replaced the com link in his belt, then glared at the Baron.

"You wouldn't know why I can't contact the task force, would you, Baron?"

"I'm certain I would not," the nobleman replied, raising one hand to his chest as if personally assaulted.

"Right."

Mars raced after his colleagues.

The Rangers had diverted from the main corridor after a second shout had sounded from somewhere deeper in the castle. Now they were hurrying along a lengthy, dimly lit passage as the Baron and his guards struggled to keep up.

Rounding a corner, Mars and the others encountered a sight they had not expected to see: Just ahead of them in the center of a broad, low-ceilinged room stood a savage-looking man in a dark coat, his long hair flying madly about him, his eyes wild.

"McCoy," he shouted at them, his voice ragged and hoarse. "One of you is McCoy, yes?"

Mars moved to the forefront of the group but stood warily, one hand near his pistol.

"I'm McCoy."

Phobos's hazel eyes flashed at him.

"The item you seek—The box! The Baron had it, but I have taken it!"

"Deimos! You fool!" cried the Baron. Then, realizing he had surely just given his game away, he took a nervous step back from the Rangers.

Mars gave the Baron a quick and accusatory glance, then looked back at this strange newcomer. He took in the man's words and understood their meaning instantly.

"Where is it?"

Phobos looked sidelong at him, suddenly suspicious.

"I have hidden it," he replied carefully.

"Where?"

"It is safe," he whined. "The Baron wanted it, but he cannot have it—but now I am not so certain you should, either. It is…dangerous…"

Mars took a step forward, his hands outstretched in a gesture of peace.

"We're with the Space Patrol. We'll see it gets to the proper place—that it is well secured."

Phobos began to back away, step by step.

"Hold on," Mars entreated him. "Just show us where it is, and—"

"No! NO!"

Phobos screamed madly, then bent over and clutched at his head.

The others waited to see what was happening now.

"No," growled Deimos as he looked up, the transformation once more complete and brown eyes now glaring out at the Rangers. "No, it's not yours. You can't have it." He whirled about and dashed away into the darkness.

"After him!" ordered Mars, motioning to Calderon. He and two of the castle guards rushed off in pursuit.

Mars whirled about.

"All right, Baron. I think the jig is up for you. Now—who was that guy?"

But no answer would be forthcoming, as Mars quickly realized—for the Baron, too, had fled.

"You two—go and find that box, if you can," Mars ordered Betty-12 and Dr. Bosco, gesturing sharply in the direction from which the strange interloper had come. "From everything I've heard so far, it's some kind of psychic thing, so you two are probably safe from it."

Betty-12 exchanged a nervous glance with Dr. Bosco, but then she instantly set her concerns aside and embraced her duty, as always. She nodded sharply and started off down the dark corridor. Bosco hesitated, his eyes flickering across the rest of the group. For almost a full second, doubt and concern dueled with honor and duty on his remarkably manlike features. Then finally he pulled himself together and hurried after Betty.

Mars turned back to the others.

"See if you can catch up to Tony and grab that Deimos guy, Captain," Mars ordered El Rey.

"Aye, sir," the other captain replied with a nod, but his eyes narrowed and his face retained the usual suspicious and dismissive expression it usually bore when dealing with his major rival in the Patrol. "And what will you be doing—Commodore?"

Mars ignored El Rey's challenging tone, set his jaw, and started back the way they had come.

"I'm going to track down the Baron," he called back. "I have a few extremely well-chosen words for him."

El Rey considered saying something—possibly objecting—but then seemed to resign himself to the situation.

"Good hunting," he called to his fellow Ranger.

Then, pistol in hand, he moved into action.

Tony Calderon ran headlong into the darkness. He had spotted his quarry a time or two, but the man the Baron had called Deimos was proving to be exceptionally quick and elusive. Calderon had also come extremely close on several occasions to smashing his head into a low-hanging beam or rounding a corner and crashing into a sealed door. Yet somehow—through sheer, dogged determination—he had managed to stay close enough that he could still hear the frantic footsteps echoing back at him.

"I'm gonna get ya," he gasped to himself as he raced along. "You're not getting away from Lt. Antonio Calderon. No way. Not after I've run this far!"

That was when the smell hit him. He'd already noted the air in the corridors growing colder and colder, but he'd dismissed this as some effect caused by being so deep in the bowels of the vast, stone castle. But the smell—there was no mistaking it, and it instantly brought him to a complete halt.

"Oh, no," he gasped. "Not those things. Not again."

From somewhere just ahead, beyond where the corridor turned another sharp corner, came unearthly moaning from many throats. The sounds grew closer and closer, and the wave of horrific odor that preceded them washed like a heavy fog over Calderon, gagging him.

He began to back away, his pistol out and ready—for all the good it would do him, he knew.

For Antonio Calderon knew all too well what sort of creatures he was about to confront.

Around the corner they came, then: the chaos horde.

Those same nightmare shapes that had attacked Mars and Flint on Artinax-2; the same ones that had infested the Black Hole; those unspeakable, unstoppable horrors were *here*, now, too.

Calderon was about to turn on his heel and flee when footsteps clattered behind him. He looked back, his face a mask of fear, only to see Captain El Rey racing up.

"Did you find him?" the captain demanded. "And—what's that smell?"

Calderon said nothing; instead, he gestured ahead with his free hand.

El Rey squinted into the gloom, then blanched.

"Oh, fantastic," he breathed.

"Captain, I recommend a strategic and very rapid retreat."

El Rey looked from the shambling creatures to Calderon, then back.

"Let me emphasize *rapid*," Calderon repeated.

"Yes, I—yes. Fine."

El Rey rushed back down the corridor, Tony just behind him—and the chaos horde at their backs.

"I fear that the same lack of humanity that gives us an advantage in resisting the box's psychic power also dulls us to the possibility of detecting and tracking that power," Dr. Bosco observed as he finally caught up to Betty-12.

"One of you is McCoy, yes?"

The beautiful lieutenant scarcely glanced back at him.

"I am taking that into account," she replied sharply. "I have adjusted my external senses to detect any extremely unusual secondary phenomena that might be associated with this box and its alleged powers."

Bosco nodded, finding himself a little hurt by her dismissive response to him.

"Of course, of course…"

A few moments later, Betty-12 came to a halt and Dr. Bosco nearly ran into her back, instead tripping and stumbling to the stone floor of the castle corridor. Rising and dusting himself off, he realized that Betty was staring intently at the mortared wall on the right-hand side.

"What is it, Lieutenant? What do you see?"

Betty-12 reached out and ran a finger carefully over the stone blocks.

"Cold," she answered. "And ice is beginning to accumulate."

"Yes," Dr. Bosco agreed as he leaned in. "And—look! It's beginning to spread—to grow thicker. Here…and here…"

Within seconds, the walls and part of the roof of the corridor were covered over in a thick layer of ice.

"I believe this qualifies as the 'unusual secondary phenomena' to which you referred, Lieutenant."

But Betty-12 was already racing forward again, a pistol unholstered and clutched in her hand now.

Rounding a corner, Betty sped up again, but a cry from Dr. Bosco behind her brought her up short.

"Lieutenant! Stop!" Dr. Bosco was nearly beside himself, gesturing frantically for her to come back. "Don't you see—can't you see what's ahead of you?"

Betty-12 frowned, turning from Dr. Bosco back to the dark corridor into which she'd been sprinting. An occasional light burned along the left wall, but otherwise the hallway appeared completely deserted to her.

"Those things!" Dr. Bosco again waved madly for her to retreat. "The creatures—from before—"

Betty-12 still could not understand what the Doctor was talking about. Had his computer mind been damaged somehow? Was this some strange delayed reaction that he was suffering, from an earlier incident she did not know about?

Dr. Bosco stood next to her now, clutching at her arm. She brushed him back impatiently.

"Doctor, we do not have time for—"

Dr. Bosco cried out, and now Betty-12 could see that the man did in fact appear to be under attack by something—something very close by. He screamed again, doubling over, and appeared to be fighting to escape the clutches of an invisible man.

"Doctor!"

Now Betty-12 could tell that something was seriously amiss, and her concern for Dr. Bosco increased dramatically. And thus, as she moved forward to help him, her vision cleared—

"Oh!"

The chaos horde surrounded them on three sides. Those massive, repulsive, misshapen bodies sloshed and gurgled as they pressed in relentlessly. The smell, now that Betty-12 could detect it, was overpowering.

Leveling her pistol, she fired a rapid succession of blasts into the faces of the nearest creatures. Unfortunately, the attack had no real effect—the beast cried out and stumbled back a step or two, but then recovered completely and advanced.

Her cool demeanor back in place, she reached an arm about Bosco's waist and pulled him free of his attacker's clutches, then dragged him back and fired again at the monster's face.

"Go back, Doctor," she ordered, emptying her pistol and reloading with a fresh cell.

Dr. Bosco stumbled away from her, coughing and gagging. His arm, where the creature had clutched him, appeared to be half-melted. Quickly he deactivated the pain receptors in that limb.

"Come on," he cried to Betty-12. "You can't fight those things alone! No one could!"

Betty fired the second charge empty, backed away a few steps, reloaded, and started on her third. The creatures shambled towards her, unperturbed.

"Come on!" Dr. Bosco repeated, frantic now.

Reluctantly, Betty-12 turned and ran back down the corridor, dragging Dr. Bosco behind her.

"Not again," Deimos cried, once again in charge of his own body. "Not again!"

He ran through the darkened corridors, cold sweat trailing down his face. He knew he had changed to the *other* again, and that somehow he had severely damaged his own chances of settling matters here on Gothika and being done with it all.

"It's not too late," he breathed as he ran. "Not too late just yet. I have to get rid of these Rangers and help the Baron to restore control here. And then—and then…"

He rounded a corner and the smell hit him, just as strongly as if he'd run into a brick wall.

"Oh no," he whispered.

Just ahead of him stood a cluster of the bizarre chaos horde creatures. They noticed him at the same instant he noticed them, and a group of them started slowly forward.

Reversing his momentum quickly, he sprinted back the way he'd come. The awful moaning sounds behind him faded after a few turns, and he was just starting to believe he was safe again when he came to a doorway—a doorway that led outside.

"Rangers, creatures, the Baron likely wanting to kill me…" He considered his situation quickly, then shrugged. "Things can't be worse outside."

Unlatching the heavy wooden door, he leaned into it and managed to force it open a few inches—just enough for his slender form to slip through. Now outside, he looked around, not recognizing at first exactly where on the castle grounds he was.

Then he looked further afield, just beyond the edge of the grounds, and saw a massive, mechanical shape that loomed up in the late afternoon sky.

"Oh," he muttered. Then, sensing new possibilities, "Oh…!"

Deimos ran for the Mining-Titan.

Having dispatched his Rangers to their various frantic tasks, Mars McCoy now found himself alone in the massive, cold stone castle of Baron Serling.

"This is pointless, Baron," he shouted, his voice echoing eerily from the hard surfaces all around. "Even if you manage to elude me and my squad for a time, we have a Naval task force in orbit! You can't escape. You'll have to return with us and face an Imperial tribunal. You know that."

No reply came back through the still silence save those relentless, flat echoes. Mars frowned. What did this man—this arrogant, spoiled nobleman—possibly think he was accomplishing?

"Baron! Come out! Cooperation is your only option now. You—"

The silence around Mars was shattered all at once as the stone wall to his right bent inward and then shattered, the stones cascading down in a storm of dust and a cacophony of noise.

Mars leapt frantically out of the way, just managing to avoid being buried beneath a half-ton of debris.

When his head stopped spinning and the roaring in his ears became somewhat manageable, Mars pulled himself out of the rubble, groaning at the pain from numerous bruises and gashes that covered his arms and torso. His gray and blue Patrol uniform had been torn across the chest and blood was seeping down slowly from a shallow wound there. Gathering his wits as quickly as possible, he gazed up through the newly created gap in the castle wall to see what exactly had hit him.

The answer disturbed him greatly.

Looming high above in the darkening Gothika sky stood a Mining-Titan, one of the tremendous, man-shaped machines that the Baron's workers used to strip-mine their world's resources. The robotic-looking monstrosity leaned over him, spotlights on its cockpit-head glaring down harshly. The grinding of its motors washed over him as the Titan took another step towards the castle and began to raise its mighty arm.

Mars leapt for cover just as the yellow-and-black-striped, solid steel industrial claw smashed down onto the spot where he had stood.

There could be no doubt now. The machine was under the control of someone—probably one of the Baron's men—who meant to kill him. Mars's mind worked frantically: how could he fight something like this?

The giant metal hand swooped down again, pulverizing the stone floor of the castle even as Mars once again dived for cover. This time he cried out as he landed on an already lacerated shoulder, then rolled for cover behind a mound of debris.

Enough of this, Mars thought as he watched the machine raise its hand again—followed by the ominous humming sound of the drilling lasers set onto the machine's shoulders whirring to life and moving to target him. *Have to find a way to shut this thing down, and fast!*

Leaping to his feet, Mars scrambled through the ragged hole in the wall the Titan had created with its first blow. Now out on the grounds of the castle, he sprinted for all he was worth across the several hundred yards of manicured lawn to the nearest corner, hoping he had his directions correct in his head.

Rounding the corner, he saw with a great sense of relief that he had been right—this was the direction of the courtyard where the Black Bird ships were parked.

As the booming footsteps of the Titan drew nearer, Mars ran for the hatch of Black Bird Five. Only a single uniformed guard had been left there by the Baron, and the man didn't see his attacker coming until Mars had dispatched him with a quick combination of punches, before he could so much as cry a warning.

Mars first thought of simply leaping into the cockpit of the Black Bird and trying to use the ship itself to battle the Titan, but he dismissed this thought instantly. The Black Bird's engines would require quite a few seconds to properly start up, during which time the Titan could smash it to rubble. Instead, Mars raced inside and grabbed hold of the large crate he'd loaded on board before they had undocked from the battleship, dragging it along behind him out of the ship and into the courtyard.

The Titan was nearly upon him now. Mars popped the lid off the crate and yanked out the rocket pack, heavy rifle, and several other items, all exactly where he'd left them. Securing the smaller items to his person, he slung the rocket pack onto his back, fastened it in place, and hit the launch button.

With a roar of combustion, Mars hurtled up into the sky, the pack on his back spewing a bright arc of flame in his wake.

The Titan appeared to react to this unexpected turn of events in almost comical fashion, stopping in mid-step and raring back its head and torso, watching Mars's trajectory across the sky. Each of the monstrous metal claw-hands took a swipe at him, but Mars managed to soar just beyond its reach.

Hovering in a stationary position for the moment, Mars unslung the heavy blast rifle he'd brought from the ship. Leveling it at the Titan's head, he fired.

The blinding bolt of energy blasted down at the machine's control cabin but struck reinforced armor and deflected away, leaving only a dark streak across the silver metal surface.

That's not good, Mars thought with alarm. *If even this gun won't get through that hide, I'm in serious trouble here.*

A second later, the mining lasers on the colossus's shoulders swiveled upward and opened fire.

Mars reacted with remarkable calm and composure to the sudden onslaught of deadly energy weaponry directed his way. Jinking his rocket pack left and right, he managed to dodge the initial barrage. Then, before a repeat performance could be sent his way, he dived straight down towards the towering monstrosity and landed on top of its head.

The Titan spun around, arms waving in agitation, as Mars clung tightly to metal rungs bolted to the surface. One of the claw-hands swiped at him, but apparently the Titan's builders had not intended for the machine to be able to strike itself, and thus the arm would not bend far enough to reach him. Mars mouthed a silent "thank you" to those far-away engineers, then quickly climbed down to the back side of the Titan's head and wrenched at the door handle.

Locked—of course, he reflected with disappointment. *Can't get at the driver that easily.*

The Titan spun around again, rocking this way and that, in an effort to shake Mars loose. After a few seconds of this robotic bull-riding, during which Mars clung tightly to the bar but felt he might throw up, the Titan turned away from the castle and then began to back towards it.

He's going to try to scrape me off—like a bug!

Mars leapt from the Titan's neck area just before the big machine crashed backwards into the towering stone wall. Down he plunged, managing to activate the rockets only an instant before he would have struck the ground. Roaring back into the air, he watched as the Titan extricated itself from the crumbled blocks and rubble it had torn loose from the castle. The big machine had scarcely regained its feet before Mars had swooped down upon it again—but this time with a different plan.

These aren't combat mechs, he reminded himself. *They're built to be tough, for heavy construction and mining work, but they weren't designed to keep an enemy out, the way a military model would be. They're designed for ease of access for the crew—for doing quick repair work.*

That thought in mind, Mars scrambled down to the lower back and found the hatch that covered the Titan's main drive engine. This hatch, he quickly discovered, was not locked—indeed, it had no lock on it. Opening the black and yellow striped door, he tossed in two of the small objects that he had retrieved from the Black Bird: grenades.

Scarcely had he leapt free and zoomed back into the air than the twin, muffled detonations sounded within the belly of the beast. These sounds were followed instantly by a dramatic change in the engine's tone: now stuttering and choking, the power plant belched black smoke into the air and then cut out entirely. It was in an eerie silence that the Titan staggered forward, stumbled to one side—and then went down hard on the grassy lawn, its steel arms gouging out great troughs of soil as it met the ground.

Hovering high above, Mars saw the rear hatch of the Titan's head pop open and a man emerge. He was the same guy Mars had encountered before, in the castle halls—slender and dark-haired, wearing a long, dark coat. Mars shot down towards him, pistol in hand, but the man leapt through the debris of the castle wall and disappeared inside before he could be caught.

Casting a glance back at the wreckage of the Titan, Mars gave silent thanks that at least he'd managed to survive the confrontation. Then, his duty and his mission clear, he landed on the lawn, unslung the rocket pack, tossed it aside, and raced into the castle after his quarry.

El Rey and Calderon hustled along the winding passageways of the Baron's castle, casting only an occasional glimpse over their shoulders at the horrors they knew to be close behind.

"I think we're lost," Tony exclaimed after several minutes of running had resulted only in their finding themselves in yet another unexplored area of the castle's labyrinthine innards. He halted, leaning forward, hands on his hips, gasping for breath.

"That's ridiculous," El Rey snapped, coming to a halt just ahead and scowling as he looked this way and that. "This place can't be endless. We just have to find—"

At that instant, both men looked up in surprise as a small group of castle guards rounded the corner in front of them. The guards stopped in their tracks, taking a half-second to realize just who they were seeing, then raised their weapons menacingly. El Rey and Calderon leveled their own pistols and readied to fight.

Before anyone on either side could fire or even speak, however, a sheet of ice formed almost instantaneously on the walls and floor of the corridor and the temperature dropped precipitously. A heartbeat later, a low, moaning sound echoed up from the corridor in the direction from which the two Rangers had come.

The leader of the castle guards looked down at the unnatural ice, then back up at the Rangers—and then beyond them, to the horrific forms shambling out of the darkness.

"By the Emperor's throne!"

The guards opened fire with their blast pistols, lighting up the shadowy hallway with vivid and blinding flashes of red.

El Rey and Calderon dived out of the way, then found themselves on the other side of the guards, who had totally forgotten about them in the face of the advancing monstrosities.

"What do we do now, Captain?" Tony breathed, eyeing the frantic guards who were firing as fast as they could pull their triggers.

El Rey pursed his lips, wrestling with the answer.

"We can't leave these men to die," he finally growled.

He stood and retrieved his own pistol from where it had clattered away in the confusion, aimed at the chaos horde and fired.

Tony sighed, knowing all too well how this was likely to end. Then he drew his own pistol and joined in the battle.

Mars was somewhat surprised as he stumbled back through a side door and found himself in what turned out to be the main dining hall he had occupied a surprisingly brief time earlier. He felt as though he had no understanding whatsoever for the layout of the castle—though that was hardly surprising, given the frantic events that had transpired almost from the moment they had arrived. Even so, it seemed as though building's very layout was being altered—warped—around them somehow.

Scarcely had he begun to contemplate such things, however, before his attention was grabbed by the heavy, oaken chair that smashed into his back and sent him sprawling.

"You are ruining everything!" came a bellowed cry. "Everything!"

Mars found himself sprawled on his back in the center of the big room, staring straight up at the elaborate chandelier that hung suspended from a long cable high above. He blinked, trying to get his bearings. Then, ignoring the pain and rolling with the blow, he scrambled to his feet just in time to dodge another attack.

"You must all disappear. That's the only solution now. All of you Rangers must vanish—as if you were never on Gothika!"

Rolling over again on the cold stone floor, Mars gazed up at the figure who was assaulting him.

He was not surprised: it was the Baron.

The older man loomed over him now, a fiendish expression masking his face, one of the dining room chairs held aloft over his head. With a cry he brought the piece of stout furniture down hard, attempting to swat Mars where he lay.

The attack missed only by inches.

Mars swept out and kicked the Baron to the floor, sending the chair tumbling away with a clatter. Then both men were up again, circling one another, searching for an opening.

Mars felt that he enjoyed an advantage, should the struggle remain at the hand-to-hand level. Years of strenuous Ranger training had elevated his physical condition and reflexes to peak performance. Surely, he thought, the Baron could not match that.

But the Baron clearly had no intentions of making it a fair fight. Instead, the older man lunged to the side and snatched up a small blaster pistol from where it lay on a side table.

Mars cursed and leapt behind an overstuffed lounge chair as the first blast speared out.

"An accident," the Baron was raving. "We'll say there was some accident—your ships collided in a storm, or—"

Mars scrambled along behind the ornate furniture as another blast sizzled past his head.

"You realize that we have a Naval battleship in orbit, right? It will only take one of us surviving to contact it—I'm sure someone already has!"

"Bah! You cannot contact your precious battleship, Commodore," the Baron retorted. "I have had this entire area—the castle and all its surrounding territory—blanketed by a signal-distortion field since just after you arrived."

More shots, growing ominously close to Mars—and he saw he was running out of cover rapidly.

"They'll send someone down to investigate!"

"You'll all be dead by then!"

Mars growled and, positioning his booted feet underneath a heavy wooden footstool, he launched the object directly at the Baron. The maneuver worked perfectly; the man brought his hand up to block the attack and in the process had the pistol knocked from his grasp.

Mars was up and on him in an instant, two sharp punches connecting with his stomach and a third crossing the nobleman's jaw.

As the older man doubled over in pain, Mars cast about quickly for the fallen blast pistol—and then cursed when he saw that it had apparently fallen through a broad vent in the tiled floor.

At that moment, the Baron—who was proving to be a much tougher and more resourceful fighter than Mars ever would have suspected—swept out with his leg and took Mars down. The two men clashed in hand-to-hand combat for a few moments, and then the Baron wrestled free and lunged for the nearest wall.

Seeing what the man was doing, Mars scrambled after him, and the two wrestled again before the Baron at last managed to reach up to the display above the fireplace and grasp the hilt of one of the crossed rapiers fastened there. The nobleman swept the blade out madly; Mars only just managed to dodge the killing stroke. Then the Ranger grasped the hilt of the other sword and pulled it away just in time to deflect another blow.

The two men squared off then, lethal blades dancing before one another's eyes.

Captain Maruwari strode back and forth across the command bridge of the *Jakarta*, his eyes relentlessly moving from the view of the planet Gothika that filled the huge, panoramic forward window to the communications officer at her station nearby.

"Still no word from Commodore McCoy?" he asked for perhaps the twentieth time in the past hour.

"Nothing, sir," the officer replied, shaking her head as she worked the radio controls. "In fact, I'm not getting anything from the planet's surface, at least in the vicinity of the castle. It's as if the whole area's under radio silence."

Maruwari frowned at that bit of news, chewed his lip, and resumed pacing. Something would have to be done, and soon, he knew. But he did not wish to interfere with what had firmly been asserted to him as primarily a Space Patrol operation, at least until he was satisfied that the Rangers were in danger. And considering that all they had done to this point, as far as he knew, was to travel down to the home of a nobleman of the Empire, he didn't feel quite right about raising any alarms just yet.

Still, this radio silence business was troubling. Perhaps…

The Captain's thoughts were interrupted by the sudden shout of the tactical officer behind him.

"Captain! Multiple null-space exit points opening—all around us!"

Maruwari didn't have to look at the tactical station display; what was happening was readily apparent to the naked eye. A dozen small-to-medium-sized vessels were emerging from null-space right on top of the

Jakarta. In less than a second, Maruwari recognized the configuration of those ships and their origins. His blood ran cold.

"Cabal!" he shouted. "We're under attack by the Adversary! Go to battlestations—*now!*"

All around, officers and techs surged to life, racing for their proper stations.

"Seal the bulkheads," Maruwari cried. "Bring up the defensive screens and order the gun crews to fire at will!"

Already the big battleship was shuddering under the impact of blasters and missiles.

"Damage on decks seven and nineteen, Captain!" shouted the first lieutenant as she leaned over the shoulders of two techs and studied their consoles, peering down at the flashing red indicator lights.

Maruwari steadied himself as the deck rocked violently again.

"I don't care what it takes," he yelled at the communications officer. "Get Commodore McCoy on the line. I want those Black Birds back up here now!"

As the *Jakarta* fired up its maneuvering engines and unleashed its awesome firepower at the wave of attackers, another ship—a smaller transport—popped out of null-space and slipped quietly past the scene of battle. Seconds later, the small Cabal transport was knifing down toward the surface of Gothika.

Beneath the heavy crystal chandelier, in the center of the dining hall of Castle Gothika, Mars McCoy and Baron Serling squared off, rapiers crossed.

"This is not necessary, Baron," Mars stated calmly, knowing the effort was probably a wasted one. "You are entitled to a fair trial. No sense in making things worse for yourself."

"You cannot think you could come to my world—to my home!—and dictate terms to me," the Baron shot back. "This is my domain! I make the laws here! And with you and your Ranger ilk gone, I will yet prevail!"

Filled with righteous anger, the Baron swung wildly, but Mars dodged it easily enough.

"This is the last time I'm going to attempt to reason with you, Baron. Don't add resisting arrest and deadly assault upon a Ranger to your list of charges!"

The Baron said nothing, instead jabbing his rapier directly at Mars's chest. This time, the Ranger was fortunate to avoid a wound at all, his desperate downward blocking stroke only barely causing the attack to go wide.

"Fine, then," Mars growled, anger creeping into his demeanor. "We can do this the hard way!"

Mars lunged at the Baron and attempted a head-cut. The older man parried it easily. Instantly Mars parried the riposte that came back at him and cut at his foe's wrist.

The Baron fell back, a look of surprise on his face.

"You look to be a decent enough swordsman, Commodore. I will give you that."

Mars gave him a nod of respect in return.

"But," the Baron went on, "do you seriously think to challenge me with a blade? I was taught by the finest swordsmen in the Empire. No expense was spared in educating me in all the ways of combat and self-defense."

He came at Mars then with a complex and multi-faceted attack that required all of the Ranger's skills to repel. At the end of this flurry of strokes, both men were breathing heavily and eyeing one another with yet more respect—and concern.

Mars thought to take advantage of his own youth and better fitness level by pressing forward while the Baron was winded. He shot forward, his blade singing as he executed a variety of moves and feints.

The Baron deflected this attack in cavalier fashion and then looped his foot under a small stool, kicking it between them. Mars brought his own booted foot up and sent the stool hurtling at the Baron's face, but it missed by mere inches to the right.

Then the Baron was on him again. Mars parried the next attack, and the Baron did likewise. Growing a touch frustrated, Mars lunged at his enemy but was deflected again, barely managing to beat off the counterattack that followed.

Mars then attempted a very fancy attack he'd studied while on leave in France, on Earth. A beat, a *feint in quarte*, a *feint in sixte*, and a lunge all set up a lightning attack on the Baron's wrist.

This time the blade found its way to its mark and the blood flowed.

The Baron cursed and retreated a couple of steps, red droplets splattering around him.

"Impressive," the nobleman grudgingly admitted, even as he sought to catch his breath. "But you'll find a few training exercises here and there cannot match a lifetime of devoted study."

"...the big battleship was shuttering under the impact..."

He lunged at Mars then and beat the Ranger back with a furious counterattack.

Mars parried the attacks as best he could, retreating step by step as he did so. The slightest hint of true concern grew in his breast that perhaps he had indeed gotten himself into a bad situation—a fight to the death with a superior opponent. Thus he began to improvise. Grabbing priceless antiques from the Baron's tables, he hurled them at the nobleman's head. The Baron pressed on, dodging when necessary but otherwise never dropping the tip of his blade from Mars's left eye.

"You're finished," the nobleman crowed to Mars. "Finished!"

A trampling of feet from down the corridor drew Mars's attention for an instant. Was it his own men, or the Baron's, coming to tilt this contest one way or the other? The gleam in the Baron's eye betrayed the truth. Desperately Mars managed to work his way backwards to the door and kick it closed, dropping the heavy bar across it just before the castle guards could rush in.

"That's but a temporary reprieve, Commodore," the Baron chuckled, pressing on with his seemingly tireless attacks.

The guards began to bang on the door.

"They will break through soon enough, and that will be the end of you!"

Mars found himself driven relentlessly back. Curving his retreat around into a circle, in order to avoid being pinned to the wall, he backed into a heavy marble table. Quickly he moved around to the far side of it, the Baron's blade just missing him with two vicious strokes.

The Baron leapt atop the table; Mars raised a boot and kicked out. The table slid across the smooth stone floor several yards, coming to rest almost directly beneath the chandelier, while the Baron tumbled off to one side and rolled.

Mars leapt to the attack, but the Baron was too quick and made it to his feet again, parrying each blow as he backed away. For the moment, though, Mars found himself on the offensive, and he pressed his new advantage as best he could. He emptied his bag of tricks, attempting every fancy maneuver he'd ever studied, read about, or seen in person.

Meanwhile, the guards had ceased their banging on the door and were now blasting at it with their pistols. Mars could see out of the corner of his eye that it would be mere moments before they shattered it and came through.

The temperature in the dining hall suddenly dropped, and ice spread like wildfire across the walls and the floor.

The Baron didn't notice this. All of his attention was centered upon

Mars, and he moved in for the kill, his own bag of sword-tricks seemingly bottomless. If anything, his blade moved faster now, despite his bleeding wound, than it had at the start.

The ice crept across the floor, and Mars could see that its main body was now only a step or two behind the Baron.

One last maneuver came to Mars's mind then, and he put it into action. Ducking and then sweeping his blade out and up, he forced the Baron to take a step back—a second one—and then—

"No!"

The Baron's feet went out from under him as he slipped on the ice, and his sword tumbled from his grasp as his hand hit the hard stone floor.

Instantly Mars had his own blade tip to the nobleman's throat.

"That wasn't fair!" cried the Baron.

"This isn't the Olympics," Mars replied coldly. "You're under arrest."

The door shattered at last and half a dozen guards rushed in, holding themselves up short as they took in the scene before them.

"Put down your weapons," Mars shouted. "All of you!"

The guards glanced nervously from one to the other, then at the Baron.

"Drop them," Mars repeated, more loudly this time. "Now!"

The leader of the guards hesitated, then raised his pistol and leveled it directly at Mars. And then the guard's head exploded.

Through the doorway behind the guards charged two huge, grotesque beings. Giant, bulging muscles rippled under pale flesh, and tiny eyes in tiny heads darted here and there, evidencing very little intelligence. From iron collars around their necks depended heavy metal chains that led back to their handlers, lurking in the darkness behind them.

Following directly on the heels of these two abominations came a pair of shorter figures who appeared to be almost direct opposites of the first. Gangly, hunched, almost delicate in form, their heads and upper faces were completely covered with dull metal helmets fastened tightly in place.

"Cabal!" Mars exclaimed, recognizing the foul beings immediately. He felt his stomach turn upside down as the psychic energies from the Psi-Clones lashed out at everyone in the room. He could see that the guards were completely immobilized by the telepathic powers being used against them. And now, surging forward and emitting bloodcurdling howls, the two muscular behemoths grasped the remaining guards and smashed them together, shattering bones and crushing skulls with wanton fervor.

A clattering noise behind him caused Mars to whirl about, and he realized that with the sudden carnage he'd quite forgotten about the Baron. The nobleman was up and racing for the far side of the room.

Mars thought to follow him—in part to prevent his escape, and in part to join him in fleeing the horrific attackers. But he found then that he could not move—like the remaining guards, he was psychically locked down.

Before the nobleman could reach the exit, however, he, too, froze in place. The howling of the Cabal Berserkers grew nearly deafening as the two Psi-Clones moved forward, each led now by a pair of Shadowmen. They ignored Mars altogether and focused their attentions on the Baron, who now had turned about and was walking stiffly—or being forced to walk—back to the dark-clad invaders.

"Where is it, Baron?" the lead Shadowman demanded, leaning forward. His dark cowl flared around his pale, pockmarked skull.

"I—what do you—I—"

"You know precisely of what I speak. This is your only opportunity to survive. Divulge the information now."

The Baron choked and gasped. Nothing articulate emerged from his throat.

The Shadowman shrugged, then gestured casually with one clawlike hand. One of the Psi-Clones was led forward until he stood just in front of the Baron. The telepath's helmeted head moved eerily from side to side, as though his neck were broken, as he reached up with gnarled talons. The Baron screamed as telepathic waves lashed at him, penetrating his mind. Blood trailed down from his nose and his ears, and he gurgled wordlessly as his eyes began to roll back.

A second later, the Psi-Clone shook his head.

"This…one…does…not…know…"

The Shadowman growled deeply in his throat, then motioned to the nearest Berserker's handlers. The huge creature surged forward, grasped the Baron by the neck with one meaty hand, and flung him bodily across the chamber. The nobleman smashed into the stonework and fell lifeless to the floor.

The leader of the Shadowmen stood motionless for a second or two, as if contemplating his next move. Then he turned—directly toward Mars.

"Ah," he breathed, the sound more a hiss than a spoken word. "The Ranger. McCoy."

Mars tried to move but the Psi-Clones still had him locked in place.

"Now," the Adversary whispered, "I am afraid it is *your* turn."

"Even if you find the box—and I have no idea where it is," Mars told the Shadowman, his flashing green eyes peering defiantly back into those of the Adversary, "you'll never get away from this planet with it. There's a battleship in orbit that will blow you away if you try to escape."

"Ah, yes—the *Jakarta*, I believe it is." The Shadowman's face, inside his tattered black hood, was mostly covered in shadow, but Mars could see an evil, jagged-toothed grin spreading across it now. "I fear that soon it will be no more. Even now, like a wounded bear surrounded by vicious and starving wolves, your vessel finds itself besieged on all fronts."

The Shadowman held up a comm link and clicked it open. Immediately a voice—eerily similar to the Shadowman's own—came across it.

"The Navy ship is burning, Dark One. Her hull is punctured in many places, and her screens are nearly all down now."

Before Mars, the Shadowman's grin widened.

"You see? None of you will be returning from this mission alive. Though perhaps we might find work for you, McCoy…in the mines."

"Their screens are all down now, Dark One," reported the voice over the link. *"We will be—"*

The transmission dissolved into static at that point, though Mars distinctly thought he heard a scream of terror just before it cut off.

The Shadowman leader's smile disappeared. He looked down at his comm link in puzzlement.

"Shadow Four. Shadow Four! What is happening? Answer!"

"Something wrong?" Mars asked casually.

The Shadowman hissed at him and stepped to one side, working the controls of the link with increasing desperation. Still no sounds came from it.

He would not be getting an answer to his question, for in mere moments everyone aboard the Cabal ships would be dead, the ships themselves destroyed. And this was not due to some Naval task force arriving to relieve the mission, or to a Space Patrol force arriving like the ancient cavalry, just in the nick of time.

No, the Cabal fleet was being destroyed from within. For, deep in the bowels of Castle Gothika, the brain in the box had awoken once more. And, just as it had sent forth its mindless apparitions to menace the Rangers in the castle, now the chaos horde was appearing within the Cabal ships themselves.

With the Shadowmen thus distracted by the sudden disappearance of their fleet, Captain El Rey and Lieutenant Calderon caught them completely flat-footed as they burst into the dining hall. Both Rangers took in the situation instantly and opened fire; Rangers understood all too well to never grant the Cabal even a moment to work their evil, for the Adversary never surrendered and always had at least two unexpected and deadly tricks up their tattered black sleeves.

Calderon took down the two Psi-Clones first. He knew that while the Berserkers appeared the more dangerous foes, the telepaths represented the most immediate threat.

With the psychic lock-down dispersed, Mars found he could move once more. Grabbing up his sword, he speared the nearest Shadowman cleanly, withdrew the blade, and whirled about for his next target.

El Rey and Calderon had by now taken down all the others save one remaining Berserker. The other had required a dozen blasts before succumbing, and this one appeared even tougher. They had the beast backed into a corner and peppered it with shots, but it managed one last lunge that sent Calderon tumbling to the floor before it finally slumped over him, dead.

Calderon groaned under the weight, then groaned again as the rancid smell of the creature's sweat washed over him. He struggled to get loose, but his leg had been caught and twisted and a sharp angle.

"Um—somebody want to get this thing off me? Please?"

El Rey stared down at him, a smirk crossing his face.

"You know you're getting a bath before you get back on my ship, right?"

Meanwhile Mars had cornered the last remaining Shadowman and held him at swordpoint.

"You don't have to die."

As if in reply, the Shadowman leapt forward onto the blade. Mars jerked it back reflexively, but the Adversary was already slumping to the floor. Before he had completely come to rest there, his body hissed and smoked—an instant later, he had completely disintegrated.

Mars stared down at the empty black robe in disgust, shook his head, then turned back to his Ranger colleagues.

"Good timing, gentlemen," he called to them with a grin.

Calderon laughed.

"Yeah, um, we had this planned all along, Mars," he replied wryly—and even El Rey had to snicker at that.

"Now," Mars said, "where are the others? Did they find—"

The doors on the far end of the hall burst open and the man called Deimos rushed in, one hand aloft. In it he held the small metal box.

The voice that emerged from Deimos's throat, however, was not that of Deimos—nor of Phobos. It was a bizarre, unearthly voice that radiated at least as much across the psychic plane as through the air. It was the voice of the box—of the *thing* in the box, at last fully awake.

"You are all my servants now," it crowed. "Servants of Zykzyxl! You who sought to use me—to shackle my powers to your own service. Foolish lesser beings! I strode like a god across this galaxy when your race had not yet emerged from the primordial swamps. And now my children will do so, as well!"

From behind Deimos emerged a phalanx of shapeless, faceless horrors— the chaos horde. The hideous beings shambled into the hall and then halted, standing in ranks as if at attention.

"My children will sweep this galaxy clean," the voice of the box droned on. "Nothing will survive in their wake. Nothing—save the will of Zykzyxl!"

Deimos, clearly a mindless slave now, shuffled forward and set the box on the marble table at the center of the room. From there, wave upon wave of psychic energy—far stronger than that of the Psi-Clones—lashed out, enthralling them all.

It was at that moment that Betty-12 and Dr. Bosco found their own way into the dining hall. At first, all they could see was Mars standing unmoving near the center of the room, with El Rey and Calderon nearby, all surrounded by the bodies of the Castle Guard and the Cabal. Deimos stood off to one side.

"Commodore?"

Dr. Bosco started into the room, stepping carefully over the bodies. No one else moved.

"Doctor," Betty-12 called out, "wait a moment. Clearly something is very wrong here. We must proceed with caution and—"

"They are machines!" screamed the voice of Deimos—or at least a voice that came from his body. "I cannot touch their minds!"

"Doctor," Betty-12 shouted, "get back here now!"

She rushed forward, catching up to Dr. Bosco and yanking him back by the collar just as Deimos shuffled forward. The possessed man moved rapidly, considering he was not in control of his own body. He swung a fist at the robotic Ranger but missed.

"I don't understand what's happening," Dr. Bosco cried, stumbling backward.

Before Betty could answer, El Rey and Calderon came at them both, knocking Bosco to the floor.

"Destroy them! Destroy them!" crowed the voice of the box, spoken through Deimos's lips.

El Rey and Calderon began kicking Dr. Bosco savagely as he lay on the stone floor.

Betty-12 scrambled to her feet, only to lurch backwards just in time to avoid the tip of Mars's sword as it slashed out for her.

"Bbbbb—Betty! Lllloooooook out!" mumbled Mars as he found himself forced to press his attack against his lieutenant again, sword slicing wildly.

Betty-12 could not both dodge Mars's blade and watch for bodies behind her at the same time, and soon enough she tripped over the corpse of a guard and fell. Mars's blade swung down and missed her head by less than an inch, then slashed out again as she crawled frantically on hands and knees away.

"Finish them now!"

Betty-12 could see that Mars was fighting whatever was controlling his body.

"Captain!" she called to him. "Mars! Resist it! You can do it—I know you can!"

Mars slowed his advance, then halted outright. He stood stock still, his body trembling, the sword in his hand bobbing up and down. Saliva trailed down from the corner of his mouth as he burbled unintelligible sounds.

"You cannot resist my power, human!" came the voice of the box. "No living being can resist!"

Yet still Mars fought on inside his head, struggling valiantly against the telepathic onslaught.

"That's it, Mars," Betty encouraged him. "Break free! I know you can do it!"

For another two or three seconds, Mars looked to be winning the struggle. Nearby, El Rey and Calderon were halted in their assault upon poor Dr. Bosco as the box redirected more of its power toward Mars.

And then Mars rushed forward at Betty again, sword held high, murder in his eyes.

With a cry, the brunette Ranger stumbled backwards, almost to the chamber wall. Just as the blade swung out, she tripped over a body—the Baron's, as it turned out—and fell head over heels.

Mars's sword blade slashed out with tremendous force—and, just as he had intended, struck the cable that was fastened to the wall, slicing cleanly through it.

The huge crystal chandelier that had been held up by the cable dropped like a plunging meteor and smashed into the marble table beneath.

On that table, the box—now half-crushed—tumbled to the floor. It fell open.

A small, purple, gelatinous object spilled out of it and rolled across the hard stone tiles.

Betty loomed over it.

"NOOOOO!" cried Deimos—and then, "Yes," cried Phobos. "Yes!"

Betty's pouty red lips frowned as she considered the strange purple object that had come from the box. She looked up at Mars, who was rubbing his face with both hands, as though just waking up from a deep sleep. She looked over at the other two Rangers, who had stopped attacking the cringing Bosco and were staggering away, clearly dazed and confused. And she looked down at the gelatinous thing on the floor once more.

Then she shrugged and brought her boot heel down upon the brain—the all-powerful Zykzyxl—and crushed it to a pulp.

Mars made his way over to Betty and put one arm around her shoulders. He rested there a moment, still coming back to himself, then gazed down at the crushed gelatinous form on the floor. He shuddered.

"Nice work, Lieutenant," he told her. "That's as ruthless and efficient a handling of a dangerous foe as I believe I've ever witnessed."

Betty pursed her lips and shrugged.

"It seemed the wisest move, given the circumstances," she replied coolly.

"You too, Doctor," Mars called to Bosco. "Nice work with drawing the thing's attention and occupying Tony and James."

The doctor, lying in the fetal position on the floor, whimpered wordlessly by way of reply.

"Now," Mars added, as much to himself as to anyone else, "let's just hope there's still a ship up in orbit to get us out of here…"

Just then, Captain No-Rah and Acting Lt. Flint Rogers raced through the doorway, pistols at the ready.

"We finally managed to escape," Flint exclaimed. "And we—"

He looked around, taking in the strange sight of the dead Cabal agents and Castle Guard, then turned a puzzled face toward Mars.

"Oh, man—don't tell me we missed out on all the action!"

"Well," Mars laughed, clapping both of his friends on the back, "better late than never, I guess."

Mars McCoy and his fellow Rangers stood on the command bridge of the *Jakarta* as the damaged but victorious craft emerged from null-space and closed in on the Black Hole.

"We're certainly glad to have you back, and we congratulate you on your great success," came the voice of Commander Verne over the radio. "Though of course we regret that not all of Task Force Obsidian is returning with you."

The fate of the *Spitzbergen* and of Commodore Crabbe weighed heavily on everyone present, and they observed a moment of silence in memory and honor of their fallen comrades.

Then Mars stepped forward and shook hands with the *Jakarta's* captain.

"I appreciate your assistance and your cooperation, Captain Maruwari."

"It was an honor, Commodore McCoy."

"No, no—Now that this business is over I'm back to being plain old *Captain* McCoy," Mars said with a laugh. "That's more than enough for me."

Maruwari smiled back at him, but then his expression turned to puzzlement.

"There are a few things I'm still not sure I understand. This thing in a box that you mentioned—?"

"We have some theories on that, Captain," Mars replied. He turned to Dr. Bosco.

"It was clearly a very ancient artifact," the robotic scientist explained, "possessing enormous psychic power. An alien—or perhaps merely an alien brain, somehow kept alive on its own. And those creatures—the chaos horde, we've taken to calling them—they were merely a physical manifestation of the brain's power. As it began to awaken, it caused them to appear somewhat randomly in a very wide area around it—even across a vast distance of space."

"The thing's psychic power, yes," Maruwari said, nodding slowly. "That was what was causing all the conflict out here—driving the various races to go to war with one another."

"We believe so, yes," Bosco said.

"And this Baron Serling—he thought to control it himself, yes?"

"He was a collector of such things—of dangerous artifacts; objects of power," Mars stated. "From what we've been able to learn from his records, he'd heard about the brain in the box somewhere in his researches, and had offered a great deal of money for anyone who could bring it to him."

"That's where that Deimos guy came in," Tony added. "And where the Cabal got involved, too, we suspect."

"We don't know much about Deimos. At least, not much yet," Mars observed, his face betraying his concern on this one point in particular. "Other than the fact that he possesses some form of psychic ability himself— though we're not entirely sure about the specifics of that—and is extremely dangerous."

"But, since he's on his way to a top-security facility this very minute," Calderon noted, "we should have some answers before too long." He smiled at the others. "I'd say this operation is over and done with—a success, for the most part—and we can all kick back and relax for a while. Maybe enjoy a well-earned vacation..."

"I hope you're right," Mars replied with a smile—but, inside, Mars McCoy knew that nothing was ever quite that simple.

The Cabal ship's timing was perfect; it dropped from null-space just as the Navy prison transport itself reappeared in normal space, a few hundred thousand miles out from the high-security station complex to which it had been headed.

Before the prison ship could fire a shot or even issue a warning, the Cabal cruiser had jammed its transmission and opened its hull with a blast of searing energy from its main gun. Through the breach flew a cadre of operatives in black spacesuits, weapons at the ready.

Ruthlessly finishing off the survivors of the ship's crew in a blazing and very one-sided firefight, the Cabal agents located the containment cells and searched through them. More than a dozen hardened criminals they tossed aside or out the breach in the hull before at last they found their man. Quickly they placed a hood over his head and bound his hands and feet. Then, carrying him aboard their ship, they separated and left the transport adrift—now a lifeless hulk, floating dead in space.

Aboard the Cabal ship, two Shadowmen shoved their target into a chair and fastened him down securely, then pulled the hood from his head. They leaned in close, their darkened faces leering down at him, the air about them growing foul.

"We have plans for you," one of them breathed, even as the other cackled madly. "Oh yes—great plans, indeed."

Deimos's brown eyes stared up at the Adversary agents—and, deep within his mind, so did the hazel eyes of Phobos.

Both of them screamed.

THE END

This has been a long time coming, folks.

Early in 2007 a conversation emerged on the Pulp Factory Yahoo group about the prospect of doing a space-based pulp hero, to complement the then-emerging stable of crime fighters and the like that were just taking shape in the books of Ron Fortier and Rob Davis. (This, you will understand, pre-dates even Airship 27 Productions itself!)

The good and great Captain Ron, in his wisdom, liked the idea and immediately drew up the basics of the Mars McCoy universe—including Mars himself, a true-blue, Flash-Gordon-esque hero in the classic mold. Ron then went a step further and opened it up to the other writers present who wished to throw in their own characters and ideas. What emerged days later was a true group effort, anchored by Ron's rock-solid core concepts, engaging the attentions and the passions of everyone involved. Writers stepped forward, story ideas were approved, and things proceeded apace right up until the very moment that the whole thing ground to a halt.

A reorganization was happening at the upper levels of (what would become) the New Pulp world at that time, and one consequence was that Mars McCoy was left floating adrift, without a publishing home. I stepped up, as publisher of White Rocket Books, and offered Mars and his crew safe haven for a time. Once again writers came forward and keyboards started getting typed upon and things were advancing. For me, that meant beginning what I hoped would be the magnum opus of Mars McCoy stories: a novel-length adventure featuring not just space pirates but monsters, evil psychics, and an overriding dark menace, along with a brewing galactic war and a whole task force of star-battleships for Mars to get involved with. For good measure I tossed in references to Buster Crabbe, and even snuck in a villain with a split personality who "orbits" Mars in his dual personas of Deimos and Phobos, the twin moons of the Red Planet itself. (Sharp-eyed readers will also note that the music playing in the governor's palace is Holst's "Mars: Bringer of War!") I got about halfway through the first draft, with things clicking along—and then the situation changed yet again.

Ron and Rob had re-emerged onto the New Pulp scene with Airship 27 Productions—something to make pulp fans everywhere rejoice. But with that dynamic duo active again, I could not, in good conscience, retain control of the Mars McCoy franchise; Airship was unquestionably where the redheaded hero of the space patrol belonged. So I offered to give him back, and Ron happily accepted. Mars was back where he belonged—but he was now in a long and growing queue with tons of other great properties, and had to wait his turn.

In the meantime, I gathered up the 120,000 words of stories turned in by five writers (Andrew Salmon, James Palmer, John Bear Ross, Greg Gick and myself) and edited the entire package into two full-length anthologies of standard Airship 27 length.   But various unexpected situations continued to stretch out the days until we could at last see any Mars at all in print.

Finally, early in 2011, Mars at last made his debut, with Ross and Salmon and Gick shepherding the good space ranger out to the public. I was overjoyed about that, but had to remain patient while waiting for my 45,000-word novel and James's story, which were slated for the second volume, to make their appearance. Given the winding road Mars had already traveled to that point, though, we all should have known there would be a few more twists and turns before that day finally arrived.

As you can see, though, that day finally *has* come, and now you are at last able to hold this book in your hands—six years after its conception and two years after the first volume hit the stands. And that's something I'm beyond elated about. Because I dearly love the story I wrote for it, and I've waited a long, long time to share it with all of you.

The only thing left to say is, I hope you found it worth the wait.

VAN PLEXICO writes and edits both fiction and non-fiction for a variety of publishers, and is the driving force behind White Rocket Books. His best-known works include the ASSEMBLED! books about Marvel's Avengers, along with the novels HAWK, LUCIAN, and the groundbreaking SENTINELS superhero novel series. His first sports book, SEASON OF OUR DREAMS, spent the summer of 2011 on the Amazon. com Best Sellers List, and his post-apocalyptic hero, John Blackthorn, won the 2012 PulpArk Award for Best New Character. He hosts the White Rocket Podcast and, in his spare time, serves as Assistant Professor at Southwestern Illinois College.

REACHING FOR THE STARS
Afterword by Ron Fortier

Events sometimes happen in a way that just naturally focus your thoughts on subjects that may not seem that related on the surface but when you dig under the surface the connections appear immediately.

I'm referring to the death of astronaut Neil Armstrong back on Aug. 25th, only a few short weeks ago as I write these words. He was eighty-two years old at the time of his death, which all the world mourned as he held the unique honor of having been the first man on the moon. In recalling the stats of his biography, I recalled that Armstrong was born in the same month in which he died, Aug. To be exact, 5th Aug. 1930.

Now if you are one of our regular readers, that year is all too familiar with you as it fall smack dab in the middle of what know of as the Pulp Era in Literature. So consider a kid from the midwest born in 1930 America growing up through the thirties and forties it then becomes rather easy to imagine what fiction heroes he would have encountered along the way.

To think that Armstrong might have been a fan of those early sci-fi pulp explorers like Flash Gordon, Buck Rogers or Captain Future is not a far stretch of the imagination at all. They would have been typical fare for an intelligent young man eager to explore both the world around him and the stars beyond. Those early pulp spacemen would have totally fired him up and been the arrow that pointed him towards his aviation military career and that eventful day when he did in reality what his heroes had only ever done in fiction, stepped on an alien world.

And so here we are keeping the faith, continuing in our humble efforts to keep pulps alive in all their many facets and genres to include the wonderful, exciting space operas as typified by our own Mars McCoy Space Ranger. Mars is the heir to Gordon, Rogers and all those other great heroes and in this his second book of adventures, James Palmer and Van Allen Plexico really put him through his paces.

Response to our first book was overwhelming positive with many of you demanding more of this high flying hero and as always we aim to please.

Still, in lieu of Neil Armstrong's passing, I can't help but wonder at all those other young minds out there, boys and girls alike, looking up at the stars and wondering why we haven't gone back to the moon. It's been too long, people. Destiny is calling us and its origin is in the stars. Armstrong and all his brave fellow astronauts pointed the way for us and we must continue their journey.

We here at Airship 27 Productions would like to dedicate this volume to all those future space men and women out there. We hope our stories will inspire them to reach upward and take up the challenge. Tomorrow awaits us all, let's not keep it waiting.

Ron Fortier
9/8/2012
(www.Airship27.com)
(Airship27@comcast.net)

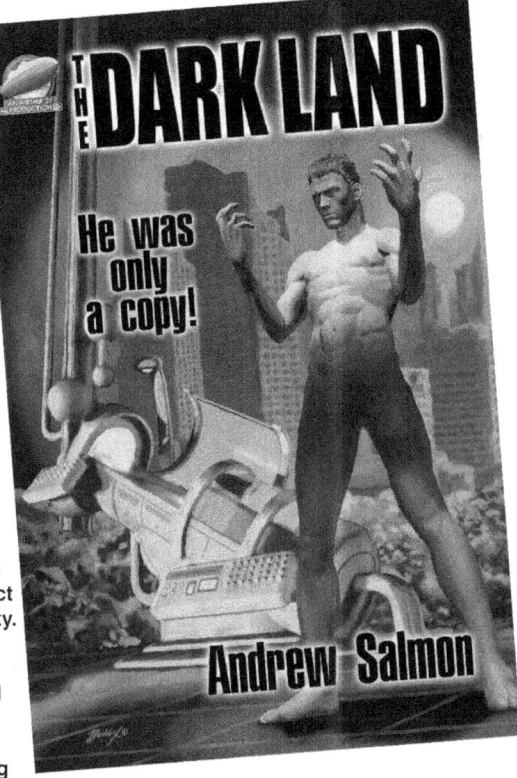

A MAN OUT OF TIME

Restaurant owner Steve Beaudine is killed in a car accident and his beautiful wife, Ava is severely injured. After months of physical recuperation, she returns to AVA'S with the desire to keep the business going. But Tony Jasco, her husband's partner, has plans to sell the eatery and split the profits. Ava adamantly refuses to terminate what had been Steve's dream. She is determined to make it work no matter Jasco's opposition.

Then the mysterious David Ehlert enters her life with a fantastic story, one straight out of a fairy tale. He claims to be a wizard and that Jasco is trying to have her killed to gain his own ends. Ava simply can't believe such a fanciful claim...until they are attacked by magical dark forces. Suddenly she finds herself the target of a twisted, dark magician and her only salvation is Ehlert, a man claiming to have been born in 1886 but still looking young and fit.

Writer David C. Smith spins a colorful, fast paced thriller that introduces a fascinating new hero in the vein of the classic golden age pulps but with a decidedly modern day twist. It is the story of a haunted man out of time seeking redemption for past sins in a world of arcane mysteries and magiks. CALL OF SHADOWS is a masterful thriller by a veteran writer that will keep you on the edge of your chair from start to finish.

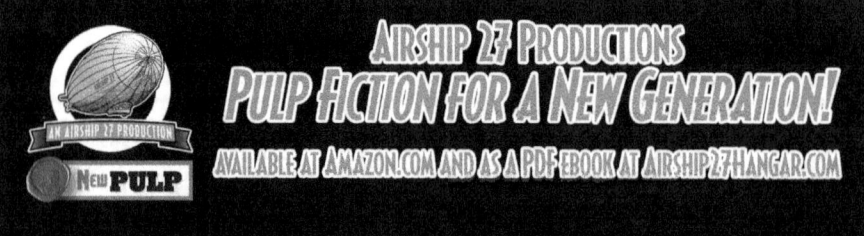

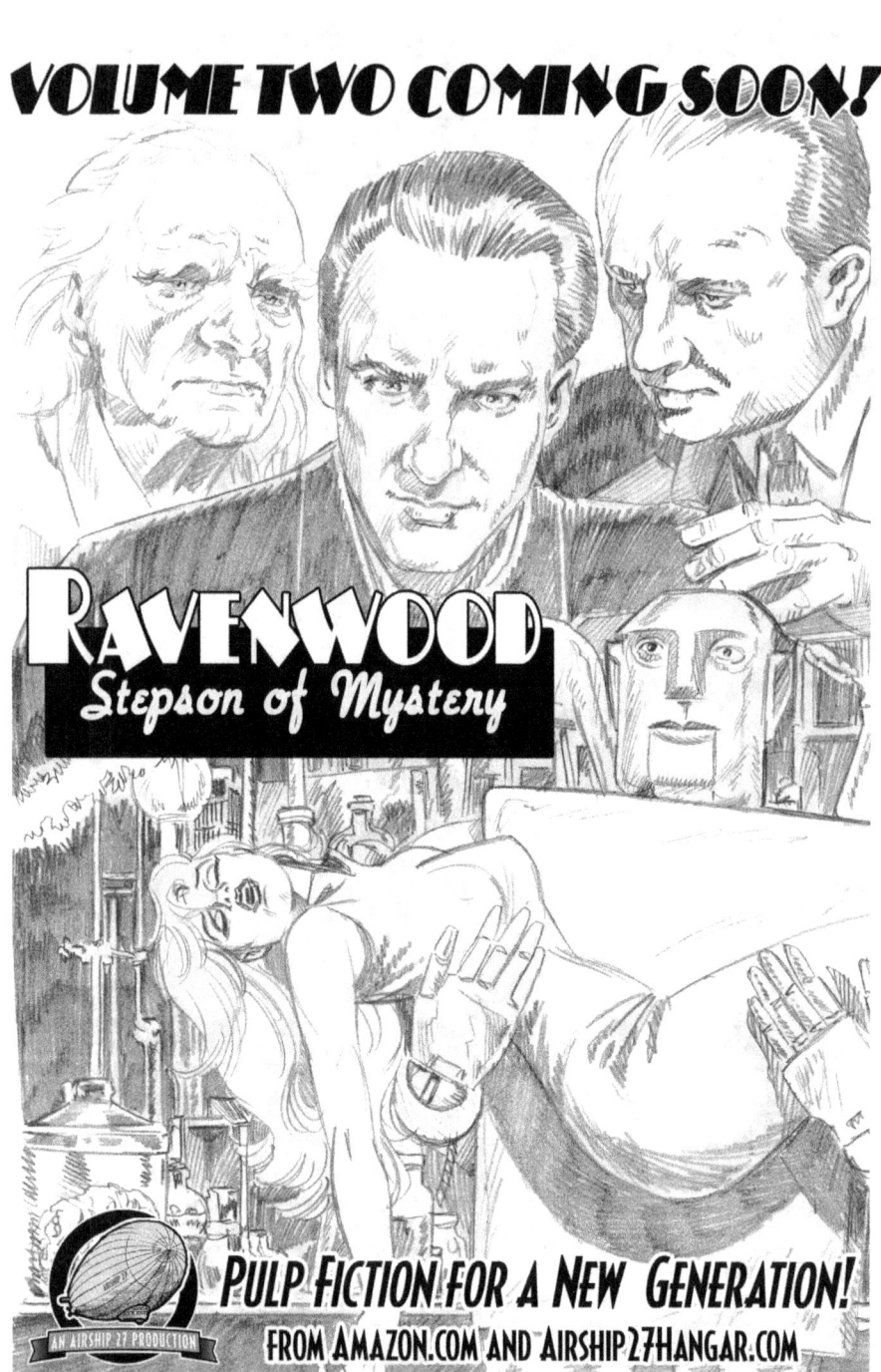